The Gikkie Dokkers
Book Two
The Aoes Shee

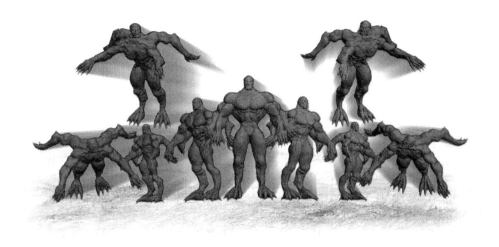

For John and Jayden
Love Is...

The Gikkie Bokkers
- Book Two -
The Aoes Shee

by Jason Conway

The Gikkie Bokkers
- Book Two -

The Aoes Shee

Copyright © 2016 by Jason Conway

Illustrations by Jason Conway

ISBN-13: 978-1500626907
ISBN-10:1500626902
www.gikkiebokkers.com
www.facebook.com/gikkie.bokker

The Gikkie Bokkers
BOOK TWO
THE AOES SHEE

Jason Conway

DEDICATION

There would be no Gikkie Bokkers if not for the wonderful
John Haverty. To him I lovingly dedicate this book.

May you cause as much mischief in heaven as you did
on earth my friend.

And to my son Jayden Haverty Conway,
the moment that I saw you I was healed from
the inside out.

'We have travelled afar from lands lost in mist,
guarding the fiend entombed in the pit,
Our origins unclear we seek to understand,
why there is so much suffering in the world of Man.

In times of old our Allies were they, now we must hide,
their world in decay, to reach out for friendship
is too much to ask yet we must take the risk before
her army does mass.

Our greatest force has lost it's way,
the curse of dark memories leads it astray.
If only for a single day his power returned
the balance would sway.'

ACKNOWLEDGEMENTS

I want to acknowledge my parents Gerry and Angela Conway for creating me and letting me loose on this planet to get up to whatever I wanted to and for raising me with such wonderful values. My beautiful Lady Warrior Wife Nicola Haverty, alongside my Mother she is the bravest creature that I have ever known and who is the furnace inside my heart that drives me onwards to create from within myself.

Gikkie Bokker salutations to my lovely wife Nicola. My brilliant sons Jayden and Robert. Mum, Dad, Anne, John Haverty, John Reddin, John Richardson, The Higster, Elaine, Stacie Theis, Derek Fox and Owen Quinn and Bo Luellen and thankyou to Darran Shaw such an awesome job at being my best man at our wedding, best day ever dude.

Table of Contents

Chapter One – A gift of power remembered

DARKNESS! It was all that he ever was, it was his home, almost tolerable. Deprived of his senses no pain could ever reach him. Sleep was all he craved, it drowned out the sense of loss haunting him. The blackness of the void and of time drowned out the feeling till it was only a hidden whisper.

Even at its height the feeling of loss had no memory, just a feeling, of what was lost he could not remember. But then… Awareness! Light! A blurred sense of reality struck him. Brief flickers of images, of different points in time. The only memory that was clear to him was that of the little Aeos Shee clan creature who reached out to him instead of running from him. Such bravery struck a chord of respect deep within.

Then a distant feeling of belonging, an identity, pure and noble fleeted by his awareness. He had helped in some way this little creature and his race, as well as a bizarre mix of creatures from another realm. The little creature was the only thing that had stayed his mighty hand from destroying everything.

Now he was awake, dazed, lost, confused, but awake. This was the second time awareness had illuminated the blackness filling his world. The habit of clinging to the darkness for a broken sense of comfort was calling out to him. So tempting, the urge was to run to it for comfort like a child towards its mother.

But the darkness of the void was only a trick, a way of existing, of making do. The awareness that had now been given back to him showed his true self how this way of imprisoning himself had simply delayed what was really happening. He was hiding!

There was now a feeling of distant menace, and more. A fear of not only what was happening in the now, but also of what he was not facing in the past.

Then the flashes of distant memories attacked him. Relentlessly pecking at him like a murder of Crow's. Fleeting sharp visions of events and places. Of creatures familiar, some beloved, some hated, yet all too fleeting to fixate on making it impossible for him to discern any detail. Just like the last time they faded, he now yearned to feel the comfort of the dark void once more... But a beautiful golden glow of light filled his mind, a new memory was manifesting.

The light should have been a thing to shun, but it gently beckoned him towards it. As his curiosity grew so did the light, it relaxed him. There were no more empty feelings, the sense of loss was replaced by a magnificent wonder.

The light grew until there was no more darkness. It enveloped him filling the dark space within him with warmth, a gentleness that he had long forgotten. He could hear faint sounds now, the sound of deep footsteps and of moving armour. There was no more void, he was within the light, he let himself go freely and began his journey.

The light guided him along a great pathway of stone and crystal. At first all around him was a golden glow of blurred scenery, but as he relaxed the hidden majesty of his surroundings gently came into view.

The glow was of a beautiful golden dawn, breath taking in appearance and gently warming. He had found himself gazing upwards at the breaking rays of light. Tickled and refreshed it made him smile faintly. The embracing rays of golden sunshine were illuminating the valley that he was walking in, exposing more detail in the path before him. The vast path of stone and crystal lead out of the valley rising upwards towards a mountain forest trail. Massive engraved illustrations of his noble race adorned the entire pathway. He noticed all the detail in them as he marched. The engravings seemed to depict stories of a number of kings holding court over a small army. Various scenes of these great figures leading their kind into battle against a vast set of armies followed.

Each battle was different and there were thousands of battles depicted along the entire pathway. He noticed that all in high command were depicted with a silver crown adorned with small horns growing out of an armoured helmet and elongated claws protruding from dark metal fists. He turned his attention to his own hands, all four of them! They too had dark metallic fists ending with long sharp talon like claws.

As he marched he became more aware of his surroundings, he was not alone!

'Be mindful of your surroundings my brave Eireannos! We may be in our kingdom but a true wrathien warrior is always aware of himself... At all times!'

The mighty voice came from his left hand side. He turned his head refocusing his eyes away from the glare of the rays of the dawn and met the gaze of the creature that had just spoke. The creature was one of his own kind, much larger and more powerful than himself yet his features were similar. He responded to his larger companion without thinking, he was outside of what was happening yet was also part of it.

'Brother, I am mindful of myself! I am ready for this task, I have trained ceaselessly for this day!' He responded sincerely to his mighty giant companion.

'Well then! If such a thing is true you are well aware of what's approaching, are you not?' The great leader's voice boomed out from within his huge chest.

'What do you mean my brother, I am well prepared for battle! I have passed all trials you placed before me I....'

He stumbled and fell over a small ornate statue smashing it to pieces and fell awkwardly to one knee. There was a large outpouring of laughter all around him as he now became fully aware of his surroundings. He was flanked by thirty companions, all larger and older who were in hysterics at his collision with the statue.

'My Battle Queen spent many nights creating that form with her own talons, the forthcoming battle shall be nothing compared to what she will do to you!' teased his mighty brother.

The entire pack broke into belly laughs at his comment. He snarled to himself embarrassed at his clumsiness and got hastily to his feet.

'My lord Gelfedaron if he is the Dark fist of the Almighty then perhaps we should turn around now and run home to our Mothers!' shouted out one of the pack - his smile revealing a powerful array of fangs.

The leader of the pack silenced his companion with one look then patted Eireannos on the shoulder shouting out playfully in reply.

'My friends, to get away from all of your mother's I would gladly run into the mightiest foe, for I can no longer endure their cooking!' The whole group broke into laughter again. Eireannos' spirit lifted. His clumsiness was not dwelt upon and he got back into his stride.

'Thank you Brother!' He whispered to Gelfedaron who amiably returned his glance.

'I was the same when I joined battle for the first time, but be mindful. Your awareness must be at its height now. Even our Queen cannot tell what manner of enemy has invaded the Siabhra domain'.

Even though Eireannos was deep in his memory he was also aware of where he really was. Sitting down on the very same ornate pathway leading out into the Selfin Mountains that separated his realm from that of the Siabhra. But the pathway like the rest of his realm was all overgrown now with vegetation, trees and vines.

The young Aeos Shee creature known as Fluke-Fluke had restored at least in part small fragments of his past. It stayed off the sadness and loss of the darkness he used to fall back into. Now at least he remembered his own name again... Eireannos - The Dark Fist of the Almighty.

He also knew he had companions and a brother, who was a King no less of his kind. He scraped off a portion of brambles and long grass on the ground to reveal part of the great pathway underneath.

The engravings dulled by earth and rock were just visible, the exposed path depicted the very same mountain range that his memory was recalling. His memory guided him back to the march he had with his warrior pack. Gelfederon was mighty indeed standing a head height above all of his warriors. He like the others had darker patterns of fine fur in the shape of Celtic knots and spirals all over his body all branded into him by his Mother Queen with the most ancient of magic.

When the light of dawn bounced off his dark fur it illuminated an almost metallic set of highlights cascading along his enormous frame. The whole pack shared these features Gelfedaron being the mightiest of them all. Eireannos noticed his older brother smiling at him...

'Now you've regained your focus! Rejoice for you shall soon feed off the power of the oncoming battle'. Eireannos felt a hunger and fire stir inside him.

'I feel my power gathering strength, becoming alive! But not like the trials you placed before me, something feels different'
Gelfedaron slapped him on his massive shoulders playfully.

'You are the Dark fist, your power is not even ripe yet. You can best all of my pack in battle if you chose to. There is a divine power beginning to awaken within you but take heed - battles are won inside the mind before they get anyway near the enemy! Your inner self and spirit are your most valuable weapons in combat!'

Eireannos thought deeply for a moment absorbing the words...
'Brother how will I know how to use this power? You spoke of new abilities manifesting from within me, how can I apply them if I do not

know what they are?' Gelfederon smiled with pride and rubbed his chin playfully in thought.

'I do not know how your powers shall manifest or what they shall be. Our Mother Queen knew what you were the moment she felt you in her pouch. All of us are blessed with divine purpose but you have been anointed the Dark Fist, a true son of Hellwrath. This battle shall awaken your powers, for only under the intensity of battle shall your fists become the tools of the almighty!'

'I know not how I shall deal with these powers but I swear I shall give my all to make you proud of me my brother. I will never leave your side!' Gelfederon nodded his appreciation proudly and thumped his little brother on the shoulder. Faint charges of energy trickled from his fist down onto Eireannos' frame faintly highlighting his Celtic inscriptions.

'I am forever proud of you already my young one. Your power is awakening. I can feel it off you, and now! We hasten our march!'

A giant amongst giants, Gelfederon turned to face his pack who all stopped their march and hunched down on one knee in reverence. He noticed that Gelfederon had stopped precisely at the end of the pathway. One more step would lead out of the valley into the neutral territory of the Selfin Mountains. The amiable King looked over his thirty two warriors. Studying them, inspecting them with a critical eye, his face became serious. 'I am truly grateful this day that you are here with me, at the border of our lands. Once you step forward out beyond this valley you become the chosen weapons of the almighty. Every action and choice you make - you make as a descendant of Dhuul-Grun-Chrom our ancient King. Make him proud. Let his spirit guide you and protect each other like a Wrathien pack should!'

The pack remained on their knees, but Eireannos could sense their energy and power rise from within. They flexed their massive muscles tapping into their own power aching to rise, desperate for a sign from their King to unleash them. 'We march onwards to our foe, begin your growl so that I may join in with you!'

Gelfederon knelt down before them and it began! Thirty two gigantic creatures along with their king manifested a deep rumbling growl from deep within their chest's shaking the entire valley and much futher beyond their kingdom.

Eireannos had passed his trials of combat and proven himself many times but all the trials tested him as a single warrior. This was the first time he was allowed into the pack. The fastest rising young warrior had no time to savour his accomplishments. Once one trial was over with he was tested again immediately. Now for a brief moment he savoured the pack and his place in it.

Just before his passion for battle peaked a gentle whisper washed along him… 'Let yourself go my son. When your Brother unleashes the pack don't hesitate, follow your instincts'.

He felt his Mother Queen gently encourage him from her temple. With that he smiled confidently to himself.

'I will Mother', he whispered to himself. Suddenly Gelfederon roared like thunder - shaking the trees throughout the valley - and leaped into a sprint out onto the mountain path tearing up soil, dust and rock in his wake. His whole pack leaped after him with a chorus of roars. The pack was now on the hunt.

Eireannos came too from his memory. Old feelings of power and belonging stirred within him. He began unearthing more of the overgrown path with his talons but, instead of facing the path out towards the Selfin Mountains some distant habit urged him to go to the opposite direction towards the old abandoned village huts. Uncovering more of the path he came across some old stone fragments of the statue that he had knocked over in ancient days. The statue was of a creature of the earthly realm, a female by what he could tell, but it was not designed in the style of Wrathien artists. The females countenance was not benevolent or wise. It seemed evil, a hateful scowl was carved into the face which otherwise would have seemed attractive. The expression stirred his memories once more. The warm light beckoned him back into recollection, and Eireannos let the light take him back in time.

He was amongst the pack, running upright in a tight arrow formation second from Gelfederon. The mountain path winded constantly upward into lush forests, wisps of low cloud evaporated over their bodies the moment it swept over them. 'Ulgathos!' shouted out Gelfederon to the Wrathien to Eireannos' rear left hand side.

'Yes my King!' shouted out the massive figure over the din of gigantic galloping footsteps.

'I have consulted with our Queen. She cannot see beyond the peak of the mountain, an evil force is hindering Her sight. We may be facing the creature the Siabhra were warning us of at the last council. Ready our pack we shall be using our living armour!' The mighty pack replied proudly in unison.

'Yes my King!'

Eireannos could sense the thoughts of Ulgathos sharing the conversation with the pack who howled in acknowledgement, Gelfederon could not share his mind with the pack until he was fully finished communicating with the queen. Then the pack reached the mountain summit. The beautiful view of the forest they sped through obscured by dense unmoving cloud. The pack was willed to stop by its leader. Eireannos wondered how it could be so peaceful this close to whatever was causing the Siabhra so much trouble. He also sensed that he was now fully part of the pack. Then he sensed something else, no one else seemed to be aware of it. He broke rank and placed himself ahead of his King. The entire pack looked nervously at each other waiting for Gelfederon to pull him back but he stood motionless watching what Eireannos would do next. Eireannos' Celtic glyph's were darkening.

A deep buzzing noise was coming from within him. The energy was charging the clouds floating around him turning them a red hue. He was about to pounce sensing movement towards him. The clouds in front of him parted chaotically revealing a silhouette of a humanoid figure running in his direction.

He bore his gigantic fangs in preparation for a killing bite but a weak voice sailed into his soul coming from the advancing figure... 'I am with you Wrathien, do not attack! save your energy for the vile evil that awaits you!'

The figure fully emerged from the glare of the cloud bank dropping to its knees in exhaustion. It was a lone Siabhra warrior. Her golden battle armour singed black along her left side and her armoured helmet badly split almost hanging off her head with dark scorch marks staining the remains of it. Eireannos immediately retracted his talons and rushed over to her gently lifting her whole body into the palm of his hand. The entire pack surrounded him facing outwards forming a protective circle. Gelfederon placed his left front hand over her and uttered a gentle incantation in Gaelic so softly even Eireannos could barely hear it.

'Oh beautiful Mother let your divine love pour into my heart and through my hand into this creature, a creation of your beautiful love, heal her wounds and wash away her fear, make it known to her that she is protected'.

The Siabhra warrior came too slowly, removing her helmet she revealed long fiery red hair. 'I must get word to your Queen! We are surrounded! She has risen!' Gelfederon's face looked grim. 'She? Who is this you speak of?'

She refocused on her surroundings trying to get her bearings.

'All I know is it once was a high Queen of the Banshee's, it was driven out of their clan for dark sorcery and it was thought it was consumed by the very magic it practiced, it was buried far away from all of our lands. But She has risen! Go and get help, you need more numbers!' Her emerald green eyes glazed over and she fell unconscious. Gelfederon looked intensely at the unconscious creature.

'She is self-healing. We have no more time. We must meet the battle if there still is one! Eireannos make a shelter for the Siabhra warrior in that clearing. We should be grateful that we at least have some knowledge of our foe!'

Eireannos gently tied four nearby treetops together bending them into each other forming a cruciform shelter of leaves over the exhausted Siabhra soldier. 'She will be fine my King' Gelfederon smiled in acknowledgement.

'Good little brother. Make sure you tend to her first on our return! They are our most noble Allies. My fellow Wrathien summon forth your living armour! We now go forth and meet with our enemy!'

The entire pack reformed into an arrow formation with their King at the front. Then thirty two bodies began to emit a deep pulsating humming sound. Their dark Celtic glyph began to glow a deep orange and red colour. The fine fur on their bodies began to reflect the light generated by their glyph in a metallic fashion, as if every strand of their fur was fashioned from steel. Then the fur grew longer, flowing and twisting over their bodies, sharpening their features becoming pronounced angular tufts of metallic hair at all of their extremities.

Angular metallic helmets formed around their skulls and all four arms grew serrated blades along their edges. The back set of arms grew massive triangular shields from out of the forearms with a giant Celtic knot pattern engraved in each shield, and all four hands grew fearsomely long black steel talons from each finger, so large that they could impale a large house. The pack erupted into a lightning quick sprint through the cloud bank cleaving a massive hole through it creating vortex of energy that wiped away most of the cloud bank obscuring the view of the descending mountain path below them.

Pieces of the path began to crumble and fell away with the force of giant's sprinting down it. But, the tree line of the mountain forest still blocked out the view of the Siabhra domain, increasing the pack's frustration at what they could be encountering.

The intense feeling of oneness imprinted Eireannos with a deep pride and longing to prove himself. Every delay or obstacle preventing him from seeing his enemy made him grow stronger, longing all the more for battle. Dust and debris flicked past his eyes but the living armour deflected any obstacles away from his vision. Every now and then the tree line dropped a little just revealing a teasing glimpse of the Siabhra domain but just enough to recognize the blue river that marked the entry way into their lands but nothing more. He felt his companions communicate with each other telepathically. Every thought was shared amongst the pack. Their Queen's presence could no longer be felt, it troubled them all. She was with them always, in domains far further afield than the Siabhra homeland.

As the downward momentum of their strides tore up the path before them, they finally cleared the tree-line and ran out onto a large overhang of rock overlooking the start of the Blue River known as 'An Gorm Abhainn'. The pack halted instinctively to observe anything unusual. 'There are bodies in the river my King, but I cannot tell of what race'. Drevathius was the pack's eyes, blessed with almost supernatural vision he could see four times as far as any of his kind.

'I also sense a foreign presence on their homeland, the like of which I've never come across, it has to be...' Gelfederon was cut off in mid-sentence by an unearthly scream in the far distance, uncomfortably shrill and piercing to the ear finishing off with a wailing moan.

'That is the vile Siren, and there is dark magic within it. We no longer follow the path, We drop off this cliff and cross the river and we do not stop till there is only the pounded dust of our fallen enemy flowing from our hands! MY PACK!!, WE FIGHT!! PROTECT EIREANNOS UNTIL HE REACHES THE SIREN!' The pack extended their fangs and thumped their massive chests in compliance. Nothing more was said. The whole pack leaped off the edge of the cliff hurtling in free fall for thousands of feet smashing through outcrops of rock that got between them and their foe.

He sat back onto the earth and grass taking a deep breath savouring this incredible memory. He was more aware of his surroundings now. Always night time where he was yet the memories were so far all in daylight. He noticed that he was still holding the head of the stone sculpture, rotating it amongst his fingers. Something made him fixate on the evil expression carved onto it. The night and this face had a connection. He did his best to relax once more, he yearned to be back amongst his pack. He scraped off more foliage from the ground revealing a small trickling blue stream running alongside the giant pathway. The moonlight increased the intensity of the glowing water, and the light took Eireannos back into his memories once more...

The Blue River 'Gorm Abhainn' in its Siabhra tongue grew vast in size, occupying most of Eireannos' vision. He was still free falling, slicing through the occasional tree and boulder unfortunate enough to be in the path of his fall. All of the pack were slightly ahead of him in a protective arc, they all could make out dark shiny bodies floating along the river.

'Fiends my King! The forbidden life forms have returned!' Drevathius roared out aloud eclipsing the loud howl of the wind lashing against their bodies. 'Yes I see it now, what malignant force is resurrecting these creatures? Pack! Reform on making contact with solid earth!' The King was acknowledged with a huge growl of triumphant affirmation. With a series of deafening booms the pack collided with the earth landing on a small cliff overlooking the great river giving them a clear view of the entire Siabhra homeland. The landscape ahead was dotted with the jet black carcasses of slain Fiend's. The Mother Queen thought Eireannos as a young Darkling that the Fiend's were a failed attempt by Dark Earth Magician's to create an invincible army to do their bidding.

A horrid breed of earth men, plant and steel contraptions that could feel no pain and could be grown on command. They turned on their masters and were eventually destroyed by the Banshee's. How they could have returned in such numbers and caused the mighty Siabhra such hardship was a mystery.

The entire pack fleeted their eyes along the shallow valley beyond the river into the Siabhra homeland to locate their allies. The valley floor was darkened with the countless masses of Dark Fiend's. The sunlight casting highlights off their bizarre bodies making it difficult to locate where the Siabhra warriors were. The wail of the Siren pierced the air into two, twice as loud as before. Drevathius located it's source quickly. At the far end of the valley just before the bronze road leading to the Siabhra city stood an unnaturally tall lone woman dressed in long white flowing robes. It seemed to be gesturing with its long slender arms controlling the army of the Fiend's through intricate gestures. Dust and the chaos of battle obscured any more detail. The pack reformed into an arrow shape and sprinted in the direction of the lone woman. It was still impossible to make out the Siabhra, a gloom of dust clouds and chaotic movement eclipsed them.

'I see them! West of the bronze road! Below the steps to the city!' Gelfederon smiled in anticipation. 'Good Drevathius! Protect Eireannos until we are near the Witch! I shall clear the path, prepare to gallop!' The whole pack ran on all four arms as well as their massive legs and leaped over the width of the great river in one jump the thunderous noise of all their limbs combined distracted the entire army of Fiend's. The Siren noticed it too, gesturing for half her entire force to break rank and head towards the Wrathien pack.

Gelfederon and Eireannos then saw the Siabhra warriors, their golden armour shining through the gaps left by the approaching half of the Fiend army. The Witch was changing her gestures. She no longer guided the Fiend's they were enough to keep the Siabhra from reaching her. Instead, the pack all noticed that she was summoning blue energy from within her body. Eireannos could make out that the Siabhra stood one hundred in number if even that. Pulses of blue energy began flashing chaotically amongst the landscape, generated from the far away Siren. The valley floor was so vast it would still be minutes before the pack would meet the oncoming Fiend army. Now every few seconds an arc of harsh white and green lightning branched outwards from the silhouetted outline of the lone woman. Eireannos was aching to leap amongst the battle and prove himself to his brothers, but the young warrior was restrained from bolting away from his rank by the watchful eye of his brother King.

Accelerating even faster the pack could now make out more detail in the battle. Their beloved Siabhra allies, a beautiful yet fearsome nation of sisters, were slaying countless masses of Fiend's as if swatting away small flies. So utterly focused on reaching the wailing giant of a pale figure. Eireannos smiled with pride, he had never encountered such beautiful rhythmic violence. Vicious and graceful all at once and carried out by such pretty and delicate creatures. Slender golden armour with silver Celtic inscriptions almost moulded onto each warriors delicate frame flashed and gleamed amongst the chaotic masses of attacking Fiend's. The Siabhra fought as one entity changing formation constantly unsettling the Fiend warriors making it impossible for them to strike at the Siabhra in any meaningful way. But then the great arc of light came again. Now closer to the battle but still descending into the valley Eireannos saw the raw power that caused the massive arcs of lightning, The energy was being cast from the crone like figure itself. Gushing from its fingertips were incredibly bright pulses of blue energy aura surrounding a bright green almost white arc of lightning.

The very air cracked in two with the deafening discharge of raw power. The pale creature kept the lightning arc flowing at a steady pace and wielded it like a whip lashing out violently at the approaching Siabhra who gathered ranks with their beautiful black diamond shields to deflect the massive charges of energy. The force of the Witches discharge of massive energy acted like an entire ocean of water collapsing on top of the Siabhra. It reeled their combined ranks backward and pressed them into the ground ankle deep as if they had just dug a trench.

Every time the Siabhra recovered, but only just in time to ward off a seemingly endless wave of approaching Fiend's. The pale Witch had no concern for its own army, hundreds of Fiend's were wiped out after every discharge yet there seemed to be no sign of their numbers dwindling. The Siabhra could venture no closer to the Witch, no matter how many

Fiend's that they slayed. Finally a sign of progress as the pack hurtled by the growing masses of slain fiend carcasses, it would be moments before they joined battle. 'Fiend' - it was just a word thought to him by his elders, but no word could describe how awful and putrid a creature that he was bounding over in droves actually seemed to him. All different in form yet all shared the same black blistering skin, shining with multi-coloured pus with huge gaping maws filled with fangs.

No earthly warrior could slay one as they could repair their own wounds even while fighting. They consisted of an outer layer of beetle like armour hung over a skeletal frame of thick red vines protecting a pale inner humanoid figure which, only existed to support the humanoid head which provided the brain power to act and think. The skull was human except for the enormous wolf like jaw and it was protected by an armoured helmet.

All known Fiend's shared these features yet it was the differences that defined them. Some had two eyes and were man like in form, yet others had a single eye with four legs and a scorpion like tail. The entire army was an almost infinite mix of deformity and unnatural features and its movement was so random and unorthodox it made any warrior's task of combating them extremely difficult. Gelfederon bellowed out in his mother tongue…

'Grudunzan notor wrathienz bullud drallouri los shale' - Divine force of Wrathiens, hammer our foes into dust!

The battle cry focused Eireannos instantly. The terrible Witch's wail and the thunderous sprint of the pack all faded away and he became a living weapon. The pack protected him, guiding his path towards the Witch who was lashing the Siabhra with ever more vicious torrents of harshly bright lightning. Suddenly there was no more time to think or reflect. The massive bulk of Gelfederon was first to spearhead directly into the oncoming army of Fiend's.

The Earth shook as his now metallic fur and armoured extremities disintegrated thousands of Fiend's in one charge. The entire pack followed their mighty King in a tightly grouped arrow formation sending thousands more Fiend's hurtling through the air with a vicious unrelenting fury.

The pack vanished into the massive blackness of the greater portion of the fiend army, creating a huge cloud of dark dust and smog created from the vaporized bodies of those fiend's unlucky enough to be in the way of the pack's path. The Siabhra finally became aware that they were not alone in the fight. The thunderous collision of the Wrathien pack into the Banshee's army stopped her from discharging her terrible lightning into the Siabhra and she glided off the bronze path rising into the air to gain a better view of her new foe.

The momentum of the pack was unstoppable. Fiend's were not even being engaged in combat. The sheer force of the pack acting as one behaved like a giant fist pounding into a small mound of Ants. The King's younger brother was telepathically summoned, it was the voice of Gelfederon, strong and clear…

'We have guided you to the end! It is now your time my brother, I now summon you forth upon our enemy as Eireannos Hellwrath! The Dark Fist of the Almighty! STOP THE WITCH!'

Eireannos was given no time to think, the silver armoured frames of his companions broke rank dispersing in different directions into the endless masses of the fiend army vaporizing thousands of enemies along their way. Eireannos was faced with the shine and lustre of a massive tidal wave of contorted dark creature's hell bent on killing him. Divine instinct took over, his dark mystic glyph's ignited fiery red all over his body channelling orange yellow streams of energy racing along the contours of his frame.

The energy flowed directly into his dark fists and every talon on his four hands glowed a furnace red. He extended all four massive arms as if to embrace the oncoming Fiend's and bared his huge fangs, his eyes blood red with Wrathien fury. The Fiend's collided with the younger warrior and were instantly transformed into dark ash. He sliced through their now dwindling ranks speeding up so fast he just noticed that he was about to trample over the desperately battling Siabhra. He took one gigantic leap clearing their numbers and landed right below the pale Banshee creature creating a deafening boom as his mighty feet struck the ground. The shockwave of his landing wiped out the remaining fiends that were attacking the Siabhra. Leaving a thousand frames collapsing awkwardly on top of each other twitching nervously on the earth, and pushing the Banshee herself higher into the heavens to oversee the carnage of her once seemingly overwhelming army.

The pack had circled around Eireannos destroying the remaining Fiend forces and regrouped into an arrow head formation but this time Eireannos was kept to the front. The massive force formed a protective line across the exhausted Siabhra army shielding them from harm. The pack looked skywards at the floating creature. Her snow white shawl and flowing robes glowing against the background of a now cloudy sky darkened by vast amounts of disintegrated fiend bodies. There was no wailing, no sound, just a morbid anticipation of what would happen next. Eireannos had time to observe in more detail the form of the risen Queen. She was incredibly tall for a humanoid female. At least twice the height of a typical earth dweller. Delicately proportioned and beautifully slim, her face was enchantingly beautiful. A pair of bright crystal blue eyes faintly luminous cast a gentle light upon her pale white face with high cheek bones and beautifully plump red lips. Her radiant face was framed by long flowing silky black hair flowing freely and gently undulating in the light breeze nearly reaching the back of her bare ankles. The sapphire blue eyes held the young Wrathiens gaze. The colour brought him back to the present moment.

Still squatting down on the ground, he gently swept his fingers along the bright blue surface of the stream he uncovered next to the ancient engraved pathway.

The face he remembered matched the features of the head of the statue that he was examining save for the radically different facial expression. He felt that there was more history between himself and this creature, more to be discovered. He got to his feet slowly following the overgrown pathway closer towards the ancient ornate hut structures at the centre of what was once his village. Using the giant talons on his feet to clear away the densest overgrowth along the path he hoped that he would uncover an engraving that would spur his memory into recalling more of his past. But he found nothing more of help on the path. Walking towards his old ornate hut as he had done for centuries his new found awareness beckoned him to study an odd overgrown ruin below the steps to his hut.

Standing equal to his own incredible height was a huge mound of earth, moss and undergrowth. He curiously swept away clumps of loose moss and vines revealing the hint of an elaborate marble sculpture. Carefully pulling away more sticky vines and brushing away loose soil he could make out the features of the sculpted piece. Still tinged with a mossy green the sculpture was a scene of a battle. It depicted a Wrathien warrior standing below the slender form of a banshee, grasping her with its right front forearm and preparing to strike her with a massive sword. Below both figures were hundreds of smaller figures, a mix of Siabhra and Wrathien all surrounding the battling pair. Cleaning away as much dirt as he could without damaging it, he saw the base of the sculpture. It depicted an army of the Aeos-Shee, adult versions of the youngling who awakened his senses. They were all raising their right forward arms into the air in seeming support of the battling Wrathien. Running his eyes over the whole depiction he welled up with pride. The lone Wrathien figure was Eireannos himself. His heart raced and his dark eyes ignited red again as he switched his gaze from the effigy of himself to that of the Banshee in his grip. The same evil snarl that was on the smaller statue was carved on this one. The evil expression held his gaze stirring him deeply and memory took him back in time once more.

The two figures held each other's gaze. Eireannos ready to deal out a killing blow if the pale creature above him moved against the Siabhra. Instead the elegant giant of a woman smiled enticingly at him, rising ever higher into the air above him. She spoke softly but her voice travelled to all below her.

'You would do so well if you rendered your service unto me. We are both kindred, chosen amongst the already capable masses we are gifted beyond your companions meagre knowledge of what power really is! Step up next to my side and claim this land for yourself, I shall be your new Queen!' He never broke the Witches gaze. 'There is no higher honour to me than to serve my Battle Queen! Your feeble attempt to supplant her in my heart with your selfish reasoning is a dishonour upon my entire race! Fight me now or surrender yourself. I shall not be merciful if you choose to act against us!'

The risen Banshee's face transformed horribly, her lips became thin and pale blue curling into a snarl which revealed a set of fang like incisors. Her eyes became yellow with red pupils and her shiny black hair became more animated. Her soft featured forehead became horribly creased with a deeply furrowed brow and she glared with utter hatred at the defiant face of Eireannos.

'I withdraw my offer of sharing power with you, go back to your ignorant masses to be slaughtered!' She glided upwards summoning the same blue energy from within her that she used against the Siabhra. The air crackled and hummed with power, the Siabhra who had lost their helmets in battle noticed that their hair was beginning to flow and gently raise with the surge of static electricity. The Wrathien pack closed ranks tightly around the Siabhra to protect them. The Witch began muttering an incantation to herself in a strange tongue. Her voice became deeper and full of menace yet the angrier she became the closer he became aware of a distant feeling of his mother Queen. The feeling grew in strength and turned from a thought into a gentle whisper.

'You have turned her anger against her. She thinks her rage is her strength but it is her weakness. Be the Hellwrath, your destiny my Son awaits you'. Eireannos felt the warmth of his mother's love seep into his heart, and he passed it onto the whole pack. Then he smiled and became the Dark Fist. Where there was uncertainty he now felt confidence, were there was anger he now felt at peace, he was ready for any outcome. His mind free of the fear of letting down his pack he became like a pool of calm water, tranquil and unresisting.

The resurrected Banshee Queen viciously hurled an enormous flowing discharge of bright energy at Eireannos from her right hand. The young Wrathien outreached his four massive arms embracing the lightning, his Celtic glyphs glowing like a furnace. The energy circled around him fiercely, his dark eyes became red again and refusing to avert his gaze from the Witch he absorbed all of the Banshee's energy. His glowing body slowly came back to its natural resting state, as confusion reigned over the Banshee's face, her snarl vanished and a very human expression of fear replaced it.

In an act of desperation the Siren let out a horrible scream and dived almost vertically downward upon the young Wrathien, her hands glowing with chaotic arcs of lightning hoping to overwhelm the Dark fist. But Eireannos saw her fear and anticipated perfectly her desperate lunge. He caught the undead Queen by the neck with his front right hand while a rapidly extended serrated sword grew out of his left forward arm ready to impale the Witch. The risen Queen cast all of her power onto the face of Eireannos in a last ditch attempt to escape. His face was battered with pulses of green and blue energy from her hands keeping him off balance and delaying his killing strike with his extended sword arm. Suddenly the beautiful green tree line encircling most of the upper vale darkened with the shadow of a till then hidden army of Fiend warriors. The pack broke away from protecting the Siabhra and sprinted towards the direction of the descending dark army talons extended. The Siabhra having time to recover sped after the pack sensing the need to keep the Fiend army away from Eireannos who had now pinned the Banshee Queen to the earth with his right hand.

Her unrelenting barrage of energy arcs were now being absorbed by the Wrathien who was feeding off the Witches fear and desperation. 'You are beaten, stop this nonsense! Resist no more or I shall feed your dark hearts energy back onto you!'

The Witch looked into his eyes with nothing but hate and spat back… 'You're not that powerful. Save your righteous pity for your friends, my army is about to devour them'.

Eireannos smiled back … 'It's over, I know exactly where my friends are, and your army is but meagre food for my pack!'

There was a barrage of roars in the distance. The pack had finished off the ambushing Fiends and were racing back towards Eireannos.

With the Siabhra army evenly dispersed amongst the advancing pack holding onto the mighty pack members armoured helmets like armoured silver saddles scattering the huge dust cloud of obliterated fiends along the way.

The risen Queen could bear no more. Summoning her last reserves she held onto Eireannos' grasping hand and rose into the air bringing the young Wrathien with her. The pack could not reach him in time as he let himself rise with the Witch as the battling pair vanished into the vortex of dark grey clouds caused by the battle. The Sun made the Wrathiens body shine brightly blinding the Banshee making her wail in frustration. Eireannos chose to end the battle and readied his sword arm to finish her but as the mighty sword shaped arm stabbed into the wailing Siren she vanished from his grasp! His gigantic body fell back into the dark whirling clouds amidst an evil sly laugh. The Witch reappeared floating above the hole punched through the cloud by the fallen Wrathien laughing aloud...

'The gift of flight was not bestowed upon your race. Fall to your death knowing that I shall butcher every one of your kind!' The resurrected Banshee parted the cloud bank completely so she could see the on looking Wrathien pack and Siabhra army.

They were all surrounding a large smouldering crater were her enemies body had pierced the surface of the earth and had buried itself from view. She laughed triumphantly and outreached her right hand pointing towards the swampy marshland to the west of the Siabhra homeland.

Steam started to rise out of the marshland. Its black water boiled, spurting mud and foam into the air until the marshland swelled. It became a thick oozing river of dark foul smelling liquid making a serpentine path towards the outskirts of the Siabhra homeland. The air became full of a hideous dark magic prayer uttered by the Banshee. Nothing like it was ever heard before, neither ancient Celtic, Gaelic, Wrathien or of any tongue that was spoken by sentient beings...

'Shill eucht drure, gar-ip carthuule, ill vhis screer, ul ip screer, brul crut screer!' The overflowed dark liquid approached the Wrathiens and Siabhra. Strange shapes rose from it, growing in height being carried along by the momentum of the floods. The flood picked up mass by collecting remnants of shattered fiend armour and machine parts.

'Regroup my warriors we shall have time to grieve for Eireannos when the battle is over, something approaches from the west!'

Gelfederon willed his pack to form a cruciform shape with the Siabhra splitting into four ranks nesting into the four wedges of the Wrathien formation. The Siabhra let loose a barrage of golden arrows at the sky bound Witch who vanished a split second before the wave of arrows were due to strike her and then she reappeared laughing behind the Siabhra archers as if playing a game.

The Wrathiens were focusing on the approaching black flood which was slowing down but increasing in height. The flood stopped a hundred yards from the pack and rose in height slowly. The dark liquid hissed and gulped and thousands of huge dark humanoid shapes rose out from the dark liquid - equipped with reassembled Fiend machine parts and armour equalling the Wrathiens in size.

'Gelfederon split your forces into two, take one half towards the Fiend's and let me lead the other against the Banshee! As long as she lives she can keep summoning Fiend's with her dark magic!'

The voice came from the most beautiful of the Siabhra warriors. Gelfederon knew her as Maeve, the Siabhra Queen.

'Agreed! You have one half! I have now willed it so! Take action and half my pack shall follow you to any end!'

Maeve nodded in acknowledgement and broke rank with half of the pack following her towards the floating Banshee. Gelfederon turned his attention back towards the vile mass of fully reformed Fiend's.

The Banshee unleashed a flood of arc lightning energy at Eireannos' half of the pack. Blinding them it created an opening for the giant

Fiend's to strike first, knocking Gelfederon' pack backwards and quickly surrounding them. As the pack struck back in retaliation the giant Fiend's were cut in two but slowly reformed awkwardly recollecting their parts but never reforming exactly as they originally had been.

Maeve the Siabhra Queen willed her half of the pack to form a pyramid shape standing on top of each other which reached halfway in distance to the floating Banshee. She then ran up onto the packs massive formation leaping from shoulder to helmet and shoulder to helmet until, at the top of Dravathius' helmet, she leaped off the pack formation. She hurled herself at the risen Banshee queen smashing into her and used her glass armoured shield as a battering ram taking the Banshee by surprise. Face to face in a death grip the Banshee cursed the Siabhra Queen and ignited herself into a mass of blue flames forcing Maeve to let go leaving her to tumble back to Earth colliding harshly onto the bronze steps leading up to her city.

'You are defeated! But I shall not accept your surrender! Die like worthless insects!' The risen Banshee Queen lashed out once more with her arc lightning engulfing Maeve's half of the pack forcing their pyramid formation to topple over falling onto the waiting mass of ever multiplying Fiend's.

With the pack split up and smothered by the Fiend's and the Siabhra all unconscious from the Banshee's dark energy, she gave herself permission to smile and gloat.

'Your world is mine you fools! I am unstoppable, I will take your

Wrathien home world next and slay your Queen!'

The crater formed by Eireannos' body exploded. A huge burst of red fiery energy erupted out of the crater and a massive shape leaped lightning quick from the crater skywards. It smashed into the floating Witch sending her body hurtling through the air, tumbling awkwardly out of control, and smashing into the Bell Tower of the Siabhra City bursting into blue flames against it and making the bell ring out loudly.

Blue aura whirled and rushed around the bell tower then twirled skywards a thousand feet into the air and the Banshee reformed, but this time she was silent, looking around herself in all directions looking for the force that had struck her.

'Come out and show yourself! Face your end!' There was a trace of nervousness in her voice, while she scanned the earth below for her attacker. She noticed a small pack of rapidly advancing creatures blazing a trail of dust in their wake heading straight for the flank of her giant Fiend forces. The Banshee had no time to approach these new attackers.

She summoned a huge arc of energy to lash out at these unknown attackers. Taking time to judge their distance, she lashed out at them but a massive body rose up in front of her with an all too familiar metallic sheen deflecting the energy arc directly back at the resurrected queen's surprised face.

The air was torn in two with a genuine cry of pain from the pale Witch who hurtled towards the ground crashing in front of the still glowing bell tower and curled up in agony.

'I killed you! You were slain! No one can withstand my power, the dark magic has betrayed me!'

The sobbing wretch shook and wrapped her arms around herself as if to comfort herself. Eireannos looked back out onto the battle just in time to see a small pride of Aoes Shee warriors tear apart the surprised flank of the Fiend army. He grasped the curled up Banshee in His rear left hand and raced over to the reviving Siabhra warriors who were huddled around Queen Maeve. He softly connected to her mind...

'I do not know of these creatures who are helping us, their armour is similar to your own so if you can make it known to them that I wish for all warriors to break off the attack so that I can have a clear path to the Fiend army!' Maeve's eyes opened to meet his gaze and she slowly nodded in affirmation. The Aoes Shee pride broke off their attack and sprinted like lightning past the ranks of the Fiend army and joined formation with the now emerging Wrathien pack leaving a clear line of approach for Eireannos. He then felt Gelfederon' presence in his mind. 'I don't know how you are alive but what are your plans my dark fist?' The pack and its allies were now well beyond the awkward gait of the giant Fiend's. Eireannos smiled...

'Don't ask me how I know I just do, I've absorbed all of this creatures darkness, why not share it with all of her army? If her magic creates them it can also destroy them! Shield the Siabhra from my attack, the power will be immense!'

The pack circled around the Siabhra while the Aeos Shee leaped

41

onto the heads of the startled pack to get a better view of what was to happen. The Wrathien summoned the blue arc lightning channelling it into his hands. A gigantic buzzing and crackling filled the air as Eireannos directed the combined energy of all the lightning arcs that he had absorbed throughout the battle into one gigantic stream of electrical violence and unleashed it upon the hulking mass of Fiends.

Blue lightning arcs penetrated deep into the Fiend's numbers jumping from one form to another disintegrating every last one of the corrupted life forms. Then Eireannos rose into the air to the astonishment of all onlookers, with the Banshee still in his hind left hand he landed at the end of the over flown marshland were the giant Fiend's took shape. Raising his front left hand high above his head he struck the dark liquid with a powerful blow, his massive fist causing a tidal wave towards the marshlands. Blue energy flooded into the dark liquid evaporating it until the marshland reverted to its natural state.

The young Wrathien looked at the pale limp creature in his hand, the Banshee's power was utterly spent, her face a confused exhausted gaze of despair. There was a huge combined roar of elation from his pack and their allies, Wrathien, Siabhra and these new creatures of the Aoes Shee race all chanting joyously in unison. The risen Banshee renegade wailed desperately with frustration, too exhausted to meet his gaze.

'If my end comes soon it won't be before I claim all that you love and destroy it in front of your cursed red eyes, damn you and your filthy race!' The pale creatures face relaxed into unconsciousness, her features softened to that of a beautiful woman once more.

He awoke from his recollection again his heart empowered with strength and pride and yet he felt desperate too, after this one climatic battle so long ago how had he come to this?, He looked at his overgrown fur almost jet black and with faint traces of a metallic sheen, far removed from the honed living weapon that he once was. And what of the overgrown ornate cottages of his great race laying in decay and ruin in this once gleaming valley of power and pride, where was everyone? His King, his brother, his companions… His Mother Queen?

A hasty nervous tingle of desperation and impatience took him. He forced himself to remember more but no more memory came to him. He roared in frustration pacing back and forth until he sank to his knees with his head bowed low in misery, tears rolled down from his darkened eyes and a deep sobbing echoed throughout the valley, he was alone, empty and desolate once more. The glowing moon cast a silver gleam upon his bent over body, sobbing quietly to himself he noticed his reflection in the trickling stream, darkness was all that he felt that he ever was, but something inside his heart begged him to hold onto hope.

The reflection in the stream cast him as a great monster but inside his cavernous heart a voice appeared faintly like a whisper in the middle of a great ocean, it was so low and calm like the gentle voice of his long vanished Mother Queen. It took all his effort to still his sobbing frame so that he could find a brief respite of peace in which to hear it. It softly whispered, more of a feeling of the words than words themselves…

'You are more than what you see before you, your eyes are tricked, your soul sees what your eyes have trained themselves to ignore. Hold on brave one. Grim happenings are near at hand yet all who scorn you now shall have dire need of you soon enough. As long as you travel by the light of your heart a monster in the eyes of all you shall cease to be'.

For the first time in centuries a voice had touched him. He stowed the feeling of company within his empty heart as if it were the greatest treasure. His great head looked up into the sky at the hypnotic moon and his tears flowed like torrents upon the earth, each tear turned to gleaming diamonds the moment they touched the soil of his land. In spite of tortured sadness as his lone companion a much needed visitor entered into his heart, the feeling of hope!

He would nurture it and grow it in the hope that his black heart would bloom once more into a mighty furnace.

'Mother do not leave me! I am not a monster! I am more! Talk to me! All I want is to hear your voice! Don't leave me alone, I am afraid! Don't leave me in the dark anymore my beautiful mother!'

His gigantic dark frame collapsed onto the ground in nervous exhaustion and he fell silent. The green valley was still save for the echo of his great frame breathing gently. The silver rays of the moon light danced and played over the solidified diamond tears left over from his sorrowful weeping and out of the dance and play of reflected light there seemed a white glowing shape of a tall woman in silver robes rising gently from the crystal gems. The wispy robed apparition looked down upon the great figure silently for a moment then approached him and flowed gently into his great chest. The giant's breathing slowed down and became placid and calm, a look of peace finally came to rest upon his face, now noble instead of fear and hate ridden. The valley gently came back to life again with soft chirpings and melodious tunes from all the creatures of the surrounding woods, for just a small time the great warrior was allowed to rest peacefully. For a time would come sooner than he realized when he would be tested mercilessly once more.

Chapter Two - A Major Grounding

'GET YOUR GRUBBY MITT'S OFF OF ME OR OILL BURST YA!'
The temple guardian took a step back from the little creature unsure of how to treat the female Gikkie Bokker. Jele-Nai was unnaturally tall for her years and her very presence commanded respect. With almond and green eyes and a flowing golden mane of wavy hair framing a sleek almost leopard like face she was the only daughter of Vraarl Uldunjen, second only to the mighty Vrool Gala in rank. But her temper and manners were anything but princess like. It took the presence of Vrool himself to keep her in check.

'Rest easy guard, she can remain as she is'. Vrool's mighty voice seemed to swell the entire chamber filling the grand space with psychic power. The guard bowed respectfully and took a step back. Few would have challenged a temple guardian and be left alive, at nearly nine feet tall and outfitted with heavy golden armour they were the elite of the elite. Even Vrool' sons Synar and Mil-Mil dreamed of being let into their ranks.

'The cheek of yer man! Did ya see the state of that guy's head? He looks like a sack of spanners balancing on a pile of steaming shii...!'...

'Enough!!' Vrool's voice ended her rant.
'Utter not this ... horrible language! You know why you've been summoned!'

His voice shook even the guard's demeanour.

'Yes my King!' Her voice became formal and respectful. The huge chamber echoed with the footsteps of three more Gikkie Bokker

47

younglings being escorted over to Jele-Nai's left hand side by another massive guardian.

Vrool sat in a throne far above them made of dark brown shiny wood carved into the shape of a leaf which curled around him acting as a comfortable grand seat. A set of bright silver sword blades protruded at either side of the seat topped off with elongated wooden arm rests.

To sit down into the throne would take some skill in itself. The entire throne hung from the dark domed ceiling suspended by a set of huge wooden Eagle shaped wings forming a 'V' shape with the throne on the bottom. All over the wood was delicately carved engravings of Celtic and Aeos Shee glyphs.

Vrool sat over forty feet high in the air looking down at the youngling Gikkie Bokkers. The domed chamber was constructed out of what looked like mahogany wood with intricate carvings of Aeos Shee warriors and battles adorning the entire structure. The light was gloomy only the throne itself was illuminated by a series of glowing white stones set in a circle on the black paved stone floor directly beneath the throne. The effect of the lighting cast creepy shadows upon everyone in the chamber. Vrool let an uncomfortable amount of silence pass by before he spoke.

'Terrible events! Great battles! Virtuous deeds and heroic sacrifice are what fill this chamber to the brim! All recorded as they happened in the living wood that never rests. The rag tag group of youngling Gikkie Bokkers looked nervously around the chamber. The carvings were ever so slightly moving, never at rest, like what they were seeing was a reflection in slowly flowing water gently undulating along a peaceful stream. The smallest Gikkie Bokker gulped nervously to himself attracting Vrool's Owl like gaze.

'Fluke-Fluke! In this chamber we discuss only matters of grave urgency. I cannot impress upon you enough the seriousness of your actions!' The youngling kept his large yellow and black eyes fixed on the ground, too ashamed to meet Vrool's gaze. Jele-Nai interrupted the conversation in defence.

'My lord forgive us our trespass into the realms of the earth dwellers, our motives are pure, we accomplished acts of kindness, surely this counts in our favour'

'Kind acts have merit', Vrool smiled gently.
'However the deed in itself is reward enough, but you exposed yourself to the earth dwellers and almost crossed paths with the wrath of Eireannos himself! You know as much as I that you are not yet immortal. One careless move would have killed you and you would have been lost to us forever!'

Fluke-Fluke lifted his eyes slowly, gently tapping his fluffy feet like he always did to comfort himself and finally spoke.

'Please Grandfather it's all my fault, but I knew there was good in Hugo. I had to help him. I was playing games hiding his belongings, just having fun… then everything... went... berserk!'

Vrool's gaze pierced into the little creatures frame, he knew that he was being truthful but had to show the little creature how serious wandering astray from their land was.

'It was you're playing games that started all of this. Hugo would have lost interest in Harry's insane mutterings and departed Wexford without issue, but your mischief spurred him onwards until he tricked Harry into leading him through the sacred portal! However I do commend you for repairing most of the damage that Eireannos had done to Hugo's home, it is a welcome beginning to a life of integrity!'

'So we can take your leave then my King?!' Asked Jele-Nai expectantly.

'No!' The carvings in the chamber moved more quickly now as if the force of Vrool's voice acted like a powerful wind pushing along the figures into new poses on the wall, everyone became very nervous.

'But I don't understand! We have apologized to you for our misdeeds, we cannot do any more than this'

Jele-Nai was frustrated and confused, Fluke-Fluke was still looking at the ground, and his companions Spongley-Mok and Tweakle-Ponk were fumbling with their long claws nervously expecting a severe telling off. Vrool stood up out of His throne raising himself to his full height,

'You've spoken words but what good are they if no action comes from them! You all did well in repairing Hugo's home but for so many of you to have left our realm and travel into the Earth peoples domain could have brought catastrophe down upon us. We guard our borders from evil that you cannot comprehend. It taxes our numbers. I will not

50

allow you to cause further disturbance inside our own borders!'

Vrool looked at them all and sighed. He loved them all dearly but could not show it, he had to make them understand how much danger that they were in and how much was at stake.

'If even one of you was captured it could mean our discovery. We are blessed to be granted this realm by our Siabhra allies, and without them we would be living in fields and hedgerows!'

'And what's wrong with that? It's fun!' Spongley-Mok had no sense of timing whatsoever. Tweakle-Ponk kicked him in his leg to shut him up from saying anything else. Vrool bellowed out crossly in reply at the cheeky little Gikkie Bokker.

'Silence, you have absorbed nothing of what has been discussed. You are to be interred at the youngling tree city until you are called upon for the trails of adulthood!' They all gasped, Vrool scowled at Jele-Nai...

'We could be on our way towards being discovered already!, For what Fluke-Fluke had caused but Jele-Nai it was obviously you who enticed Fluke-Fluke to travel to the city of Dublin to make repairs. Your obsessive fascination with that city is utterly mystifying to me! Learning to speak not only their confounded language but also the hideous slang speak they use is an affront to all we hold dear as Aeos-Shee Warriors!'

'But it could be a hundred years before we are ready for the trials! Please reconsider!' The fiery Jele-Nai began to sound desperate losing her regal composure.

'You are all Gikkie Bokkers! If you wish to grow into the armour of

51

an Aeos-Shee Warrior you will have to earn it! You are all reckless and silly. In the youngling city you will learn discipline and honour, prepare to leave immediately!'

'Oh no!' Nervously whispered Fluke-Fluke to Spongley-Mok and Tweakle-Ponk.

'Here it comes!' They all looked over at Jele-Nai and slowly took two steps away from her arousing the curiosity of the two temple guards standing behind them.

'Ah… JANEY MAKKERS OIVE had enuff of yur CADSWALLOP! There's nutin wrong wi da way Dubliners speak! It's deadly so stop givin mee grief ovur their language, yur seriously wreckin me buzz!'

Jele-Nai had completely lost it, the guards looked at each other baffled by her indecipherable slang, then looked up to Vrool for guidance.

Vrool roared angrily at her unsettling even the temple guardians… 'Cease your offensive mutterings and leave my sight! You are all to depart at once to the Youngling Tree City effective immediately'.

Vrool nodded at the guards and leaped from his suspended throne in disgust at her outburst. Upon landing lightly on the floor he ignored the group of young Gikkie Bokkers turning his back on them and marched out of the chamber through a large set of silver armour mesh curtains.

'Grand-Dad!' Whimpered a teary eyed Fluke-Fluke.
'Stupid gasbag! We were deadly and in all and anyways he should be thanking us for what we did!' Jele-Nai muttered under her breath.

Fluke-Fluke was very upset and trembling being consoled on either side by Spongley-Mok and Tweakle-Ponk. 'All I wanted to do was have fun and look what I've done, I'm lucky I wasn't thrown out of our land, I'm sorry I asked you all along to help!'

'Watcha talkin about? I was the one who decided for us all to come along to Dublin, you just got in da way and messed things up, now we are grounded for a hundred years ya mad scratty eyed git!'

The guards placed their hands on Jele-Nai' shoulder gently to silence her as everyone walked through a stone corridor out into a large set of marble steps that flowed down into a busy courtyard full of Gikkie Bokkers going about their business.

'Get your hands off me or I'll burst ye all ye smelly freaks!' Jele-Nai had endured enough of the guards placing their hands on her shoulder. The entire courtyard looked up at the escorted group on top of the steps to see who had shouted so loudly.

'What are you looking at? Ya nevur seen a Princess before?' The courtyard paused for a moment in curiosity then carried on as if she was not there. One of the guards returned to the temple chamber while the other spoke… 'Your behaviour does not tally with your title. Start acting like a princess before that honour is taken from you'.

'Ah well hello there! So mister fancy pants has a voice after all!' Jele-Nai mocked slyly.

'I am not permitted to speak in the chamber but out here you shall hear me if need be. I am Zarn-Hurad and I am your teacher until Vrool releases you from the youngling City. Your days of play acting and nonsense are over! Your journey to becoming a fully fledged Aeos-Shee warrior has begun!'

The youngling Gikkie Bokkers looked at each other with a sense of dread, even the fiery Jele-Nai was now at a loss for words.

Chapter Three – What to do next

'You've rarely lost your temper before! Even when war was upon us! They are such brave little ones, Fluke-fluke above them all. They are too young for the journey you place in front of them. Don't you remember how painful it was for you?!' Four delicate loving hands placed themselves on Vrool's huge shoulders trying to calm him. He closed his eyes and held onto her hands gently, savouring the comfort.

'I... can find no other way of protecting them from what's coming. It's all play and fun to them, and how do I teach them that our existence hangs by a thread without destroying their spirit? There is also something else on my mind. We still do not yet know how Reginold's servant Yardal was able to obtain a guardian amulet to open the portal and track Hugo. Even after being with Reginold I cannot get to the truth. Yet, he honestly has no recollection of how Yardal managed to come across one or how he followed Hugo and Harry out onto the stout marshes, and we sensed nothing! I feel like I am losing my power'

Shard purred at him in sympathy, 'We cannot attach ourselves to things that we could not have prevented or are beyond our ability. All the more reason to continue with our spells of concealment. We cannot be everywhere at once. Let's just work with what we know. I believe the truth will present itself to us in time. Regarding Fluke-Fluke and his friends, just let them be. Sometimes you have to let go of your ideas on how they should behave. Fluke-Fluke nearly died out on the lakes. He is learning and shall pass his wisdom onto the others'.

She let her golden mane drape gently onto Vrool's shoulders as she leaned over him and gently embraced him from behind. He smiled, grateful for the comfort and soothing manner of her voice. 'It's his wisdom that I am most afraid of! I've never seen his like before, nervous and timid yet when danger arises he becomes strong and resolute.

Jele-Nai is a bad influence on him. The trials will temper their rashness with good judgment'.

'Perhaps but let it be ten, or even five gatherings from now. They are too young. The horrors of your trials still haunt me! I nearly lost you, don't you remember your suffering at the hands of the inquisitors?'

He winced at the memory of them. The Inquisitors: a strange sect of priests that every creature wishing to become a champion, including the Siabhra, had to approach to be tested and vetted according to their ancient ways. To protect the lands of the Aoes Shee, the Siabhra and its allies, this race of Inquisitors would put forth trials of combat and quests that were so harsh many creatures would perish trying to accomplish them. But Vrool had passed the trials more powerfully than any creature before him. His prowess still provided little comfort when remembering the ghastly tasks that he had to accomplish.

Vrool turned his head into the cradle of her left arm and closed his eyes. She stroked the long scar on darkened fur on his right cheek and growled gently resting her head against his. 'Shard?' He whispered gently. 'Yes my king?' She softly replied.

'I have witnessed horror no living thing should be permitted to see, and still in spite of this when I look into your eyes you give me the strength to wash away the sadness and face each blessed day with hope and joy'. Shard smiled warmly with her eyes and tightened her hug around him.

'Let's leave them under Zarn's watchful eye for a few days. That should be enough to teach them a lesson'.

He held onto Shard's embrace savouring the tenderness then took a deep breath and turned around to face her. Tall and delicately feminine shard was beautiful, not only outwardly but also from within. He stood up slowly letting her step back a little to allow for his huge frame to stand upright. She was wondrous to behold, a diamond jewel of beauty with a soul of kindness that radiated tender love and peace. She faintly glowed with a wonderful magic unique to her alone. She wore a silver robe decorated with delicate gold glyphs of Celtic spirals and knots and an emerald green silver cloak that constantly undulated even when she remained at rest.

This was the only outward hint of the huge well of power she possessed as Queen of her kind. Vrool placed his front most hands on top of her slender shoulders and smiled. He knew the power she possessed was only possible to wield because of her strength of mind and kind heart.

He remembered many a time in the past when fearsome warriors with evil intent underestimated her power and paid the price. Most of all he was proud, for with all the power that she had she always chose to use it for good, to honour the forces of light.

'You make me proud to be your life mate! To whatever end that plays itself out I shall be the golden flame of love that encircles your heart for eternity'. The depths of his heart opened up and embraced her words. For to be an Aeos Shee his word was as solid and powerful as the ground that they both stood upon.

'Our little grandson will be fine. After listening to you I realize how proud I am of him; mortal and fearless, bold and intrepid, it shall be a bright day when he becomes aware of how powerful that he really is'.

Shard smiled back at him looking into his eyes deeply, then she smiled and winked playfully at him. 'You didn't just do that did you?' Vrool asked her curiously with an inquisitive grin.

'Yes I did and I think it's very suitable to convey my mood!' He stood over her trying to understand the gesture so alien to him.

'What do you call it again? The thing that you just did?'
Shard laughed playfully…

'It's called winking. You wink at someone and the best thing about it is that it can mean different things in different situations'.

He stood still in thought, his eyes focused into space trying to find a time in the past that he could have used it. 'I cannot understand this winking, forgive me but what are you intending you're… err… wink to mean?' She smiled coyly back at him and walked away gingerly, her gown and cloak flowing as if she was in flight.

'That my dear is for you to find out'. She turned her head around towards Vrool and gave another playful wink. 'Humans' he sighed, still trying to work out if he would have a use for this earth gesture.

'Don't forget my love to speak to the human called Drake. The forces of light are upon him, more than the others. I shall have the second spell of concealment ready for casting by the time you finish speaking with them all. I must also tend to the one known as Hooknose, Mister Harry Corbett. His mind is clearing at last and I'm so glad of it'.

She glided out of the room leaving Vrool in a state of amusement at her winking and admiration for her ability to focus on the second spell in such a relaxed and playful way.

Vrool then focused on the task at hand, to ask for the aid of the humans who were unwittingly enticed into his realm. He closed his eyes and spoke to his sons Synar and Mil-Mil through the dark ether.

'The Morgannis? Has she been found?' He felt his words echo around the chamber room and then flow into the earth below him.

His two sons spoke together as they always did when communicating through the dark ether with their father.

'It is moving father. I feel a chasm is growing underneath us. The creature is making ready plans to move against us, and all that dwell upon the surface!'

Vrool shuddered slightly.

'I feel it too. Have you sensed Henry? Is there any sign of him?' The reply took some moments as his sons searched for him.

'He searches endlessly. She is hidden from him. Your words of entombment have imprisoned him forever, and our salvation lies in those weakest amongst us! Father you must hasten your plans!'

Vrool readied himself to leave.

'And what of the creatures massing on our eastern borders? Have you intercepted them?'

'Yes father we have only finished questioning them. We have never encountered their like before. They call themselves the Heratii, an exiled race of monks and scholars fleeing with their families from a land far beyond our borders. They are completely covered in dark shawls but seem peaceful. We have arranged provisions to be sent to them, when time permits you should meet with them'.

Vrool left the chamber pondering to himself about the timing of this new races appearance but asked one more question of his sons while making his way to meet the people of earth who were still on his land.

'Finally my sons have you met Larn on your ventures? It has been over four gatherings since he last appeared at our borders'. Vrool felt the dark scar on his cheek begin to heat up as he spoke.

Another pause followed as two elite temple guardians escorted Vrool out of the chamber room onto a beautiful moonlit garden overlooking the stout marshes. 'We scouted out his tracks. They vanished into brittle valley but that's what lead led us to the Heratii refugees, and they claim they have never seen him'.

'Thank you my sons. I am on my way to meet with the remaining humans. Meet up with me as soon as time allows'.
Striding confidently he moved in unison with his guards, his form was serious but he secretly savoured every little detail of his surroundings.

The dark majesty of a lush land bathed in moonlight. He feared for his realm and what was to come. Shard and himself were the only two strong enough to find a way to keep the Morgannis entombed. Yet, despite their power, the outcast Banshee Queen still found a way to seep out some of her dark influence onto their realm. She had hundreds of years of earth time to plot against them, and while she could not physically escape, her malice and trickery was still able to affect in some way the minds of the earth creatures. Creating the unfinished spells of entombment was already exhausting him and his wife Queen but the spells were the only way that the Morgannis could be utterly contained within the mountain tomb for eternity.

Vrool put aside the worry and focused on his environment, the air was sweet and rich and a joy to inhale, brightly luminous fire bee's danced around him and his guards then darted into the trees on either side of the great marble steps spinning around branches in a game of tag. As they descended into the forest bizarre fur covered flying creatures (affectionately known as 'Flarpz' by the Gikkie Bokker younglings) began tweeting and chirping in the forest canopy welcoming Vrool and his guard's presence. A pair of Glowing orbs contained in a sculpted marble set of talons resting on a small silver base illuminating the pathway into the dark forest guiding Vrool and his companions deeper into the lush forest depths. Emerging from out of the dense forest the marble path ended with a large pair of crystal and stone pillars gently glowing with a faint white light and emitting a soft tingling chime. The pillars were a warning for any creature not of the realm of the Aoes Shee to dare not venture further up the mountain. An teampall sliabh barr an tsolais! The Mountain Top Temple, a place where even the Gikkie Bokker younglings would fight to the death to protect.

Vrool prepared himself to speak gently and dampen his power so as not to hurt the humans. The very act of an Aeos Shee Warrior speaking aloud was a medium to communicate with higher beings, his language was magic in of itself. When he spoke his soul and mind and heart all aligned fusing into one force. His intention and spirit drove the words that he uttered so that whatever language he chose to speak in would become infused with the power in his soul. Mere words became power to be used in whatever way he chose but he had to be constantly mindful of who he spoke to as his words had the ability to kill or destroy.

A large plateau of ornate glowing gardens with fountains of frothy magical stout and stone statues lay before them illuminated by the full moon colouring every delicate thing in pale blue, The King could see a group of human beings at the far end of the plateau surrounded by ten Aeos Shee warriors. Even from a mile away his raptor like vision could make out the smallest detail on them. He found even the mightiest of them hilarious to his sight, pale flesh and only four limbs with minute patches of hair on their bodies, he wondered how they had existed on Earth for so long without being conquered by another life form. The tallest of them would warrant special attention, the human named Drake. He alone faced the crazed Eireannos attempting to reason with the Wrathien and was prepared to trade his life for those of his men.

And he did. A stray projectile from one of his men's weapons pierced his heart, then something magical happened that he could not explain. The human known as Barney placed the stolen guardian amulet on top of Drakes chest and it melted into his body and revived him. He had to speak to Drake one more time if he could and hopefully find out more about how this had happened. Vrool and his escorts quickened their pace swiftly and silently covering the distance between themselves and their human guests, the time to beg for help had come.

Chapter Four - Reflection into the past

Hugo stroked the leather bound diary's spine, rolling his fingers over the gold embossed letters of its title … THE LOST LORE OF THE OTHER PEOPLE – DIARY TWO, ALASTAIR MAC NIADH.

The diary was over a hundred years old and yet, well preserved. Delicately gilded in an ornamental gold framed cover the red leather of the cover had become soft leaving impressions of Hugo's thick fingers wherever he touched it.

He had read through the entire first diary, completely engrossed and amazed. He knew small pieces of one of the languages that the Gikkie Bokkers spoke. He also knew how they came to arrive in Wexford and the playful nature of the creatures. It was now time to read his ancestors second diary, but the book remained tightly shut. He could not see any hint of a device or process that kept the diary firmly closed.

He sighed with disappointment as he loved all that he had learned and discovered. But in spite of encountering magical realms and creatures and also having being charged with the protection of them from the outside, world his thoughts were firmly on the whereabouts of his long thought dead father. The moment he thought of the word 'Father' his amulet buzzed faintly and he felt the amulet warming up like the feeling of a large warm hand placed straight over his heart. The warmth flowed into every part of his body soothing him.

For a moment he felt that he was rising up from his comfortable bed. It was the second day of taking the magical glowing carrot's that would reverse the altering effects of joining with the Gikkie Bokkers.

Hugo picked up the silver face mirror off his bedside cabinet and checked his reflection. Only a few short whiskers and a slightly elongated sweaty nose were left. One more day and the glowing Bokwana carrots would put things right. He was very fortunate, so he was told, to have survived so many close encounters with the Gikkie Bokkers, particularly with the massive Aoes Shee Warriors. Touching them had led to his current predicament. Despite the most fantastic adventure of his life so far had ended and that he had made friends with an amazing array of unearthly creatures he felt alone and very empty inside.

'Daa, where are ya? Give me some sign that you're alright, please!' He held his guardian amulet lovingly like it was his father Henry's very own hand. Once more the amulet buzzed with power but something more than mere magical vibration flowed into Hugo's body. Somehow through the obstacles of time and space Hugo felt his love being returned. The amulets golden glow became stronger until it tinted the entire bedroom with its light. Hugo closed his eyes, shut tightly with emotion, overcome by its strength the love had no name or sound but it unmistakably came from his father Henry. The sensation was as if he had embraced Hugo in person the moment Hugo had called out for him. Hugo's eyes filled with tears, his hard man image had no place in this room. The sensation of the love contained a message. Words could not carry the feelings, this love spoke directly to the heart, and only another loving heart could understand it. His father was alright! Hugo smiled.

His eyes still shut. The love changed its message slowly. Another feeling was being communicated through the amulet, it was still soft and loving but also final and direct.

'I have to go!' And that was the end of the message. His amulet stopped glowing and the bedroom returned to its natural colour.

He took a deep breath and wiped his eyes dry and began to roll his bedcovers away from him to get out of bed. Hugo was halfway out of the bed when the bedroom door opened...

'Hugo MacNiadh! Get back into bed! How many times do we need to tell you to be still you massive rascal!'

'Err, ah sorry love I wasn't thinking straight. Just give me a minute, I will er sort meself out!' He sighed and kept his eyes on the floor, unable to look Eimhir in the eye.

'Hugo its Henry isn't it? He was just with you'.

He grunted and got back into bed pulling the soft warm quilt over himself and remained still. Eimhir looked intently at him, being mindful of his feelings. He was not himself, sad and sensitive. She knew what he was going through but it was Hugo who had to deal with the feelings and come out of the sadness by his own doing - if he was to fully heal.

'My dear fellow don't despair. Rest yourself and let your father's love in. Don't try to cling to it like it's going to vanish into thin air forever'. She held onto his hand, the ancient power and strength of her race seemed to be behind her words, giving them extra strength and meaning.

'It must be a mighty love your father has for you, such that it passes through rock and stone, through time and the fabric of dimension itself, all in the hope that his warm heart reaches yours'.

Hugo remained motionless his eyes fixated at the end of his bed. Eimhir felt his grip tightening on her hand, then tears sparkling with light rolled down his eyes and landed on their joined hands. His eyes slowly rose and he nervously met Eimhir's gaze.

'That love my auld man has for me, it counts for something doesn't it?' Eimhir smiled at him unwavering in her gaze. 'Yes, yes it does. It counts for an awful lot. What you feel is a power beyond any magic that has ever been crafted, in time you will see the bigger picture'.

Eimhir's eyes were not an old ladies anymore. They had transformed into a wonderful jet black colour, shiny and hypnotic in their complexity.

Her eyes had as much depth as if he was looking at the stars in the heavens and they communicated in their own way expressing what words were unable to give meaning to. 'You are getting younger me dear'! He winked at her playfully, rising from his sorrow. Her smile grew larger. He noticed that her once grey white hair had started to darken right in front of his eyes. 'We grow stronger! Recovering from our battle wound's. Being with you and watching you grow in spirit hastens our healing. A day more and you can venture back into the outside world. Hugo's energy seemed to rise, his body perked up in the bed. 'Where's Brianag?' He asked expectantly.

'She's feeding your darling Alice, that creature never stops eating. Keeping her in our backyard is only going to work for a little while longer'. Hugo smiled. 'Yeah, if she grows up to be like her mother I will have to hand her over to the Spungle to take care of her'.

Eimhir's smile faded. 'If we ever see him again'. Hugo grew puzzled, 'I thought he was back to his old self, what's happened now?' Eimhir looked worried.

'Spungle! The word is ancient Wrathien for Outcast or Wildman, you must know this firstly. It is what the great warrior known as Eireannos became when he went mad from grief. Fluke-Fluke helped him for a brief time to see his true self but, unless Eireannos comes to his senses by his own hand, he will never escape the madness that haunts him and will remain the Spungle forever!'

Hugo felt sadness and pity but tried to uplift Eimhir's spirit. 'At least he is powerful as a Spungle, we can still use his help'. Eimhir became grim faced. 'As a Spungle his rage is unchecked and wild, it does not have a fraction of the strength of Eireannos! And none of his wisdom. His power could be swayed to evil as well as good in the blinking of an eye. Vrool and his Queen shall have need to seek him out very soon. We can all sense the Morgannis is about to make a move. Can you see now how powerful and dangerous she is? It's not massive power that makes her lethal, it is her dark trickery. Her power to twist meaning, to deceive and create fear and mistrust that is her most powerful weapon! Never underestimate her, the very soul of darkness itself has taken hold of and guides her'.

Hugo sat up fully alert clenching his fists. 'Boginold, Claudia, Vinnie and the kids! I need to keep them safe! We've got to get moving!' Hugo leaped out of the bed surprising Eimhir and made a dash for the door in his pyjamas. There was a blur of dark colour and a thud. Hugo found himself back on the bed in the blinking of an eye. 'What the? How did I get? What did ya just do?' Eimhir was standing over him by his bedside, her weak old frame was gone, her bent posture and frail figure had straightened up and her physique appeared to be that of a healthy woman in her thirties.

'Hugo, until such time as you are healed, you're staying put! Do not test me on this!' Still confused and amazed at the same time he chose to stay put. 'Alright and all! I'll stay still, ya didn't need to do the ninja warrior thing, just concerned over me loved ones!'.

'Boginold is more capable than you think, we need to bring him in and become a guardian as well. There are evil influences in your world too, who unwittingly do the bidding of the Morgannis, but right now your friends are very safe'.

Hugo growled back. 'And you're leaving me here to do nothin! I'm like a molly coddled spoiled brat trapped in a coal house!' Eimhir sighed disappointedly, 'You could have died sharing so many times with the Aoes Shee. The more you move the longer healing takes, and you're not ready yet. One more day Hugo is all we ask, then you are free. I really am having doubts about you being appointed a guardian, if you cannot control your emotions'. His face became still and pale.

'I'm sorry Eimhir! Didn't mean to be rash, I will keep meself in check in future but how do you keep so calm under all of this danger?' Eimhir placed a comforting hand over his heart. 'The mind is not your ruler, it is simply a part of you like your big toe. It has a function like any other part of you. It's only when you yourself as a whole - working as one being - becoming aware of everything inside and around you that you really see how wonderful you are. Yes there is evil, but there is so much more good and light as well. Trust in me, your friends are safe'.

Hugo relaxed back into bed only to be startled by the bedroom door opening rapidly. 'Okay mister Grey Bear it's time for your soup, Alice has been fed and you've only the day to recover!' Brianag had speedily shuffled around Eimhir to the other side of Hugo's bed and placed a wooden tray of soup and bread on his lap. 'He's done it again hasn't he? His whiskers are growing back from not being still, cop onto yourself old timer!' Hugo noticed that Brianag was still looking old, a little more spritely looking than when he had first met her but far short of the amazing improvement in Eimhir. Before he could speak Brianag caught him off guard. 'Some healing takes longer when it is your heart that has been broken Hugo! My strength shall return in time'.

Brianag spoke to him using her mind and he sprung to attention with embarrassment. 'Er sorry Brianag I didn't mean to pry, please take no offence!' Her eyes glistened a little and a very brief shiver of emotion passed over her. 'No offence has been taken my friend, get some rest' and she shuffled out of the room. Hugo looked over at Eimhir unsure of what to do. 'Please tell her I'm sorry I didn't mean to offend her, what happened?'.

'Siabhra are forbidden life mates, there are no men amongst us. She rebelled against tradition falling in love with an outsider and was expelled from our order. Then when the Morgannis waged war upon us she went to the aid of her kind along with her beloved and he was slain in battle. It's the hurt which takes the longest to heal, she will catch up with my rate of healing in time'.

He wished that the ground would have swallowed him up. 'I walked right into that one didn't I? How do I help? Please forgive my ignorance, tell me what to do!' Eimhir sat down beside him and lovingly touched his cheek. 'Start by getting some rest, you have many teachings that will need to be absorbed' and she stood back up and left the room.

Eimhir forgot to close the door behind her. Intent on finding Brianag she walked through the cottage corridor and into the living room parlour. Brianag's bent over frame was very busy dusting the old sofa and table.

Eimhir walked purposefully over to her and placed a comforting hand on her shoulder. 'Brianag forgive yourself. This has gone on long enough, it's affecting your healing and Hugo is a handful to manage as it is without me having to worry about you too. Brianag walked away from her pretending to be busy, but tears dripped onto the floor betraying her emotions. 'There is nothing wrong Eimhir, simply so much dust in the room it's making my eyes water!' Eimhir took her hand gently and spun her around to face her. 'I need you, don't shut yourself away from me. I can't reach you when you make yourself so wrong for nothing'.

Brianag's eyes were flooded with tears, her arms and body trembling with emotion. 'And you expect me to just move on and find another? Like my lovely Fionn? A man who should have been a king! No man in this world or the next is fit to even clean his armour. He could have united the land instead I enticed him away to mine and he paid so dearly for it! My selfishness cost him his life and now look at the nation that was once his, in ruin and trickery, run by imps and slugs, my selfish heart has caused this!'.

'NONSENSE!' - Emihir's voice spoke from within her soul slicing through Brianag's hostility like a cold sharp slap in the face.

She grasped Brianag by the shoulders, 'You have let your sadness rot into bitterness and resentment, none of this was anyone's fault. Fionn made his own choices as did you. The Morgannis was the cause of your Fionn's death, be mindful of that, you will see love again I promise, but forgive yourself first!'.

She relaxed her grip and embraced her tightly, it pained her to see her sister so weak, but she would be there for her no matter what would come. Eimhir let out a tear of affection and her embrace was returned, the room lightened up with a golden glow and they both could feel the healing begin anew.

The old paintings of long dead friends drinking in their pub in times gone by shook gently on the rose patterned walls. The vibration grew stronger causing the furniture to rattle and the chandeliers to swing. The sisters let go of each other and stood back to back posturing to defend their home. The rumble remained steady in the earth with no sign of

74

relenting. Hugo ran into the room to check on them still in his pyjamas but the sisters ran outside the house into the front garden. Hugo raced out after them surprised by their speed until he realised that his new pet Alice was around in the back garden.

'ALICE! I will go check on her then be right back ladies!' The lady guardians swiftly nodded without saying a word both sensing a second deeper rumble approaching from beyond Grandane village. The second rumble arrived with a deafening roar, shaking the whole village and the surrounding peninsula violently. Hugo ran from around the other side of the house with Alice, his baby Hippo, in tow behind him squeaking and crying with fear. Just before Hugo reached his friends he lost his footing on the soil and fell to the ground just behind the sisters with Alice landing on top of his head. Getting up and about to speak his breath was taken away from him as another deep roar surged deep beneath his own feet and then rumbled on past the group in the direction of the old dirt road leading to Reginold's newly acquired mansion. The tremor was fuelled by an unseen sinister force taking every old wooden telegraph pole with it, sucking them all underground as it sped away from them shaking leaves from the trees on either side of the old dirt road.

Then all the rumbling ceased leaving only the sound of startled cattle and horses in its wake. 'WHAT IN THE NAME OF GOD WAS THAT?' Shouted Hugo placing Alice off his head and getting to his feet. Brianag responded with a grim tone. 'She is making her move, it's started, we must rally everyone to our aid!'

Eimhir responded quickly. 'Vrool has sensed it too on the other side. He is about to reason with the earth dwellers for help. Hugo I know rest shall reverse the side effects of your sharing with the Aoes Shee but I'm afraid you must endure them a little longer. You must escort us to the mountain temple. We all must meet Vrool to help him with his spells of concealment!'. Hugo eagerly nodded. 'Better than staying still in bed all day folks' he grinned cheekily.

'And what of my good self you forgetful miscreants!!' All three figures looked behind themselves in surprise. 'Reginold bleedin Newtkicker! I thought you were still inside the pub! How are you out and about?!' Reginold looked fresh and completely healed from his crushing injuries from the Spungle, grinning confidently under his grey moustache he looked like the old good humoured man he had once known as a close mentor and friend.

'I suppose you didn't bother to check in my room and rescue me had I been there Mr. MacNiadh you scallywag! However you did manage to rescue your baby mutant Hippo thingey. I was indeed lucky to be out shopping for supplies for these splendid ladies while the commotion happened, we've a lot to talk over my old friend!' Hugo was amazed, the magic liquid in the Gikkie Bokker gardens had done amazing work. Reginold was as close to death as anyone that he had seen in his life, yet to see the old man in a tweed overcoat and cap with a push-bike full of grocery supplies was a joyous spectacle to behold. 'Reginold we must all depart for...' Brianag paused for a few seconds before finishing her sentence. 'Vrool has asked for us to meet him outside the portal entrance at mid-day, he will speak to us when he is done with the Earth Dwellers'.

'Earth Dwellers?!' Snarled Reginold. 'His magic liquid concoctions may have saved my life but I find that phrase highly insulting!'.

'Reginold! Vrool does not mean to be rude. Earth Dweller is a literal translation of the word they use for anyone who is human. Believe me, there are plenty of other phrases human's go by in the lands that Vrool protects that are far from savoury'. Eimhir was smiling very slightly when she was speaking, remembering a few herself off hand. Reginold got off his bike mildly annoyed and pushed his bike into the garden. 'Well I shall be bringing the matter up with him when we meet, I am not amused in the slightest! So mid-day it shall be then'. Hugo raised a playful eyebrow at Eimhir and Brianag who followed Reginold to help him with the shopping.

'What's another word for humans in your land?' Whispered Hugo to Brianag while they unpacked Reginold's shopping into the kitchen. 'Bhulugir-Mruk-Pucker', she whispered. 'Ha ha, what's the literal translation?' Queried Hugo. 'Bog Wallowers' She replied smiling.

'That's a highly toned down translation my dear!' Laughed Eimhir. 'We've just had a bloody huge earthquake and you imbecile's are making fun of mankind? Pah!' Reginold stormed from the kitchen into his bedroom.

'Go talk to him before we meet Vrool, you have a lot to catch up on'.

Brianag guided Hugo gently in the direction of Reginold's room. The old man was still muttering to himself not aware of Hugo standing directly behind him. 'Those village throwback's don't even have caviar!' And as for fois gras! I might as well have been talking about nuclear physics, stupid backward oafs!'

Reginold had tunnel vision and his frustration blinkered him. Even unpacking a borrowed suitcase from Brianag was getting the better of him. Hugo looked on in mild amusement at his old mentor who was still in full flight ranting and raving. 'And where is Yardal and Larrymond? Good for nothing lazy blobs, don't they know how to use a phone? I shall halve their wages when I meet them!' Hugo politely coughed to make his presence known mildly wincing in expectation of a telling off. Reginold spun around in a rage meeting Hugo's gaze but to his surprise Reginold calmed down when he saw him.

'I'm sorry my boy I've let my temper get the better of me yet again! I know we must depart and meet Vrool but I am eager to get back to my new house on that nearby hill and see what those two servants of mine are up to!' He resumed packing his suitcase. 'No harm done aul pal, been through a lot we have so just glad to see you are up and about'. Reginold looked back grinning gratefully, a humble look was not a sight that Hugo had ever seen before on the old hunter's face.

'Er yes, I'm grateful to the ladies and even that giant cat, bird, owl thingey-majig whatever his name is, he set me straight on a number of things. Hugo my boy I'm sorry for my actions, I know I am a narkey cur at times but doing what I did in those marshes, following you and hunting you and your friends down, threatening you all and trying to kill that little creature, it was not me. I mean that was something I would ever do now. It was like someone else was taking the reins and controlling me. I'm really sorry, I will put things right'.

Hugo smiled in amazement, his old mentor had just spoken to him in a way that he had never done before. 'Reggie my old friend, it's fine.

I've seen first-hand what that mad witch can do, it controls your mind if you let your temper get the better of you. She or it or whatever you call the thing nearly caused a war that we wouldn't have survived! It's okay. When you are calm that amulet will talk to you, it's already working it's magic on me'.

Reginold looked away pretending to pack. I've neglected to wear their charm! I don't trust it! Never liked voodoo you know!' Hugo sighed and walked over beside him and looked into the suitcase.

Reginold's guardian amulet was wrapped up in a kitchen towel about to be covered up by a pair of old slippers. 'Now Reggie come here you nutter! Let me show you what you're supposed to be doing with that. You took an oath and this is a gift, trust me, this doesn't control you! It helps you! Now put it on!'

Hugo quickly unwrapped the amulet and placed it around the protesting Reginold's neck. Reginold ceased struggling and became still. 'Nothing's happened! I thought it was magic?' The old man was puzzled but calm. 'It is magic Reggie, but it's up to you to summon it.

I told you it does not mess with your head, it's like their version of a sheriff's badge. They told me it gives you powers when needed but it takes time to learn how to use it!' Hugo patted him on his shoulders respectfully.

'I know we are heading to the Bay soon and it's serious but I'm looking forward to meeting up with auld Harry Corbett again. He will be able to show us a thing or two about using our amulet's! Provided the aul buzzard has all his marbles back'.

Reginold felt his amulet tingle a little and his body glowed a gentle golden colour for a split second then reverted back to its normal state.

'That works! I don't feel threatened by it anymore. I will give it a go for your sake and see how I get on, after all it would be most impolite of me not to after only recently pledging myself as a guardian!'
Hugo proudly smiled at him. 'It's good to have you back on speaking terms my friend, let's get ready, no more time to be spent on packing! It's time to speak with those mighty furballs again.'

Chapter Five – Some explaining to do

'I told you before, I'm not trusting myself when I'm around this place!, What on earth was I spouting off about when I placed that amulet onto your chest? You need to get out of here and get to hospital quickly, nothing makes sense Drake!'

Barney Jibblets was sweating heavily in the tropical heat of the Gikkie Bokker forest over-looking the stout lakes. His Garda uniform top was completely opened revealing a white vest and a bulging belly.

'Just relax Barney, we are way past hospitals at this stage, what happened to me over in the Bay? Who knows? But I have my mission to fulfil we must leave here at once, besides our chaperones are not exactly the most talkative of hosts!'

Barney looked at the huge Aeos Shee warrior escort standing five strong on either side of his group that Drake was talking about. 'Yes me lad I know what you mean'.

'I feel fine Barney, stronger than I have ever felt. I can't remember that you said anything and definitely can't remember an amulet disappearing into my chest but in a way I feel grateful. I can't explain that either, typical of this place! Everything just leads to more and more questions!'

'Then ask your questions, I am a grateful host!' The voice surprised even the Aoes Shee Escort. Directly in front of the huge general stood the King of the Aoes Shee, protector of the Gikkie Bokkers and his two escorting guardians. Barney became uneasy. He was stumbling for ages through the tropical heat with his gaze firmly fixed on the forest path beyond him. How on earth did the three huge creatures appear out of nowhere directly in front of him?

Only Drake had the composure to return conversation, the rest of the group caught their breath from the long march. 'We wish to leave, why have you not shown us a way out of here?' Vrool lowered his head looking down upon Drake with sympathy in his glowing eyes.

'Forgive me I shall release you from here shortly, I only ask you consider my plea before you depart!'

'Plea? You are pleading with us?' Vrool motioned for the Aoes Shee guard and escorts to return to the temple and walked over to a fountain of luminous water sitting at its edge.

'I need... Desperately your help! In return you may ask what you want of me and I will do my best to ensure that your request is granted.

My world and yours are about to hurtle into an awful Armageddon'. The General looked around at his companion's faces all who looked amazed and confused. He paused for a moment looking up at the massive creature then laughed under his breath.

'After all the carnage and unearthly events that have taken place here, how you've managed to hypnotise the world into thinking that this place doesn't exist, and that nothing has happened, and now you are asking for our help? It's bizzare.'

'Yes, help us, become our ally'.

'How can we be of help to you?'

'The amulet that bonded with you, it gives me a window into your world. If you give me permission, I can see the influence of the

Morgannis in your world without travelling there myself, giving me time to cast my spells of concealment on this place which in turn will contain the creatures power forever'.

'In spite of how my life was saved and the fact that you are a non-hostile force I still have my orders to secure that spire structure and render it's power inert! It's already caused chaos and set in motion events I doubt even your power can conceal, the answer is no! Release us and I will give a favourable account of your actions to my superiors. That's all in my power to grant. I'm sorry'.

Drake turned away from The Gikkie Bokker King feeling conflicted and powerless. Barney, Bill and Borris wiped the sweat off themselves and without a word hastily followed the general secretly in fear of the Aoes Shee King's potential reaction.

'I wish it were so clear and defined Andrew Drake but the artefact that has bonded with you belongs to the line the Siabhra, caretakers of this realm. It lives as you do. Forgetting that it exists and carrying on with the life you knew is impossible. Besides, if you leave here and return to your clan you know that they will make you attempt to come back setting more conflict in motion!'

Drake kept walking but Borris slowed down and turned around to face Vrool, but the Irish policeman's friends rushed over to him and escorted him away from the creature. 'Can't this all just end? What's going to happen to us when we go home?'

'You've crossed over two realms of the same world. In doing so not only do you bring part of my realm into yours but you leave some of yours in mine. You all will be sensitive to events that happen here till the end of your days, but I need your blessing before I can see through your eyes when needed!' Borris shouted over at the Aoes Shee King as he was escorted away.

'And what do we get if we help you?'

Vrool stood up from the fountain and caught up with the departing humans in three short steps. 'I will provide protection to you all and manifest wealth upon you, wealth in gems and metals - providing you aid me in being my eyes and ears in your world when called for!'

Bill Stump chuckled to himself as he restrained Borris from leaving the group. 'So it's a payoff?! Don't listen to him Borris. I'm sorry no deal, show us out of here and the best I will do is to never speak of this place to anyone ever again!'

The great King said nothing in return and walked a few steps ahead of the group, silently and slowly leading them away from the Gikkie Bokker gardens and marched without a breath or a sound across the stout lakes towards the portal entrance.

Everyone felt hurt and awkward inside. The King's appearance was fearsome but he showed nothing but respect and gentleness to his companions. Finally, after a very uncomfortable journey, the great creature gestured for a portal of energy to appear overlooking a small line of moss covered hills that the humans could easily walk up towards.

'Farewell and kind blessings be upon you', spoke the King softly.

The group said nothing and walked awkwardly up into the glowing portal, vanishing in a flash of turbulent energy. The marshy moss and misty bay became silent for a moment until Vrool could hear the distant roar of the Spungle, startled by the portals activation.

His two sons Synar Chro and Mil-Mil-Ulthu appeared out of the mist placing themselves by his side silently awaiting his next command. The King reached out into the dark ether realm and connected with his beloved life mate.

'My love, before you finish the second spell seek out Eireannos. The humans have rejected us! He is all we have left!'

'Father, will they not help us?'

'Worse than not helping Mil-Mil. All are too fearful to answer save one, the one who must help us most, he would see the Morgannis' influence before all others but his oath to his clan is drowning his reason!'

'Then what's to be done now?'

'We follow them out to their world, meet Eimhir, Brianag, Hugo and Reginold and formulate a strategy, and hope that our interaction with them inspires Drake to rethink his choice before he has a chance to depart for good!'

Synar Chro placed a hand on his father's shoulder to comfort him.

'Come Father. Let us accompany you, we may be fewer in number but those who remain are true and strong!' The King smiled and looked over his shoulder at his sons with fondness.

'Indeed! Let us depart'. Vrool summoned the portal to open and the three noble figures vanished up into its shimmery glow.

Chapter Six – A nice quiet stroll

'If you seriously think that a mutant Hippo is going to be of use to us on our journey then I have clearly given you far too much credit Hugo, will you please leave it behind in the garden for goodness sake!'

'Nah! Alice is coming with me, she is terrified after the earthquake. I'm not taking any chances, besides I will leave her back at the house after we talk to those Gikkie Bokker fellas! She's coming with us and that's that!'

Hugo lovingly cradled the pudgy infant Hippo in his stocky arms, mindful of tripping over any fallen telegraph poles that littered the winding dirt road leading up to Grandane Bay.

'Look, the closer we get to the Bay the less damage from the earthquake, like whatever caused this is resting at the Bay'.

Hugo was leading his companions slowly towards the water. They were just past the old haunted church which looked rather pleasant in broad daylight. Eimhir and Brianag brought up the rear of the group and seemed to be getting younger and more robust all the time.

'Eimhir my dear, if we are meeting your mighty hosts again then what is stopping the outside world from picking up the energy of the portal yet again? Is he going to cast yet another magical spell?'
'A long as Vrool opens the portal himself the power is concealed, only Shard his queen and Eireannos have the same ability.' They all came to brow of the hill looking over the huge Bay and the lush peninsula. Reginold's eyes were fixed on his newly purchased mansion perching on top of the hill overlooking Grandane beach directly opposite the Bay

to the east.

'When this meeting has concluded I shall pay a visit to my servants not one peep from them since I gave them the keys to my house, lazy auld sods of men!'

Hugo said nothing, content with babying the hippo he saved from his distant past. A brief flash of light much milder than usual swept out from out of the portal area and four figures emerged from it walking slowly onto the dirt path overlooking Grandane Bay.

'That's the army lad and the local police, must be finished with the Vrool fella then.'

Drake and his companions barely acknowledged Hugo's group and walked timidly passed them as if they had done an awful deed.

Hugo was about to go after them when the portal blazed into action one more time.

'Ah the flea bags have arrived lets be movin you lot.' And Hugo upped his pace to walk down and greet them. To his surprise Eimhir and Brianag got to the Aoes Shee first hugging Vrool and his sons with great fondness. The mighty King looked over his lady allies directly at Hugo.

'Blessings of light be upon you my friends. Now permit me to speak directly, as time grows short. We have felt the source of the earth tremors and they have ceased around this area. My sons are here to investigate and in particular examine your new home Reginold!'

'What? I mean what are the odds of my house being the epicentre of a malevolent earthquake? It's bad enough having useless servants! Pah!

Well let's be getting on with it then, follow me Your Highness!'

Hugo placed Alice down onto the ground and she sat faithfully beside him. 'And what of your army chap and the local policemen? Are they not helping?'

'They have chosen to go their own way Hugo. I cannot make them stay. Come Hugo, I apologise for my haste but I sense her presence, her hand is at work here!'

Reginold walked up to the overgrown footpath leading up towards his new home followed by his companions. He wished that he had got more time to start repairs on the old house. Smaller than Hugo's mansion but far more angular and gothic it always looked out of place on the hill top. The black iron rusted gates shrieked open and everyone walked through scouting the area for anything unusual.

Eimhir and Brianag stayed at the front of the garden looking out at the sea to their right and the haunted church with its volcanic cliff face reaching up to its boundary fence to their left. Everything seemed peaceful but Vrool paced around the house with his sons curiously as if something was out of place. Hugo decided to bring Alice up with him and the baby hippo eagerly sniffed around the back and front lawn, sampling the long overgrown grass and munched some blackberries off the many bushes littered along the iron spiked garden fence boundary.

Alice cared little for the weather beaten stone gargoyle statues that were partially concealed in the hedges, but one small statue was getting in her way of a huge bunch of juicy blackberries. She started to butt the statue gently to see if it would fall over so she could get stuck into some very tasty berries. She finally toppled over the statue and eagerly munched into the berry bush with relish. Hugo spotted the overturned statue and picked it up, curiously wiping off the moss and weeds from it. The statue was unlike any figure that he had seen before, a slender woman's form in a one piece shawl but the head needed some work to uncover the mud and moss that was obscuring its face. Still, it was an interesting find he thought to himself and he held onto the statue for a later time.

He looked out towards the direction of the Grandane Inn. The tall soldier who he barely had time to greet was leading Barney and his friends briskly up the dirt road. He sighed to himself as he expected more from the policemen. Leaving and not offering to help was something he thought was out of character for them as they never missed a chance to help their community, but he did not know enough about the soldier to chance a guess as to why he would leave without offering to help the Gikkie Bokkers.

Hugo then turned around to face the front door. It was a gothic arched double door painted jet black with an ornate hooded porch to give some shelter from the elements, more fitting for a small castle than a stately home it only enhanced the out of place look of the house.

Vrool was talking to Reginold at the front step leading up to the large doors with a look of concern. 'May we enter your home? I'm sorry but I have to be sure, something is not right here Reginold!' The old hunter sighed but without a word took the key out of his pocket and opened the large black wooden doors.

As soon as the door swung open a wave of dust and cobwebs flew out of the hall way and covered Reginold's face making him cough and splutter. Hugo laughed to himself but hurried up the pathway to the house and caught up with his friend with the strange statue still in his hand. 'Yardal! Larrymond! I distinctly remember telling you both to clean the whole house, get out here and face me immediately!'

There was no reply save for the loud echoes of his raspy voice. 'Imbeciles! You are both going to be sacked for this!' Hugo smirked to himself and stayed in the hallway waiting for Vrool and his sons to bow their heads and hunch down so that they could fit inside the doorway. Hugo noticed that in spite of their size they did not disturb any dust and they made no footprints either. The Gikkie Bokker King and his sons illuminated the whole hallway with their luminous eyes revealing a ruined interior of a house with no sign of anyone having spent any time there at all.

'Seems like your mates never bothered showing up at all!' Reginold looked back at Hugo crossly but said nothing. Even Eimhir and Brianag walked inside the already packed hallway leaving Alice outside to do some sun bathing. Everyone was waiting for the very concerned Gikkie Bokker King to speak.

'Your friends are here Reginold but someone is hiding them from us, everyone save my son's must leave immediately, hurry now, dark mischief is afoot!'

Hugo felt the statue in his hand tingle and he instinctively raised it close to his face and began to wipe off the remaining moss and dirt that obscured its head.

'There is no time for trinkets Hugo, remember collecting things not belonging to you was what got you into trouble in the first place!' But then Vrool paused, looking down at the statue with a painful expression of recognition... 'Go now! Run! Everyone!'

The mighty creature grabbed Hugo and Reginold by the scruff of their necks and flung them out of the hallway leaving them to land in an awkward mess outside on the garden path.

'Why you ignorant hairy Git! Cumere and I'll show you a thing about manners!' Grunted the bruised Hugo. Eimhir and Brianag leaped from the hallway with surprising agility leaving Vrool and his sons behind with their claws and talons at the ready for battle inside the old dusty hallway. Brianag shouted over at Hugo as eyes turned jet black.

'Hugo, there's no time to explain, get up and leave here with Reginold and Alice at once, run as fast as you can!'

Reginold came to and slowly crawled off Hugo revealing the statue still in his grasp. 'OH NO, NOT NOW!' Shouted Brianag in despair as if recognising the statue. The front doors slammed shut amongst a loud set of growls of surprise from the Aeos See warriors. Hugo looked down at the statue in surprise. The moss and grime of the garden was wiped away during his landing and a contorted face of evil sneered up him from the statue.

Even though it was a mere statue in his hands the face and expression were unmistakably familiar. Hugo felt his chest heave with fright at the memory of those hideous eyes that he had seen in his vision in the dark ether, those same piercing orbs were looking up at him with utter hatred, alive and full of venom, as if expecting something evil to happen.

Chapter Seven – The Puppet Master

'Wake up you filth! I command your bulbous frame to be my instrument of vengeance!'

The shrieking voice rattled the old glassware in the dust covered antique cabinets on either side of the ornate fireplace.

The stocky frame of Yardal, Reginold's head servant was draped on a ruined red leather sofa, a trickle of red wine dripped from the corner of his mouth. He slowly came too squinting his eyes at the afternoon light poking through a gap in the old grey heavy curtains in the living room. Yardal and his understudy, the nervous Larrymond Underling were to make repairs as best they could to the house to make it presentable for Reginold's arrival.

They had been surprised to find that the house was immaculate and pristine and decided to take advantage of this and plundered the wine cellar getting very drunk.

But he could not remember anything after that, and now awake in the same room but to find it in ruin was a harsh wake up call. All of this crossed his mind and also an erratic sense of fear, the fear of what Reginold would say faded quickly but the memory of a harsh shrill voice stayed put. His memory jolted him back to the present and the realisation that he and his understudy were enslaved to be servants of a vile creature.

He stood up in an instant and a nervous sweat dripped down from his forehead and splashed onto his bulbous nose.

'I'm awake my highness, I mean your highness, highness-Ness-Ness, what is your bidding?'

A hiss of triumph filled the room, the creature took great pleasure in the fear it had induced in the man. 'Awaken your timid assistant, you are to command a dark spirit I have summoned to crush the intruders, I need both of you to control it.'

A loud snore interrupted the conversation. Yardal looked around the room for his understudy. Under a mound of rotten mice covered cushions was a pair of protruding bare feet. He leaned over and grabbed Larrymond's feet dragging him from out under of the old cushions. 'Get to yuur feet! Lazy lump like you are, she is commanding you!'

The startled Larrymond leapt to his feet alongside his boss. The startled man had no time to adjust to his surroundings and went ashen white from the fright of watching the room become damp with a cold mist and a mocking cackling laugh echoing throughout the house.

'You will be its eyes, you will be its fists, you will enforce my will through its strength, leave no soul alive, we make war upon the surface and you shall be my generals!' Larrymond shut his eyes with fear and hugged Yardal tightly.

'And how we supposed to that?' He shivered.

'Shut yur trap, just goe along wid itt or wee are toast!'

'I promised you wealth and riches, now go forth and earn them willingly causing harm to everything you encounter, be ready to lead my forces and spearhead an assault on this village of traitors. Fail me and you will suffer endless pain. I summon my Deamhan, manifest in this space, Steal an foirgneamh, a dhéanamh do chorp, Bain úsáid as a chuid fothaí mar do airm, obey mo seirbhísigh, fág aon cheann beo!'

The house vibrated furiously as slabs of plaster and mounds of dust fell all around the terrified Yardal and Larrymond.

'How did we get ourselves into this mess? We have to leave!' Yardal looked down at Larrymond shaking with fear but could not answer him back, the spell was cast and a ghastly transformation began.

Brianag grabbed Hugo and Reginold with unearthly strength and dragged them upright and lead them into a sprint out of the garden back down the path towards the portal entrance area with Eimhir closely behind with the squealing Alice in her arms.

The whole house was shaking and shuddering, the sound became deafening with vibrating roof tiles and floorboards snapping and bending, sharp slivers of glass from the hauntingly arching windows started to crack and snap off and fly at great speed towards Hugo and Reginold who quickly dived to the earth to avoid a barrage of them.

'We have got to go back and save them, the house is going to collapse!' Hugo desperately got back up off the ground and attempted to run back to the house but Eimhir dragged him back forcefully, 'It's too late for them, we need to get out of here now!'

The rumbling and groaning of the house became unbearable shaking the surrounding earth and causing ripples and wavelets in the nearby bay. Then an even louder noise drowned out the din as the front door of the house was forcefully ripped off its hinges as Vrool and his sons jumped out onto the front lawn but instead of running over to Hugo's group they turned around to face the rapidly vibrating house as if to expect something further.

Hugo and Reginold refused to be chaperoned any further and turned around pleading with the Aeos Shee to run down to them but the creatures stayed put, there was one last huge rattle and crack of tortured wood and the houses foundations collapsed and sank the height of a man into the ground amidst a huge blinding cloud of dust and debris.

The Bay became silent as if even the local wildlife were observing the unfolding events. Vrool and his two sons remained at the ready. Clouds of dust swirling around them and the gleam of their extended claws shimmering when rays of sunlight broke through the fog of debris and reflected off them. Then a voice ripped through the air that had not been openly heard by human kind for hundreds of years, the language beautiful but there was no mistaking the malice that drove the words. 'Scriosadh iad go léir, tús a chur le do chara máistreachta iar, a dhéanamh iad a fulaingt!'

The house ruins began to shudder again and the house moved, rocking to and fro, the wooden beams and iron girders contorted and twisted in an unearthly manner. Parts of the house seemed to implode while sections of its roof tiles began to scurry and slide around the structure like giant cockroaches reforming into strange shapes that were mostly obscured by the huge clouds of dust and grit generated by the house tearing itself apart. Snapping planks and imploding furniture created an intolerable mix of harsh noise, grating and scratching innards rolled and cracked reconstructing themselves into a massive hideous form.

Vrool, Synar and Mil-Mil looked upwards as the large house started to grow ever upwards towering growing and contorting into an awkward menacing behemoth with humanoid proportions, the groaning of wood and iron and house innards never ceased making speech impossible to be heard. Vrool and his sons remained in contact through their minds easily filtering out the sound but they feared for their friends safety, they stepped back until they could see over the huge cloud of dust to get a sense of how large the entity was.

A shape resembling a head but formed out of the front porch and hooded doorframe with the bay windows of the front parlour as eyes stared down at the Aeos Shee warriors. A horribly angular mouth and jaw, made from broken timber frames and plumbing parts, scowled down at them from high above. As the cloud cleared away it revealed a massive set of roof tile lined shoulders decorated with gothic spikes and intricate flourishes.

The monstrosity rose even higher above the cloud and slowly climbed from out of the shallow crater created from its own collapse. Even Vrool had never seen such a sight before and was not sure of what action that he should take. The beastly form was nearly completely free of the debris cloud. Broken sharp wooden planks grew out of its dark stone walled back and along its forearms and every time that it moved it made an abominably chaotic mix of smashing wood and grating metal sounds.

Vrool was given no more time to take action. As he was about to summon a destructive word the form of a very tall pale woman in shawls appeared from out of the portal area and immediately attacked him with glowing surges of energy from its finger tips.

Startled at first, the Gikkie Bokker King deflected the energy away from himself and directed it out onto the beach behind him in a steady stream. The pale figure was pushed back into the air by the force of

Vrool's deflection but maintained a constant surge of power from her hands casting an eerie blue light over the nearby bay and the beach front. The apparitions jet black hair flowed with a silken grace but the face was anything but graceful.

Hugo and Reginold were shielded by Brianag and Eimhir. The surge of energy from the apparition's fingertips was getting dangerously close to them but they dared not move away from the protection of the elderly ladies. The monstrous demon house seized its chance and while Vrool was occupied it struck out its huge arms at Vrool sons attempting to spear them right through with its massive clawed fingers. Both sons darted like lightning out of the way but the monster kept a ferocious pace after them attacking with wild swings and stabs of its fists and chaotic lunging stomps with its huge stone feet, swiping huge mounds of earth away where Synar and Mil-Mil had briefly stood. The sandy path leading up to the overlooking beach front cliff was laid waste. Deflected surges of evil energy turned mounds of sand into molten glass and the whole side of Reginold's land facing the Bay was littered with craters from the monster narrowly missing Vrool's sons.

Vrool began to push back at the ghostly apparition, forcing the entity to rise up into the air. Realising it could not harm the Gikkie Bokker King it redirected it's evil energy towards Vrool's sons.
Both Synar and Mil-Mil evaded the energy streams from the creatures fingers and began fighting back at the house demon, slicing man sized portions off whatever limb the monster attacked them with. But whatever

damage they inflicted the house demon readjusted it's form, reshaped it's damaged limbs and pressed on with its attack.

The apparition kept attacking the young Ages Shee warriors to assist its attacking demon house. Vrool took a tremendous leap into the air and landed in front of his sons and deflected the apparition's energy streams once more, causing a shriek of frustration from the ghostly woman. Vrool then uttered an ancient spell emitting deep roars of an unknown language and gestured towards the attacking house demon with his hands. The massive creature was knocked off its feet causing a huge boom as it collided with the ground. The hulking form got back up quickly but retreated back into the crater that was the houses foundations attempting to gain some time to recover by hiding in the clouds of dust it had stirred up. Vrool and his sons sped after the monster ready to tear the enemy to pieces but at the last moment the monstrous entity leapt out of the crater as Vrool and his sons jumped in to slay it.

The frustrated floating Witch saw its chance and hurled a massive stream of energy at the base of the crater and the whole foundation of the crater collapsed completely and caved in submerging the warrior Gikkie Bokkers beneath hundreds of tons of earth. The house demon had landed just out of reach of the collapsed crater and now readjusted its course bearing down slowly and awkwardly from its wounds on Eimhir and Brianag. They stepped away from Hugo and Reginold in the hope of luring the monster away from them. The floating witch then sped past the fighting group with a worried look on its face, momentarily depleted of its power it desperately floated over to the marshy Bay and began chanting, more to itself than aloud its tone more nervous than commanding. A mist appeared over the shore of the Bay and the marshy water began to bubble and hiss. A twenty strong formation of humanoid forms made from mud, reeds and rotten marsh plants began to rise from the marshy Bay limping and clambering towards Hugo and Reginold, while Brianag and Eimhir struggled to deflect the recovered witch's latest attack of surging dark energy. Hugo clutched Alice tightly, slowly backing away from the advancing mud creatures but Reginold stood his ground and pulled an old but very large revolver pistol from out of a concealed holster underneath his tweed jacket.

The old hunter fired a single shot into the nearest six creatures to him but it only slowed them down for an instant. Hugo then placed Alice in a mound of reeds behind him for protection and then charged straight at the nearest mud creatures bringing down three of them in a powerful rugby tackle. Reginold rushed over to the nearest advancing creatures and wildly swung his pistol at them knocking off bits and pieces of sloppy mud from their extremities but the two men were now surrounded by the remaining mud wraiths. Just before the monsters had a chance to grab Hugo and Reginold, a huge soldier and three burly Irish police men tackled the surrounding mud wraiths from behind knocking four of the mud wraiths to pieces.

Hugo rose to his feet after thumping his tackled enemies apart and dived blindly into the middle of the remaining twelve mud wraiths disappearing from view. Incensed at his friends potential sticky end Reginold flung his creaky frame right after Hugo, vanishing amidst a gang of flailing mud ridden limbs. Drake and the policemen made a beeline straight for the mud wraiths who were too busy hammering their foes to take notice of them and paid a heavy price for ignoring the humans. Drake's huge arms ripped two mud creatures apart in seconds while his policemen companions flattened a single creature each. The odds were evening now as even Alice charged from out of her protective bed of reeds and tripped over two mud wraiths leaving them vulnerable to Hugo and Drakes huge fists. After a few short moments the only thing that remained of the mud wraiths was a groaning mess of muddy limbs.

The group shook off the cuts and bruises of the fight and focused on Eimhir and Brianag who were at the base of the hill leading up to Reginold's property and gasped with amazement. The old women were no longer old and frail and were dressed in sleek gold and silver battle armour slicing away at the massive house demon and deflecting the floating witches energy streams with intricately decorated black glass diamond shields. The floating witch was outraged at its inability to destroy its enemies and ceased its attack on the no longer old ladies and with a sly grin from its dark lips cast a huge plume of white and green energy at Hugo and his friends.

Drake jumped in the way of the blast absorbing most of the attack but even then the remaining muffled energy knocked the group off of their feet and rendered them unconscious.

The witch laughed out loud mockingly and turned its attention back on Eimhir and Brianag who had witnessed what had happened and were already sprinting away from the house demon towards their friends. The witch laughed again filling the Bay with a horrible echo...

'Too late my Siabhra sisters, they are dead! And you are next!'
Brianag and Eimhir reached their friends but were too blinded by grief to notice the rapidly advancing house demon rising up right behind them and were bashed to the ground just short of Hugo's fallen group landing in a dazed state unable to defend themselves.

The mud wraith's began to reform and hulked over the fallen people. Raising their arms to bash their enemies to death amidst the mocking wail of the witch who, in turn, raised her hands readying a huge surge of power from her fingertips to ensure that there would be no trace of life left in her enemies.

There was a large cracking noise behind the witch and a deep groaning din of pain from the house demon. Startled the witch turned around and saw her creation topple over to its knees and three Aeos Shee warriors erupted from the creature's chest ripping out pieces of the demons innards with them.

The house demon fell over landing with a deafening thud causing a cloud of debris to lash against the floating witch which protested in a vile wailing moan of frustration. The floating menace sunk to the ground and chanted one last time injecting all of her power into a desperate chant of resurrection. The house demon slowly rose back to its feet again and collected its decapitated parts together and gave out an eerie roar of triumph at its magical repair. As it towered over Vrool and his sons it sneered with its dark broken mouth raising its huge arms to spear them to death but there was a huge flash of light erupting from the portal area startling the house demon. It's energy blasted the nearby floating witch hundreds of yards away leaving her in a crumpled mess on the shore of the marshy Bay. Out of the portal light leaped the colossal form of the Spungle talons and claws fully extended, reaching towards the house demon. There was a blinding flash and an incredibly loud clap of thunder as the Spungle roared with rage and launched itself straight into the body of the house demon! Turning it into a million chaotically exploding splinters, scattering it in every direction, by the massive shockwave of its vicious attack.

The Spungle landed gracefully and rapidly spun around on the ground ripping up huge sections of earth aiming itself directly at the petrified witch. The two beings exchanged looks. The Spungles vicious expression became even more outraged as it remembered deep down from its past the face that it was staring at. It hurled itself at the witch all four arms outstretched to embrace her with a death grip. The terrified witch screamed and vanished in a flash of portal light making the Spungle collide with the shore of the marshy Bay, causing a huge tidal wave that roared out towards the direction of the nearby mountain range.

Hugo came to first, looking skywards his eyes met the Spungles. His amulet began to glow faintly repairing his wounds but there was another sensation deep inside his chest and inside his head. He almost felt like he could read the Spungles emotions. Instead of rage he felt sadness and compassion from the creature but also great confusion, like it did not know itself or rather that something was blocking out its memories. Eimhir and Brianag rallied around the creature and spoke soft words of comfort to it while Vrool and his sons saluted the giant beast bashing their chests with their fists in unison.

The effort was not in vain as the Spungles mood eased for a moment. Its dark faintly metallic fur began to become a faint dull silver colour reflecting its mood and it looked down at Vrool Gala.

'By battling the evil here you have spread its presence into their realm. More outsiders will attempt to cross over now. They have ways to see our energy. What magic trickery shall you use now to conceal this event from the earth dwellers?'

Vrool was surprised at the accusation coming from the beast. Even he could not predict the Spungles emotions, and it switched from being the unbalanced Spungle to becoming a brief hint of the mighty Eireannos so randomly it was hard to reason with it.

'I ask forgiveness of you, I am exhausted from fighting so many battles. My wits are no longer keen and sharp, but we all owe you thanks for appearing but we have further need of you, I...' The briefly calm Spungle let out a mighty roar interrupting Vrool and kneeled down deeply to look down upon him.

'My concern is no longer with your kind. The kingdoms we swore to protect are fading away and you meddle with my mind with your slippery spells. You and your kind are merely pets adopted by the Siabhra. Show me what you hide from my mind's eye and perhaps I may lend my strength to your cause.'

The humans were dumbstruck with amazement at the mighty quarrelling creatures.

'Eireannos, I beg you, there is a plan of war already in motion against us. This fight I fear is only a sample of what is awaiting us if we do not unite once again. I sense you are fading back into the shadow of the Spungle. Do not waste your existence as a wild beast, you can return to your full glory!'

The beast stood upright in disgust turning its back on the King and looked at the startled humans and the Siabhra.

'You all profess to care so much about my plight when you need aid but recoil from me when I ask the truth from you. I have seen brief instants of myself in brighter times, when this land was not cast in permanent darkness. Without any help from you I have recollected this, fight as you are for you shall have none of my help!'

Hugo hung his head in sadness unsure of himself. Staring up at him in the battle scorched soil was the small statue figure that he uncovered with the help of Alice. The face was sneering at him, alive with red and yellow eyes. Eireannos fading rapidly back to his Spungle form spotted the figure and something stirred within him, the figure was the same as the one that he had uncovered in his own village ruins. 'Earth dweller

Hugo! Where did you get that stone figure?'

Hugo quaked in his boots at being interrogated by the beast but Alice nudged him from behind with her snout causing him to stumble forward.

'Well..., I accidentally uncovered it in what was the front garden of that mansion before it turned into a monster, it's alive somehow, look at it making faces at me!'

Drake walked over to Hugo along with Eimhir and Brianag staring at the figurine in amazement while Barney and his men stayed put in fear of how the Spungle would react. Drake's chest heaved with disgust at the statue and the statue looked back at him as if surprised by his face.

The Spungle growled in hatred at the statue turning to face the sweeping view of Grandane Bay. 'How did you not sense this evil? Vrool your powers are lapsing, it is not a statue. You know full well what it is. Destroy it and do not attempt to follow me!'

Eireannos willed the portal to open and leaped through at great speed causing a deep rumble in the ground. Vrool calmly took the statue out of Hugo's hand and it began to hiss emitting a foul black gaseous vapour. 'What is it if it's not a statue?'

Vrool sighed to himself disappointed with his own abilities.
'It's a conduit, a conductor that aids the Morgannis in spreading her influence across great distances. She used hundreds of these during the time of Terun-nill-vath-doom, the last great war, but this is the first time that one has been seen in the realm of Earth!'

Vrool crushed the statue into dust with his powerful hand while Hugo shrugged his shoulders in disgust and then turned to General Drake.

'You soldier boy! It didn't like the look of me at all but I swear it looked surprised when it had a gawk at your big square head!'

'I really can't add anymore to that conversation! I've never seen anything like it in my life so it must be just coincidence. By the way I don't like your mocking tone so why don't you watch your words in future and we will get along fine okay?'

Hugo looked the general up and down and then sniffed at him disrespectfully.

'I will speak to whoever I want in whatever manner I like. You look like an toy action figure strutting around here and you must have got into those policemen's heads to convince them to leave here! Ya barely redeemed yourself by jumping in at the last minute to help us out. Go on and rat to your superiors about the place like your job orders ya to, you are just as much a part of this mess as we are but you're going to bugger off and bring more soldier boys back with ya aren't ya?'

Eimhir got between the hefty men attempting to make peace but Drake was determined to respond to Hugo's challenge.

'I've got my orders, you have no idea what it is to serve your country, the sacrifice and the pain. If something breaks free of here and goes on the rampage it will be my kind that will confront it. I am wasting time talking to you, get out of my way!'

The general stormed off in the direction of the Grandane Inn.

'Don't walk away from me I've got a few words left for ya big man!'

Hugo was about to rush after Drake when the powerful hand of Synar-Chro restrained him.

'You are better served assisting us in looking for more of the Morgannis' conduits, we cannot leave here until we are sure that none remain!'

Barney stepped forward away from his friends.

'We will lend a hand as well, we are sworn to keep the peace but I think the best way to do that is to help you as best as we can. I think we acted in haste following the General, I mean to put that right if it's fine with you all!'

Bill and Borris stepped forward reclaiming their place at Barney's side and placed their hands on Barney's shoulders in support. Bill smiled confidently at Synar.

'We feel the same, let's find those statues'. Vrool stood forward and smiled back at Bill with appreciation.

'I have another task for you three! Please give me permission to see through your eyes when needed. You shall stay put in your village and act like nothing out of the ordinary has occurred and go about your business as usual, you will be my advance guard to warn me of any outsiders with hostile intentions. For this alone you shall be of great help to us!'

Borris met Bill's gaze nervously. 'So do it then, let's get this over with, go on and cast the spell!' Vrool laughed mightily.

'There is no spell man of earth, just give me your word that you will help and that is all. I can already see through your eyes if I wish but I would never dare to do so unless you allow me to of your own free will, it is our way!'

All three Gardai, staunch guardians of the peace in Grandane Village for years agreed with Vrool to be his eyes and ears and then left for the Village police station ignoring a very agitated American General as they walked briskly by him towards the village station.

Heated conversations began amongst the remainder of the unlikely alliance with the exception of Brianag who seemed to be fixated on the lone figure of Drake walking sternly up the pathway away from them. She cleared her mind of all the background chatter from her companions and focused intently on the General who was nearly out of sight just reaching the brow of the hill leading down onto her house.

'Man of Earth! Awaken from your anger!' The voice that Drake heard was felinely sweet and yet stern. He stopped and turned around to face the person who was addressing him but there was nobody there. The nearest person to him was what looked like the elderly lady whom he had overheard went by the name of Brianag but she was nearly one hundred metres away from him.

Confused but still angered he turned his back on the lady and increased his pace. A hands gentle touch on his shoulder sent a warm relaxing wave deep into his body and he spun around quickly in surprise. In front of him was a flame haired porcelain beauty of a woman with incredible emerald eyes and beautifully expressive red lips. His heart raced in surprise, a most welcome surprise at that but the bruises and scratches of battle quickly brought him back to his senses.

'Who are you? Are you Brianag's daughter? If you are looking for her she is at the bottom of the hill... Look!' And he pointed his arm back towards where he thought he had last seen her but she was not there.

'Sorry, I thought she was there she must have returned to the others, forgive me I must be on my way!'

'I am Brianag, why do you think I am a daughter of hers?'
Drake blinked his eyes tightly and refocused them on the young woman claiming to be Brianag hoping that he had taken one too many punches in the battle with the mud wraiths, but the woman stood resolutely in front of him with a serious expression on her face.

'Well... for one thing you are a lot younger, I'm a little worse for wear and my heads not feeling great so perhaps you were always young and I have just been imagining things.'

Brianag's cheeks blushed bright red in embarrassment as she realised that her body was recovering more quickly and she was returning to her normal appearance.

'It is I who must ask of your forgiveness General of earth, this is how I really look! My appearance was altered when my sister and I fought in the last terrible battle with the Morgannis! Our energy was drained so much we became old but finally it looks like I have just caught up with my sister in healing myself'.

'General of Earth?'

He chuckled to himself modestly.

'I am no General of the Earth, just my own country mam. Please excuse me I must leave there is a mountain of chaos that I have to confront and right now I can't even think clearly!'

'Then taking action based on unclear thinking surely is an omen of chaos don't you think?'

Drake paused momentarily and wiped a layer of sweat of his forehead looking at the ground in confusion.

'You were an old lady back there with your sister and you changed didn't you? Please say what I saw was the truth. I'm only coming to my senses after getting blasted off my feet by that witch creature, I am not really feeling... very... well right... now, I think I may need to rest and...' The General's eyes rolled up into the back of his head and he fainted but Brianag swiftly caught him in her arms.

Chapter Nine – Who needs enemies with friends like these?

'Say whatcha want and ya can cleave me head off me shoulders for sayin it but I think we need to get General square head back here before we go any further. The man is goin to rat on all of us and your goin to have a war on your land before the sun sets!'

Hugo was wiping the clods of mud off himself from the battle with the mud wraiths as he stood before Vrool who listened but had his gaze fixed on Brianag who ran quickly after the American General.

'The General shall not be going very far, he absorbed a fatal amount of dark energy from the Morgannis! The only thing that saved him is the amulet that is now part of his being! Brianag has sensed this and will take care of him for the time being!'

Eimhir looked at Vrool understandingly and began to follow Brianag back up the hill but then stopped looking back at the King.
'Vrool, which amulet did the General absorb?'

'Fionn's, from the battle of the living sword'.
Vrool's sons responded by closing their eyes seemingly in pain at the mention of the event.

Eimhir exhaled heavily and resumed her march up the hill speaking to herself as she turned away from Vrool.

'It would explain why my sister was fixated on the human!'
Vrool placed a finger on Hugo's mouth to keep him from interrupting the conversation.

'Eimhir tend to the General with your sister but for now prevent him from leaving till I gather more knowledge about how the Morgannis prepared this attack on the human realm!'

'It is the wisest approach my friend, when you return I shall visit my Queen and re-join her army. I sense as you do deep currents of evil at work here, all kingdoms shall need to be awakened!'

Eimhir dashed up the hill towards Brianag who had caught the fainting General in her arms and slung him over her shoulder like a ragdoll, leaving Hugo with a rewarding smirk on his face. 'I love those ladies. I'm going to go after them and help them look after the square head, let me know if ya need me!' And with that Hugo attempted to march off after the sisters but a massive hand placed firmly on his chest blocked his departure.

'Too late for frolics with the ladies Hugo. You are joining my sons to investigate this area further and report back to me as soon as you find anything. All conduits must be destroyed. I must now leave to aid my Queen in our spells!'

Hugo sighed knowing full well that he would have had immense fun mocking and teasing the American General. He could tell if a person took himself too seriously and the General stood out like a beacon asking to be teased.

'I used to work in construction for a time! You know building houses and the like. I've met his type before stuck up and begging to be made fun of. You know once I…'

Mil-Mil Ulthu picked Hugo up with one hand and spun him around to face the biggest pile of house wreckage.

'Search the wreckage Hugo, do not delay my father's request!'

Vrool smiled back at Mil-Mil and beckoned his two sons to approach him closely and wrapped his arms around them both.

'After the conduits are disposed of join me back at An teampall sliabh barr an tsolais. We need to awaken our forces. Hugo and his friend are now under your care. I know how you feel about the earth dwellers but remember who Hugo's father is. In time he will rise from his current state and find himself fully, till then teach him about his amulet!'

'Hey don't be talkin about me like I am not here, I'm right behind your flea bitten arses!'
Vrool looked back at Hugo disappointedly and gestured for his sons to take care of the belligerent hunter.

'I wish I had more time my friend, to talk and to teach you, but there is no time left!'

'Right then, I'm looking for the conduits. Come on Reggie our auld hunters eyes shall spot these things soon enough. Talk to ya later Vrool but remember this! I need to be gettin back to Boginold and my friends by tomorrow at the latest otherwise they will suspect that something's wrong!' Vrool nodded his head respectfully and beckoned for the portal overlooking the Bay to open and vanished into its shimmering light.
'Look Hugo I found one! And there is another one outside the garden entrance, amazing! I never noticed any of these when I walked this way before, all the same, vile looking effigies the lot of them!'

Reginold placed the two figures into his jackets largest pocket and made a bee line towards the end of the garden path entrance and stared in amazement at the size of the sunken crater where his newly purchased house stood only minutes before. Hugo caught up quickly with his friend and spotted another figure hidden under a large patch of moss and dead tree roots and tried to pull it out of the grasp of the roots but it was firmly gripped and would need a great deal of effort to pull free.

Synar and Mil-Mil walked past Hugo and Reginold and discovered two more conduit figures barely six feet from where they stood. Reginold got down beside Hugo and helped him pull on the last few rotten tree roots entangling the conduit figure.

'Reggie did you notice that there's a pattern that these figures have been placed in? They all seem to be encircling the house foundations!' Reginold grinned with satisfaction after snapping off the second last tree root holding onto the figure.

'Well spotted my friend, this was a trap to begin with and planned out with some degree of precision. Forgive me my mind is not a sharp as it once was we need to rest soon and we can figure this conundrum out, what do you think yourself?'

Hugo grasped the last root and snapped it free of the conduit figure and sat back on the ground overlooking the huge sunken crater. 'I reckon Reggie me boy that the banshee queen freak has some help outside of these lands and it's not furry! I think there's human hands at play here but I don't know anybody in this area well enough anymore to guess who it is, that is if it's anyone that is local'.

'That is a most honest observation earth man'.

The shadow of Mil-Mil darkened the ground around where the two men sat. 'We have found all the conduits in the surrounding area, it is now time to focus on the wreckage of the house itself!'

Hugo looked up at Mil-Mil and sniggered in disbelief.

'Do you by any chance have a giant vacuum cleaner to sift through all of it? Your Spungle friend left more dust and splinters behind than wreckage and let's not forget to mention that a set of climbing gear and rope ladders would come in handy to search what's at the bottom of that bleedin crater!'

The dark Gikkie Bokker grabbed Hugo by the arm and placed him on his shoulders and jumped down into the sunken crater without uttering a word.

'Why ya mad bag of mongrel dog hair you could have killed me! That was over a hundred feet deep at least!'

There was a high pitched shriek of alarm high above and then Synar Chro landed alongside his brother and placed a terrified Reginold onto the ground.

'My good man would you kindly refrain from performing acrobatic endeavours with me attached to you, my lunch needs to be re digested because of it and believe me its most unpleasant a second time around my system I can assure you!'

The Aoes Shee warrior did not reply, instead they walked to opposite ends of the sunken crater and started to scout the area for leftover house wreckage large enough to conceal any of the Morgannis' conduit figures. Hugo squinted trying really hard to see through the rolling clouds of dust and powdered stone that covered the ground that they were all standing on.

'This is going to be impossible. That witch could have arranged for thousands of those statues to be all around us and we would still not be able to find them all!'

'Those who say that a task cannot be done should not hinder those who carry out the task, search or stay out of our way earth dweller!'

Hugo could see Synar's piercing gaze through the mist and cloud from over one hundred feet away scowling at him bitterly. Hugo smiled back sarcastically at the fuming Synar and started to randomly kick up plumes of dust and debris into the air with his stout hunting boots not at all convinced that anything that he was going to do would be of any help in finding more conduit figures. Reginold was more sincere in his efforts but after ten minutes he resigned himself to defeat.

'Pointless, absolutely pointless, my good fellows there is nothing else here that is worthy of our efforts, let's go home and have some tea, I am parched with all of this dust, far too much of it to see what's hidden'.

Synar and Mil-Mil looked over at each other from opposite ends of the crater floor pausing for a moment, then turned to face Hugo and Reginold and spoke into the humans minds taking the tired ex hunters by surprise with a powerfully spoken warning.

'PROTECT YOUR EARS!' Hugo quickly glanced around the crater

floor until he spotted Reginold fifty feet away in the mist locking his gaze in surprise and they both quickly covered their ears tightly with their hands.

A deep growling noise came from beneath their feet shaking up the dust and debris around them causing a ghostly echo around the enclosed crater walls. The growl morphed into an immensely loud howl for a few seconds causing the dust cloud to rotate and collect more debris as it began to circulate around the inside of the crater. Then there was a moment's pause when even with hands closed over their ears the men could sense that the Aoes Shee were breathing in to let out an even louder sound. A high pitched shriek like a falcon's cry pierced the dust, lifting the entire dense enveloping cloud of debris high into the air to be scattered far away from the crater in all directions. The intense piercing shriek ceased as soon as the massive dust cloud vanished over the crater walls leaving Hugo and Reginold speechless. The floor of the crater was in clear view now revealing dull moist earth decorated with grey boulders and most importantly four large piles of house wreckage partially embedded into the southern end of the craters wall.

The Aoes Shee spoke together again into the men's minds, sparing the humans any need to hear a sound with very sore eardrums.

'Hugo, Reginold! Follow us, we shall free the wreckage and you may search through it!'

Hugo wiped the dust from out of his eyes and massaged his ears briskly with his fingers grunting to himself.

'Well thanks very much, that's mighty considerate of ya, a bit more of an advance warning the next time ya bark that loud again wouldn't go amiss either!'.

Reginold took his glasses off which were shattered from the huge shriek and with a trembling hand placed them in his breast pocket.

'Not the most pleasant of experiences but at least we are closer to finishing our task!'

The old man staggered towards the embedded house wreckage with Hugo placing a supporting grip on his shoulder to prevent him from falling over. By the time the two men reached the wreckage the Aoes Shee brothers had dislodged the wreckage from all four mounds and were already sifting through the first two mounds themselves. After an hour of exhausting hauling and moving broken bits of masonry Hugo and Reginold sat down onto the ground and rested.

Synar and Mil-Mil gathered all of the conduit figures that they had found placing them into a single pile on top of a large mound of rubble left over from the houses destruction. They sniffed in disgust at the sight of the conduits but instead of destroying them immediately Hugo observed them pondering over what action to take.

'Why don't they destroy them now? I thought this was going to be straight forward?'

'I don't know Reggie they seem to be aware of something that we can't pick up, they don't look like they are in a talkative mood right now, best not to press them on anything, lets rest until we are needed!'

'Very well my good man, that's fine with me. I can't exert myself any further. I am not the man that I once was, but that amulet thingey must be working behind the scenes. I could not have done that amount of work even twenty years ago. I just might be taking a shine to it after all my boy'.

Reginold noticed that the Aoes Shee were looking at himself and Hugo, after a moment they spoke in unison directly into their minds but in a much softer manner this time.

'Step away from the conduits, we shall destroy them now but their combined power is concealing something from us, be on the ready for the unexpected!'

Reginold and Hugo quickly got to their feet and clenched their fists tightly preparing for a fight. Synar swiftly swung his left leg high above his head and forced his leg back down rapidly like the downward stroke of a mighty axe landing his talon armed foot on top of the pile of snarling Morgannis conduits. There was a huge crack of thunder and an explosion of jet black dust erupted from the crushed carcases of the once snarling statues. Everyone present expected an event near enough of this nature but nobody expected the remaining mound of rubble that was piled up there to start moving slowly. Mil-Mil Ulthu was poised to tear apart whatever was to come from out of the mound and flexed his body readying his talons and claws to unleash an unearthly wrath upon whatever he was about to encounter.

There was a groaning and deep moaning sound coming from what seemed to be underneath the mound. It was shaking loose the top pieces of loose rubble and broken slates and window frames of the mound. Synar readied himself and stood beside Mil-Mil readying himself to pounce at whatever emerged.

Just before the brothers leaped onto the mound Reginold ran in front of them blocking their attack. 'Please don't attack, I recognise those moans well enough, only two creatures moan like that in the whole world and I am the poor old sod unlucky enough to know them!'

The Aoes Shee looked puzzled but relented and stepped back from Reginold giving him space to take action. The old man stumbled around the base of the mounds remains carefully examining the base and homing in on the moaning sounds. A moment later he smiled and thrust his right arm deep into a mess of broken planks and rubble and pulled out a short stocky man with a bulbous nose and jet black hair who in turn was holding onto another man who was taller and of slimmer build. They both landed roughly in a clump on top of each other knocking over Reginold in the process. Hugo reached down and pulled a surprisingly cheerful Reginold back onto his feet.

'You may be sacked and incompetent beyond belief but I'm glad to know that your lazy hides are alive!'

The two men on the ground did not answer back but slowly sat up and rubbed their heads looking very disoriented.

Hugo remembered Yardal from his younger days with Reginold and reckoned that the other man was under Yardal's employment. He didn't like the guilty expressions on either of them. Before Hugo could open his mouth Synar grabbed both of the dazed men and held them high above his head sneering at them in disgust.

'I smell the dark magic off the both of you! You controlled the contraption that attacked us, let us see if you fare better in battle against us without it's help!'

'Now now don't be so hasty my man, they were never that quick off the mark on their best of days. They were more than likely hypnotised by the witch don't you think?'

Synar looked over at his brother who calmly nodded in agreement. He let their whimpering bodies fall to the ground roughly and walked off in disgust.

'Oim soreee we didunt meen to steer the monster, it made us do it. She is the scariest thing oive ever seen and she said she wud kill us if we didunt do her bidding!'

Hugo looked over at Reginold in surprise as his old mentor had a tear of pity in his eye looking at his servant. 'Now now my dear chap don't be upset. I have learned over the past few days the kind of evil that's afoot here, you will be very safe with me now my boy, don't fret our task is nearly done!'

Yardal stood up slowly and helped his servant Larrymond to his feet.

'Can we go back to yur old home sir? I want to bee az far awaye as oi can from here!'

Reginold embraced his head servant taking him by surprise. 'I'm sorry old bean, I changed for the worse over the years and let our friendship dwindle, forgive me. Let's start anew back in my old mansion!'

Hugo had never seen his old mentor as warm with anyone before but noticed that Yardal's companion Larrymond was getting gradually more unstable on his feet as time went on, and was staring blankly into space not taking any of what was happening on.

Mil-Mil approached Larrymond gently and looked deeply into the man's dazed gaze.

'Can you tell me all that you know? Share it with me, I can remove the pain from your memory, trust in us, we shall protect you both!'

Larrymond slowly refocused his eyes and returned the Aoes Shee warriors gaze with a quiet look of gratitude.

'Please, take the pain away. So much fear, I will tell you everything!' He leaned over Larrymond and extended his glowing eye stalks letting them brush over the exhausted man's face. Larrymond went limp as Mil-Mil gently caught the trembling man in his arms. Everyone focused on Mil-Mil who remained completely still. A shadow covered the whole crater bathing everything in so much darkness that the Aoes Shee' luminous eyes were the only thing visible. The air in the crater floor became ice cold and a dull grey mist rose from the soil giving some light for the humans to see a dim view of their surroundings. The mist swirled round forming a vortex around the humans and the Aoes Shee warriors then sank to the ground and swirled up again but this time only around the motionless Mil-Mil.

It rushed up and over the dark Gikkie Bokker's frame creating a rotating sphere about a man's height above his head. The sphere began to show a vision, a series of events that were happening through the eyes of a human, Reginold instantly recognised that the vision was of his former house on the hill before it was corrupted by magic into a demon. 'We are seeing through Larrymond's eyes, look Hugo there is Yardal!' Hugo nodded without saying anything, too engrossed in the spinning ball of mist displaying Larrymond Underling's memory.

'Yardal, Yardaaal! Where are you? I'm not putting up with your sense of humour anymore. I am scared, lonely, sore and tired. No job is worth this. You are a strange-strange strange man. Did you put something in my drink? Do you hear me Yardal? Stop this messing. You can tell the boss why I am going. I'm leaving!'

The sphere of mist showed Larrymond looking around for Yardal who had vanished and then to everyone's horror the carpet underneath Larrymond undulated and swallowed him whole sinking him into blackness.

'Yurr not quitting on meeee yet old bean, har har har! We are in this together!'

Yardal's voice was menacing coming out from the darkness but he did not show himself. Hugo stood dumbstruck at the vision unfolding before him. 'So that's what happened to them while we were wrapping things up with Vrool after the soldiers invaded!'

'Silence Hugo! Mil-Mil must not be disturbed!' Commanded Synar grimly. The vision showed through Larrymond's eyes was vivid and stark, he was free falling in utter darkness with manic laughter echoing around him until a horrible voice pierced the nothingness.

'The selfish nature of man is setting me free. So easy are they to manipulate with promises of wealth and abundance. The world is now mine to rule once more! No one can stand in my way! The realm of the dead shall rise up and reclaim its rightful property, the souls of all human kind on earth!'

The vision then showed Yardal materialising a few feet from Larrymond's view hissing and laughing with a set of fangs and a slithering tongue like a monitor lizard but the ghastly features faded quickly until Yardal was his normal self and as soon as his mouth became normal he screamed in terror.

'It took me Larrymond, it's trying to teach me to be evil, to do things, please! Oim all riot now, please help me!' They both tumbled into nothingness accompanied by a shrieking crone like voice.

'Dim witted idiots! You are too weak to contain the powers I can grant you, still you can serve me. I have ways to make use of you yet but enough of you both for now, get out of my sight slime!'

The vision vanished from the rotating sphere of mist but the voice remained although much fainter.

'You will be its eyes, you will be its fists, you will enforce my will through its strength, leave no soul alive, we make war upon the surface and you shall be my Generals!'

Mil-Mil opened his eyes and set Larrymond down into the arms of Yardal who supported him gently onto his feet.

'Well thank god that she thought that you two were not up to the job of getting super evil powers whatever they would have been! I will take you back to Reginold's old mansion in Dublin once we have finished here, come on lads, time to head home!'

Hugo slapped Mil-Mil playfully on the back but got a stern glance from the Aoes Shee warrior who then ignored him and walked over to Synar Chro.

'We must return to the temple my brother! Our foe is far more advanced in her plans to wage war and she does not intend to strike solely at our realm. She is going to strike at the realm of earth as well!' Synar Chro closed his eyes and attempted to reach his father through the dark ether but could not find his presence.

'She is in motion right now, we must leave here immediately! Be thankful that you are alive after being in the service of the Morgannis, you are not leaving with Hugo! We have need of everyone right now and you shall redeem yourselves by sharing everything that you know to our father at the temple!'

The floor of the crater became clear as all the mist vanished but it left all the soil and stones covered in a coating of clear slippery slime that smelled of rotten meat, while the crater floor itself began to tremble from a loud voice from above.

'Alas for you my Aoes Shee puppets this is the last place that you shall reside! Say goodbye to your father! I shall send him to your tomb once I have slayed him and your self-righteous mother!'

Directly over the surprised men and Aoes Shee floated the pale apparition of the Morgannis. 'And as for you Hugo son of Henry! Die in the knowledge that your world and all you hold dear in it is next!'

The Banshee shimmered into thin air with a mocking laugh as the crater floor cracked and vibrated violently. Mil-Mil Ulthu and Synar Chro used their massive frames to encircle the humans to provide protection from the earth quake, in the hope that it would pass quickly. But amidst the rumbling the faint drone of the Morgannis chanted in ancient curses echoing around the high walls of the crater.

'How can she reappear? We have destroyed every single one of the conduits, this is it then, she has outsmarted us again! And for the last time! She has won!'

Hugo looked up at Synar and Mil-Mil who both returned his stare and most surprisingly in spite of what was happening smiled at him.

'May you meet death swiftly and with honour if this is to be your end heir of Alastair!'

Hugo felt a lump in his throat doing his best to keep his composure, none of the Aoes Shee had smiled at him before and it felt that at last he was accepted by them which filled his heart with joy.
'Thanks my friends, maybe now I will be able to have that pint with my dad after all!'

He closed his eyes shut as the rumbling turned into a deafening roar drowning out the screams of fright and shock of his human companions.

'Dad! I'm coming home!'

The crater floor violently collapsed with a huge unearthly crack sending thousands of tons of soil, rock and boulders hurtling down into a gaping hole that sucked all of the light into it masking any sign of any living thing that was once there.

Chapter Ten - Lead astray

The Gikkie Bokker Mountain Temple seemed so small and far away in the distance. None of the Gikkie Bokker younglings had ever been this far away from home despite being all highly adventurous characters in their own right.

The familiar marshy swamp and tropical forests that they played around every day was fading away leading onto a large plain of tall golden grass that went on nearly as far as they could see. Fluke-Fluke could just barely make out the hint of a wide forest at its end but guessed that it would be at least a day's travel to see it in more detail.

'Where are we Jele-Nai? What is all this yellow grass? It looks way too neat to be growing wild!'

Jele-Nai did not respond immediately. She was too busy observing her surroundings and mapping a path in her mind in case she decided to make a break and run for it.

'This is all your fault scruff bag, don't come looking to me for help when they put you in the trials!'

Fluke-Fluke sighed and lowered his head wishing that the time would fly by so at least they could look at something other than tall grass. A little hand gently held his caringly taking him by surprise.

'Don't be minding her Flukey Wukey she can be really mean sometimes!'

It was Tweakle-Ponk, his friend Spongly-Mok's sister. She always had a way of making him feel better about himself when Jele-Nai got into a foul humour.

'I heard that Tweakle-Ponk. It is his fault, he is useless, and do you want me to show you how mean I can be?'

Jele-Nai broke rank and marched over to Tweakle-Ponk towering over her in anger. 'Leave her alone you lanky plank of misery!' Spongley-Mok darted in between the two female younglings jutting his chest out and huffing and puffing to show how serious he was.

'Enough little ones, cease your quarrelling!' Everyone went silent. Zarn Hurad took off his golden helmet and placed it over his shoulder resting it onto an extendable shelf that jutted slightly out from behind his armoured neck then turned around to look down upon the younglings. *Cool!* Fluke-Fluke thought to himself, he loved the Aoes Shee warriors armour, dreaming of one day becoming one of the elite guard.

'I appoint this hour as resting time!' Zarn unsheathed a small silver dagger from his left leg and drove it blade first into the ground in front of them creating a startling yelp from Fluke-Fluke and Tweakle-Ponk.

'You have till the shadow on the side of the blade moves around to the side facing me! That's not long so make use of the time little ones!' He sat down in front of them legs crossed and stared up at the moon. Everyone was silent as they saw Zarn's face fully now. His right eye was covered with a silver eye patch that was securely fastened to a silver head band that had a vertical strut behind his head that fastened itself to the rest of his golden body armour. His cheeks had two deep scars on either side of his face piercing his golden fur.

'Forgive me, my appearance has startled you. Let it be a reminder to you that even in our lands danger can appear from out of nowhere! However let me also warn you that my apologies shall cease once we reach the youngling tree city, for it is there that your training shall begin!'

'How? How did you get those injuries?' Gulped Tweakle-Ponk nervously.

'Fiends little one! All thought to have vanished long ago yet two of them mauled me! If it was not for Jele-Nai's father Vraarl Uldunjen they would have quickly eaten me before I had become immortal!'

The younglings froze, captivated by Zarn's tale. The Aoes Shee guardian leaned closer to the younglings menacingly.

'Do you know what happens when a Gikkie Bokker youngling is killed before it ascends to immortality?'

Fluke-Fluke shook his head so rapidly in fear that Jele-Nai smacked him on the back of the head to calm him down but even she was feeling a nervous cramp in her tummy, she never knew that younglings could be killed but she was the first to respond.

No I don't! What happens to them?'
'Well!' Sighed Zarn as he slowly rose to his full height and placed his golden armoured helmet back on.

'Its soul is lost and it wanders aimlessly like a headless bird unable to return to its body!'
'That's not so bad, I'd love to be able to be invisible and move through

walls and the like!' retorted Jele-Nai defiantly.

'That is only the beginning fiery one! Once slayed, your soul is like a beacon of purity, attracting evil from all around. The Morgannis will feel your presence quickly and will seek you out herself, and then…'

He paused for effect knowing full well that he had them all engrossed. 'Your living soul is used to power a master fiend, the most deadly of all the creations of the Morgannis. Now you become the living dead, not only suffering eternal pain but also fully knowing that you are powerless to resist her commands as you attack your own kind, trapped in a hideous body... for eternity!'. He looked directly at Fluke-Fluke.

The little youngling gasped in terror. Tweakle-Ponk and Spongley-Mok huddled around Fluke-Fluke to comfort him while Jele-Nai scoffed.

'You are just yapping your trap to scare us all, try another story I'm bored already!'

Jele-Nai got up and walked past Zarn quickly but as soon as she passed him she did her best to hide a whimper of fear deep inside her while the huge guardian gruffly bellowed out an order.

'Our time is over, we march on!'
Spongley-Mok's belly rumbled as he stood up as if in protest.

'We just got here! And what about something to eat? I'm starving, just cause your immortal and don't need food and water, did ya bring anything to eat for us?'
Zarn marched onwards ahead of them observing a strange trail parallel to their own.

'Your next meal is in the youngling tree city so march quicker and your belly shall be satisfied unless you feel like chewing on the grass all around you, and you are most welcome to it all!'

The march was quiet save for their footsteps and the light fresh wind sweeping the golden blades of grass into gently undulating waves, but as time marched on the younglings witnessed something that they had never seen before.

Fluke-Fluke noticed the moonlight fading away slowly but instead of darkness engulfing the land ahead of them, the moon light was replaced by an evening sunlight which made the golden grass become almost a rusty bronze.

'I thought that the sun never shined in our realm! How is this possible?' 'It is possible because we are not in our realm anymore! We have cut across into neutral territory which cuts days from our travel! The curse of Terun-nill-vath-doom does not affect this place little one!'

'It's beautiful! I wish I knew about this place before, we could have so much fun playing out here!'

Zarn marched determinedly ahead but Fluke-Fluke noticed that he was looking from side to side in a distracted manner.

'These fields are hunting grounds for creatures that crave youngling flesh! We find our way through here and with my guidance you shall remain unharmed! But you will pass through these fields soon enough without me as one of your trials!'

Jele-Nai interrupted them.

'You have got to be joking me! I'm headin back to the temple, you're out of your one eyed mind, cumon guys let's go!'

'Wait! Be still!'

Everyone froze in their tracks. The younglings could not notice anything other than the monotonous sound of the grass swishing all around them. Zarn corralled everyone into a circle and he paced around them slowly.

'Vrool, of all the times to do this why did you choose to have me escort younglings now?' He muttered to himself.

A dark shadow launched itself in a blur directly at Zarn's head knocking him off his feet causing the younglings to scatter in all directions away from the fight. By the time Fluke-Fluke had refocused to see what was attacking Zarn he saw his fiery companion Jele-Nai balancing on top of a dark shape that was furiously pummelling the Gikkie Bokker Guardian. The claws on her long fingers were fully extended and she was slashing viciously at the strange dark creature causing it to moan and roar in a deep guttural frenzy. Zarn took advantage of the distraction grabbing the dark attacker and rolling backwards sending the creature hurtling over his head along with Jele-Nai who growled in frustration at being flung unexpectedly off the attacker and into the featureless grass. The Gikkie Bokker guardian rolled back onto his feet and unsheathed a huge silver sword and leapt into the grass after the creature and Jele-Nai vanishing from sight.

Fluke-Fluke darted straight after them but skidded to a halt as he heard Tweakle-Ponk let out a cry of pain. He swiftly changed direction and ran off towards the sound amidst the deep growls of an ongoing battle and collided with Spongley-Mok head on leaving both skidding along the ground in a daze. They quickly got up and ran side by side towards the sound and ran out into a small clearing in the grass and were grabbed by the neck by a set of dark shiny hands lifting them high off the ground.

The two younglings could not help but lock eyes with the creature who stared back at them. The hairless face was human in shape but deathly pale with faded almost white eyeballs and a dark protruding jaw with black lips and wolf's fangs. But the face was the only human like feature of the creature, the body resembled an upright cockroach but with four arms and two clawed legs very much like a Gikkie Bokker. The creature examined them closely and hissed at them in contempt but was distracted by a noise below its feet.

Fluke-Fluke looked down at the creature's clawed feet and saw Tweakle-Ponk pinned to the ground in pain and powerless to escape. The beast looked back up at Fluke-Fluke and gave him a filthy smile.

Two jagged swords slid out from its two hind arms and poised themselves to stab the two younglings with Tweakle-Ponk underneath roaring in defiance.

The younglings closed their eyes in despair and heard a deep booming thump and felt themselves falling to the earth but they never made contact with the ground. Too much time had passed for them to be slain and they opened their eyes slightly to see what had happened.

Zarn was standing over them with a youngling in each hand and the lifeless body of the dark creature underneath his clawed feet with a triumphant Jele-Nai standing on the beasts head trying to pull Zarn's massive sword out of the beast's body. Nothing was spoken for some minutes till the younglings could catch their breath and oddly to them Zarn did not speak either. Jele-Nai finally managed to dislodge Zarn's sword from the creature's body and handed it back to him.

'If that's one of the tests I'm gone! I'd rather take my chances doubling back on ourselves than go any further!'

Zarn quietly accepted his sword back with a look of concern.

'This was not a test, my test was going to be far less harsh and only intended to shake you all out of complacency. This my young ones... Is a Fiend! And a new faster more powerful breed at that! You are lucky that you are all alive!'

Fluke-Fluke wriggled free of Zarn's grip and dropped to the earth and examined the carcass. On closer inspection he could make out that the beast had a shiny beetle like body protected by multiple plates of black iron with spikes jutting out from random angles and the arms and legs were supported by what looked like slimy dark vines wrapping around the limbs acting like sinews and muscles. The head had a strange cage like helmet only protecting the back part of the skull and even though the creature was dead he could hear a slow hissing of steam coming from inside the body.

'It smells like its rotting, urrgh! Disgusting!'

'Fluke-Fluke they are born rotting and never stop! The only thing that delays their decay is an infusion of dark magic by the agents of the Morgannis to repair the devices inside them that provide locomotion!'

Jele-Nai spat at the carcass in contempt.

'They are cyborgs then! That's awesome, lets open one up and have a look see!'

Zarn held her back from the remains and turned to pick up Tweakle-Ponk placing her onto his massive shoulder.

'You did well little one to have lasted so long in the clutches of this thing but where one fiend lurks an army is never far away! Let me carry you all till we reach the borders of An Ghlean glas den saol, you have suffered enough this day!'

The rest of the younglings eagerly jumped onto his back and held on tightly as Zarn adjusted his posture to run on his four arms and two legs so the group could nest in the cradle of space created along his back by his huge shoulders.

'I thought all the fiends were slain long ago, this doesn't make sense! My granddad told me stories about them!'

'Fluke-Fluke we can reminisce about why it was here or you can merge your thoughts with your grandfather right now and tell him yourself! Your link to him is strongest!'

'Why can't you merge with him? We all have the gift and this is an emergency!'

They all found themselves hanging on more tightly as Zarn accelerated swiftly through the featureless grass with surprisingly little noise.

'Because something is blocking my merging! Vrool should already know that we are in danger and have made his presence known to all of us but I feel nothing and I did not sense the fiend until it was far too late! Something is horribly wrong here!'

There was a dark liquid gurgling chant echoing in the distance that unsettled the younglings. Fluke-Fluke did his best to hold on bouncing up and down along with his companions as Zarn accelerated so fast that the wind swept Tweakle-Ponk backwards along Zarn's back and into Fluke Fluke's arms. He felt a tickle of awkwardness and embarrassment as their eyes met but had to quickly reposition her to his side to prevent her from sliding completely of Zarn's back while Jele-Nai climbed over Spongley-Mok to get closer to Zarn's head to speak with him.

'Their coming after us aren't they?'

His eyes darted briefly over to her acknowledging the question.

'Yes!'

'How far?'

'Maybe a thousand gallops and closing!' The awful gurgling chant was getting much louder now.

'What can I do?'

'These fiends are fast, much faster than I remember, they will reach us before the start of the forest valley. I will confront them and you must escort your friends to safety. We shall reach a nest of underground caves in less than one hundred gallops. I shall leave you there. Follow the small stream in the caves and it will lead you out to the edge of this grass plateau. There is a large drop down to the valley so be careful, I will reach you as soon as I can. Prepare them! We are nearly upon it!'

Jele-Nai shimmied down Zarn's back and wrapped herself around her three companions in a protective arch to their surprise.

'We are going to leave now on Zarn's orders, trust me! On my mark let go of Zarn's armour and tumble with me into the grass!'

'You're mad Jele-Nai! I'm going nowhere!'

'Spongley! Just do as I say or we will all die!'

Spongley-Mok gulped with fear and went quiet.

She looked at Fluke-Fluke and Tweakle-Ponk.

'Ready yourselves!'

As she spoke a group of twenty dark shapes burst out from the blur of grass directly behind them gurgling and panting furiously to close in on Zarn and his companions. The younglings screamed in terror at the ghastly forms but had no time to catch their breaths as Zarn deliberately bucked causing the younglings to hurtle high into the air and back over behind the dark pack of ravenous fiends. Fluke-Fluke tumbled out of control, spinning and twisting in the air by instinct to right himself before he collided with the ground, but Spongley-Mok and Tweakle-Ponk had panicked and broken loose from Jele-Nai's grip and bumped off him sending him into a harsh skidding tumble along the sharp grass. There was a few moments that all of the younglings could not account for as they slowly came too.

Fluke-Fluke could hear the fiends still in pursuit off in the distance but could not focus his vision properly. He could hear the muffled sound of his companions moaning and grunting but could not respond yet. As he tried to stand up he saw the shape of Jele-Nai helping Spongley-Mok and Tweakle-Ponk to their feet in a small clearing of a path made by the galloping fiends. He could barely make out that they were talking amongst themselves.

'It's here somewhere! Zarn told me that we would be right on it, keep looking but keep your voices down!'

'What's the opening supposed to look like? There is no sign of anything other than grass and it's getting dark now!'

'For the last time Tweakle-Ponk keep your yap quiet, just because we can't hear them doesn't mean that they are gone!'

'What about Zarn? Do you think that they killed them?'
'I don't know. I was only told tales of the battles that used to take place all over here. I've never even seen an Aoes Shee fight before. I don't know what they can or cannot do, let's hope he managed to outrun them. I think we will be safe enough once we do what he asked of us.... Aha! There it is, right under our noses. Look - you wouldn't in a thousand years think that you could hide it so well with just...Wait! What's that awful noise?'

A dark shape burst out of the grass and leaped high into the air over the younglings and extended its dark slimy arms towards them.

Fluke-Fluke felt himself helplessly slip back into total blackness.

Chapter Eleven – A deadly diversion

Vrool materialised out onto the bay and immediately broke into a blinding sprint leaping over huge areas of swampy marsh and small islands littering the stout lakes. He could make out the magic aura of the Spungle long departed from the area and roared in frustration.

'Eireannos! Why do you hide from yourself? We need you!'

He then concentrated deeply and reached out to Shard his queen.

'My love!' She answered back immediately.

'Yes my King, I have felt it. We are being taunted on multiple fronts, being toyed with until she is ready to make her primary attack. I could not sense you out in the earth dwellers realm, come quickly I sense more deception afoot'.

'Mil-Mil and Synar shall return soon after they cleanse the Bay of Morgannis conduits and have arranged to meet with the Heratii refugees. I suggest that we postpone our spell creation and go seek Eireannos ourselves. We are too weak to complete them until he is present. Are we agreed my Queen?'

'Yes my love, I will call for Vraarl Uldenjen to take command of our temple until we both return. I shall meet you at the entrance path to the Spungle village, come quickly'.

Vrool bounded one last time clearing an entire stout lake and landed onto the shoreline of the awaiting forest path leading up towards his realm. Sprinting on six limbs up the path he prepared to clear the plateau leading to the Gikkie Bokker ornate gardens and was taken off his feet by a concussive explosion sending him reeling backwards off the plateau and back down onto the end of the forest path. He picked himself up off the ground and refocused his vision. The only noise was the echoing of the explosion and he could smell the explosive devices of earth dwellers. The same smell as when the battle between the Spungle and Drakes army had taken place.

Human explosive weapons! He cursed to himself.

'How is this possible? None remain, I saw to the task myself!'

He peered over the last step on the path to the plateau to locate the attacker. He could see and sense nothing. What troubled him most was not sensing any life presence at all. No entity living or dead was beyond his detection in his realm. The echo of the explosion had gone and only the familiar gentle breeze through the forest below him and the singing of its creatures remained. He stood fully upright and breathed in the life energy all around him. The explosive stains on his sacred clothing vanished and he prepared himself to walk straight into view of whatever had attacked him. The moment he placed his foot onto the plateau in front of him a huge boom ruptured the air around him and another concussive blast hit his body full on obscuring his body in dark cloud and fire. But this time the King was ready and stepped out of the fog of the diminishing explosion without a mark and judged the location of the attacker by sensing the angle and height of the projectile that struck him He charged directly in front of him at a speed so great that he cleared half the distance to the end of the plateau in a second and collided with a massive invisible obstacle sending a deep shocking impact into his body. In a tenth of a second the King spotted ripples of a shape in the air in front of him and, judging the shape and size in his mind he regained his footing, and leaped over the object while somersaulting at the full height of his leap slashing with all four of his claws and the talons on his feet. His attack caused a deafening buzzing hum and a discharge of blue electrical energy from the invisible object below him.

As he landed gently the object appeared slowly and awkwardly out of a haze of electrical arcs and black smoke. It had the form of a tank similar to Drakes forces but was painted in a reflective black casing and had a crown of strange antennae around the circumference of the turret. Vrool had sliced through most of the antennae which seemed to be rendering the tank invisible to him moments before and the front of the tank was bashed in from his head on collision with it. The turret did move however and swung its cannon directly at him discharging another round. He reached out one of his hands and deflected the tank shells explosion directly back at it causing the entire chassis of the vehicle to explode apart into fist sized chunks of molten metal. As soon as the vehicle was blown apart he could sense a group of ten humans behind the wreckage running swiftly towards the end of the plateau hoping to reach the cover of the first level of the Gikkie Bokker gardens.

All he could feel was a sense of outrage at this unprovoked attack and the King of the Aoes Shee roared so loud it shook the earth below the attackers lifting them off their feet causing them to fall heavily onto the ground unconscious.

The King approached cautiously towards the nearest human. The human was dressed in a strange reflective black suit with a much smaller set of antennae similar to the tanks forming a crown on top of its helmet which resembled an ants head. He pulled off the human's helmet revealing a dazed young man staring back at him. Vrool could not sense the man's thoughts with his mind, he reached out to the other humans and they all felt the same, empty and hollow and dark.

What is this? He spoke to himself in frustration. The young man came to and looked into Vrool's piercing eyes and instinctively reached for his sidearm and pointed it at Vrool's face.

'Pull the trigger human if you think it will serve you to escape! I guarantee it will only assure you swift passage to the afterlife!'

The young man gulped and dropped his hand gun refusing to meet Vrool's gaze. A distant lion like roar signalled that the Aoes Shee guardians at the temple had now detected Vrool's plight and were closing in on his location.

'My love I am at the Spungle village and shall await your presence. I sensed the battle, remove the helmets from all of the humans, I suspect something!'

Vrool slung the dazed young man over his shoulder like a rag doll and walked over to the two humans nearest him and removed their helmets while the Kings two Aoes Shee guardians arrived. He ordered them to remove the remaining human's helmets.

'My Queen, what do you sense?' He looked over at the remaining human prisoners who were still unconscious.

'Allow a few moments to pass, focus on the human's hearts, not their minds. It will come!' He peered into the energy that the human's hearts were emitting. 'They are trapped! Yes I sense it now! Once the helmets are removed their thoughts and minds start to slowly return to normal. What manner of trickery is being played out against us? These are just pawns delaying us yet again!'

He dropped the young man onto the ground and examined the uniform that he was wearing. The only visible detail on the man's clothing was a white triangular breast patch with an eye in the middle and the initials B, M and H along the sides of the triangle.

Vrool's face looked upon the symbol and he grimaced in disgust.

'My Queen, they have returned!'

He ripped the patch of the man's uniform and turned to his Aoes Shee guardians and commanded them to bring the humans to the temple for interrogation and sped off without a word towards the Spungle village to meet with Shard.

'My love no matter how many of them are here and what they intend to do we cannot let it interfere with finding the Spungle and reasoning with him to reclaim his true self! We shall deal with the intruders when the time is right, our land can be hostile enough to the unwary, visible or not, this alone may hinder their plans long enough for us to catch up with them as time allows!'

'Yes my love! I sense the Spungles rage even from here, he knows of the human's presence as well, we may meet him sooner than we think! Stay put I am only moments away from you!'

He skirted around the borders of the first level of the Gikkie Bokker gardens with tremendous speed running up onto the boundary wall so quickly that he ran horizontally along it for over a hundred yards then leaped off the end of it vanishing into a sharp dip in the forest terrain.

Shard could now see her King appearing out of the dense tree line off away to her west at the top of the lush forest valley. He moved so swiftly the trees bent and swayed from the wake of his sprint. He spotted her and with one final leap cleared the valley descent and landed directly in front of her.

'They are so brazen they bare the mark of their order with no intent of concealment! Look!' He showed her the crest of the human that he had ripped of his uniform.

'They return my love at a time to crucial to be merely a coincidence! That's why I beckoned you to help me locate the Spungle, it will be our greatest task to awaken him but also our greatest reward, come! We must not delay any longer!'

'I do not sense my sons! Nor Fluke-Fluke or Zarn, or any of our younglings, her cloak of darkness extends everywhere!'

'Now you know what is like to be human! Even for a little while, my King, and yet they still manage to accomplish great things despite being unable to see all. Have faith in all of yourself as a whole entity not just one of your many senses!'

She ran off on all six limbs and he followed her swiftly down into the valley towards the path to the village of their once loyal ally.

Chapter Twelve - Refuge

'My lord! Our King encountered these intruders and left them with us for interrogation!'

Vraarl Uldunjen eyed the bound humans with contempt but became curious when he attempted to read their minds. Any human that he had ever came in contact with would have a very erratic and excited mind from seeing an Aoes Shee warrior, particularly him. Almost as large as Vrool and with a hauntingly fierce face he was a ferocious site to behold. However, these humans had a very weak and calm thought pattern. As he looked into them deeper he could only notice little trivial things.

When will we get fed? What time are we going to be released? When can I get my side arm back and go home?

No matter how deeply he probed he could find nothing else and they did not react at all to his psychic probing. He rose from his meditation seat and walked over to them.

'Kurn! Bralnar! You have done well, leave them alone with me!'
He stared for a moment looking at each one intently, then detected the leader and fixed the dazed young man's gaze.

'What have you done with the younglings? Answer me or you shall remain here till you waste away!'

The man lowered his gaze from Vraarl and just stood still along with the rest of his companions. Their hands were bound with steel rope leaving their feet free to walk around yet they made no attempt to move at all.

I cannot interrogate these fools until I consult with my queen, they are liable to die under my questioning. He sighed and sat back down onto his seat. Ignoring the motionless humans, he blocked out the arched meditation chamber that he was sitting in and the silver room faded away into blackness. He searched for his queen.

'I cannot get answers from these earth dwellers. Even if I were to harm them, their minds have been tampered with, so I shall keep them locked away until you return'.

'Thank you Vraarl! You are the only one that I have been able to reach from the temple! We shall be some time negotiating with the Spungle upon finding him and it may still go very ill, but I am thankful that you can reach us. Have Synar-Chro and Mil Mil-Ulthu returned from their mission?'

'No my queen, only Kurn and Bralnar with Vrool's captives'.
'Please take Kurn and Bralnar with you and meet with the Heratii refugees. See to it that they have more provisions but also spend the evening with them and learn more about what is exactly the nature of their plight. Be on your guard! The Morgannis energy is everywhere'.

'Yes my queen! Does my king have any orders for me?'
'Awaken the rest of our Aoes Shee warriors! The Morgannis has moved on multiple fronts against us. Her primary attack is imminent!'

'But they are not ready to do battle! They are still weak from the battle of Terun! As are the Siabhra!'
'We are all weakened, awaken them none the less! Otherwise we may not get a second chance to summon them! Once awakened double the

guard on the entrance to the Morgannis Tomb and send word to the Siabhra as well! We cannot sense them at all!'

'I can get to Maeve of the Siabhra right after I consult with the Heratii. The Heratii camp is only half a day's march from the blue river'.

'Very well Vraarl! Reach out to us if even the smallest issue is amiss!'
'Yes my King! I already move!'

He marched out of the meditation room, locked the solid silver door behind him and beckoned Kurn and Bralnar to come with him. They marched down to the armoury area and equipped themselves with scouting battle armour and exited the small building structure out onto a large courtyard that fell under the soft shadow of the massive magical spire overlooking everything below it.

'Why only scouting armour my lord?'
'We must not alarm the Heratii refugees, the armour is just a precaution. We won't need anything heavier than light scout armour to tackle what comes our way if anything'.

Dozens of Gikkie Bokker younglings hurried around oblivious to the huge warriors and gingerly darted out of their way. They carried on with their daily task of delivering shining buckets of magical liquid, that they processed in the ornate gardens, taking it up into the spire building at the top of the Mountain Temple.

Vraarl looked down on the youngling Gikkie Bokkers with envy and admiration.

I wish I could go back to being like them, a life of nothing but joy and playfulness.

Vraarl and his escorts marched out of the courtyard and down a large meandering flight of stone steps. It lead into a ceremonial tunnel decorated with bronze statues of Siabhra warriors in battle poses, down onto a large spiralling staircase that could fit a small deployment of warriors. After a swift descent the base of the staircase opened out to a huge descending bridge road of white stone, pointing like an arrow towards the Spungle Village and beyond that the Selfin mountains which overlooked the Siabhra realm. Two Aoes Shee warriors stood guard at the mouth of the bridge. 'Lidana and Orofey! Leave your posts and awaken our sleeping army, our King and Queen command it so!'
The guards answered in unison proudly. 'Yes my lord'.

Vraarl and his escorts moved past the departing guards and emerged into the open. They readied themselves, looking back at the towering mountain temple one last time before they departed for duty.

Its lush green forests were decorated by faint glowing orbs of light from Gikkie Bokker younglings carrying the glowing stout from the lakes and gardens and a melodious chime carried itself through the air refreshing the spirits of even the weary. They sprinted now, the battle hardened warrior and his escorts racing down the long stone bridge.

They eventually descended onto a level plain of glowing gardens that ended in a white stone cliff face which, they leaped off landing far below on the forest valley floor.

Racing along tirelessly they passed the Spungle Valley and detected the residual energy from their King and Queen who had already made their way deeper into the Spungles domain. The time passed by quickly for them. Every feature of the land they sped through was imprinted into them from ceaseless marches through every crevice of it. So much so, that their journey was more trance like than lucid. They stopped suddenly after spotting a huge dark mass of Heratii refugees off in the distance much sooner than expected. Vraarl signalled for his escorts to crouch behind a large boulder while he leaped into a tall densely covered pine tree to examine the creatures. Hundreds of miles nearer than expected, they had obviously left the Brittle Valley encampment and had made their way past the Siabhra City. Marching slowly across the Siabhra Vale towards the blue river they seemed to be swelling in numbers like a plague of dark Ants on the march. Vraarl dropped from the tree and conferred with his escorts.

'The Siabhra did not even send a messenger to us about these beings, this is not in keeping with their ways!'

'My lord should we return to the temple and warn our forces?'
'No Bralnar, it's best to meet them head on before they reach the river. We confront the Head of their order and ask them to go no further until they have explained themselves. Besides, our forces are only awakening. They won't be ready - even against a minor attack!'

'Shall we hold back and provide cover for you my lord?'
'It is not necessary Kurn. Look at them, misshapen and awkward, there must be thousands of females and children amongst them. I prefer

openness and an honest conversation. We shall politely greet them. March with me now!'

Vraarl moved swiftly down the cliff face with his escorts skidding down the steep decline and stopped just short of the banks of An Gorm Abhainn - the Blue River. They swam underneath the swiftly flowing surface of the water and emerged on the far side of the river bank in minutes. Slowly emerging from the water, they gauged the distance between the massing Heratii and themselves to be around a thousand yards. They walked slowly forward with their weapons sheathed.

The dark mass of refugees slowly trod onwards in their direction, featureless and grim. Vraarl gestured for his escorts to stop.

'There is no point in approaching any further, I cannot begin to guess where their leader is. Let's wait for them to approach us!'

Minutes passed and the Siabhra vales golden pastures darkened under the shadow of the refugees. The massing dark collective reached the Aoes Shee warriors but instead of stopping they walked past them silently with stooping frames and bowed heads covered in featureless black robes. No part of the creatures was visible and there was no hint of speech or even breathing from them. Kurn looked sideways at Vraarl and Bralnar with a puzzled look. Masses of the refugees silently walked around the Aoes Shee warriors with no regard for their presence.

'People! Who is your leader? I must speak with him!'

There was no response, the dark shapes kept moving past them quietly.

'You are passing through lands that are not safe, we seek an audience to help you! We are not your enemy!'

From out of the dark masses limped a tall but huddled over figure equal to Vraarl's great height. The creature gave out a quiet slurring drawling set of mumbles that Vraarl could not understand. Seemingly frustrated at its attempt to speak, it composed itself once more and with slow but muddled gestures it seemed to him to be trying to force itself to speak aloud.

'Yurr place is dear to yuu!'

'I beg pardon of you friend, please speak again, I am unclear of your message'.

Silence passed between the Aoes Shee warrior and the creature. It breathed in deeply and seemed to be forcing the words out.

'Wu-eeee seeek home, du yuu have home?'

'Yes we have a home! And where is your home?'

'Umme... landz ov mist beeyund vallee ov daggurs, takin ovur, tall wumun, nize ad furst... bad latur, turn peepole straange, life brokin, saad, want frieend, need home, safety!'

It pointed to the smallest of the dark figures slowly shuffling along in a hopeless looking stupor. Even the battle hardened Vraarl felt his hearts sink with sadness.

'None are safer than in the Siabhra City, why do you ignore it?'

'Sense eveeil there! Not saafe! No evil frum yuuu! Bee friend, stay with friend! Heart! Inside… Know yuuu kind! Friend! For my children!'

The Aoes Shee Commander was brought back to memories of when he and his kind were imprisoned by humans before Hugo's ancestor Alastair had freed them. The refugees plight was far worse. Vast numbers of dazed dark figures stumbling along from an unknown land, he could feel the suffering in them like it was a living thing leeching onto them.

'My friend, our home is not ready for you! I am sorry! But because of your plight I can be of help to you! Look beyond the river!'

He pointed towards the winding pathways leading up to the Selfin mountain range.

'These mountains are neutral territory and are dwelled in by no race. There is abundant food and shelter in its forests and streams of clear water for you!'

The entire dark robed mass of refugees looked up all at once towards the mountains.

'Yuu make saafe? No tall wumun there?'
'No tall woman there my friend! Please stay there and camp with me for the evening, we must talk further. I wish to know of the... tall woman!'

'Yur maakin self bright und happeee, we stay in friendlee mountains, must move there now, will settle and talk with yuu there!'

'Agreed my friend, I will assist you in making camp!'
He turned and smiled in relief at Bralnar and Kurn.

'Go back to the Temple and arrange for all of our Gikkie Bokker younglings to assist us here. Ask them to bring provisions in our stores for making camp and food. They will need to bring a pack of Fíochmhar steeds with them to carry everything. Hurry now as we need to return to the Temple. If the Morgannis is on the move we cannot leave these refugees unprotected, at least in these mountains they have half a chance until time allows us to return to them!'

'My lord what of the Siabhra? If this creature senses evil from their domain should we not investigate?'

'Bralnar our vision is compromised. The Morgannis has found a way to infect the dark ether void in which we communicate. If the Siabhra are in distress then we shall need our total force to come and help them. If we go as we are then we would be overwhelmed. Best to bring these creatures to safety then regroup with our King and Queen, once they have returned from speaking with the Spungle creature!'

'Yes my lord, be careful. We shall be back soon!'

Bralnar and Kurn raced off through the dark masses of refugees.

At least these creatures are not the hostile force that I feared, its days like these that I am most thankful for.

Vraarl turned to speak with the leader of the Heratii and assess what needed to be done to make camp.

'My guards shall return soon with help and provisions and a means to make shelter from the elements, what is your name friend?'

'Shlaar! Shlaar Spirinos! I am head of my kind, thanks be with you fur help yuu give!'

'As much as need drives me to be elsewhere I cannot let your people dwell by the river - these lands are no longer safe. The Siabhra City is however very safe, what is this evil that you sense there when even I sense nothing?'

'Seee de evil - Nooo! It is hiding from my eyes, siteee is in danger, I feel the tall wumun, shee is laughing! Like shee laughed at my people when she got not pretty. Mountains feel safe, tall wumun not like mountains. Shlaar find new home in mountains to bee safe!'

'On my guards return I shall bring you to meet my King and Queen. They will be able to help you. Please ask your people to rest, help shall arrive soon my friend'.

'Freeend! Thankss bee upon yuu'
Shlaar signalled for his numbers to sit along the bank of the blue river and with barely a rustle of clothing the entire mass of robed figures gently sat down.

'You are welcome! In time we shall teach you how to fight, how to defend yourselves!'

'Shlaar knows fighting noo gud for tall womun, trick us by speech. Use words we not know so shee learn us, not much water in our landz. Tall wumun tell us these words are magic and can help us, once we learn words they worse than swords! Words enslave us, we turn on each other. Tall wumun sit back and laugh at us. We fight back but own peeple fight us, not awake, still under power of bad words. We leave behind our peeple who are not awake! Me hope peeples awake and join us, no more fight, all big trick'.

'I am sorry my friend, I need to know more of the tall woman! She is our enemy too, how did she make herself known to you?'

'Tall wumun appear from small statue outside our landz. Waz not there before, look pretty, look like she know much. Said she help us, then began to trick us!'

'You said that she does she not like mountains, how do you know?'
'When wee fight her shee kill many, we flee, only place left was mountains. Shee never follow us but our mountains have no water, we must move, shee curse us. Say shee find us and not rest till shee kill us all, said shee is coming over the blue river! She knows we are here!'

Chapter Thirteen – A new path

His fur felt cool and a trickle of water dripped on his nose making him open his eyes. My poor head hurts! Eergh! What's this place? Jele-Nai! No don't hurt her! Leave us alone!'

'Be still ya bag of nerves, I'm alright! Here Spongley-Mok help him up will ya?'

Fluke-Fluke felt himself being raised to his feet but it took a few moments for his vision to completely return.

'I saw a fiend attack you! How did we end up here?'
He looked around and found himself in the middle of a large damp gloomy cave that was faintly illuminated in green by strange glowing fungus spores that grew out of the slimy walls. The cave had five jagged openings around its circumference leading out into other eerie caves. One of the openings had a small stream trickling through it.

'She battered the mad git around the place like it was a puppet, I saw it, there is no use pretending it didn't happen Jele-Nai!'

'Spongley!, I got lucky that's all, I got out of the way just before it could get it's claws into me and it fell down the opening into the cave and smacked it's head off the cave floor, and that's it! It's time to move now so come on and all and let's get moving!'

Fluke-Fluke looked over at Tweakle-Ponk for confirmation, she discreetly shook her head denying Jele-Nai's take on events and Spongley-Mok swiftly got to his feet walking past Jele-Nai defiantly.

'Well if ya look at da state of the fiend's body Fluke-Fluke you will see that what she's just said is a load of bum fluff! Go on Fluke-Fluke, have a ganders at it!'

He pointed over behind where Fluke-Fluke stood. Fluke-Fluke turned around and spotted a dark figure propped upside down embedded in a mossy green boulder with its legs pointing awkwardly up towards the cave roof.

'Janey mackers! That's gross! Bleeh! Wait a minute I have an idea!' He scurried over to the carcass and vanished behind the boulder. Jele-Nai rolled her eyes up in the air in frustration.

'Will ya just get your scuttle butt over here, we have to make it through these caves and there is no telling what's happened to Zarn and we need to reach the youngling tree city to warn the rest of our realm so we've got our hands full enough without you playing doctor with a dead fiend carcass!'

Fluke-Fluke ignored her and was quietly grunting and puffing and panting behind the mossy green boulder.

'There! Now we have weapons! Look!'
He jumped on top of the boulder proudly brandishing a pair of fiend serrated cleavers that he had dismembered form the carcass. His friends exchanged glances with each other in cheerful amazement.

'Fluke-Fluke! It's better than a weapon! It's evidence! We can show this to the Aoes Shee warriors at the tree city, it will prove that the fiends are back!'

'Spongley's right, nicely done Flukey Wukey!'
'Ah janey mackers I'm gona throw up! Fair enough we've got something

to show them but let's be goin before the fiends notice that we have given them the slip! Come on Flukey Wukey ya silly sap!'

Fluke-Fluke walked past her disappointedly hoping that for once the fiery princess would give him some credit.

'Wish you would be nicer to me Jele-Nai! I'm only trying to help!' He sniffled to himself wiping cold droplets of water off his face that came from the moist cave roof.

'There we are! Zarn told me to follow this stream! It will lead us to a way down into the green valley! Come on will ya?'

They all huddled together in the eerie light, occasionally slipping on the slimy stones that littered the spongy soil. The stream trickled gently along gradually getting wider and deeper the further that they ventured into the cave tunnel. Tweakle-Ponk grabbed Fluke Flukes hand.

'Why would Zarn leave us? I feel very sad, are we not worth saving?' 'Ah Tweakle-Ponk he knew what he was doing, don't be sad'.

'It's just we could have tried to help him, I know I'm a girl and all but I would have fought alongside him'.

Jele-Nai placed a hand on her shoulder in comfort.
'He had no choice buddy, he knew he would have had no chance against them if he had to defend all four of us, leaving us somewhere safe left him free to fight with no distractions, I guarantee if we stood and fought they would have killed all of us except one and used that one for ransom to get Zarn to surrender and who knows what they would have done to Zarn then! The thought makes even my skin crawl'

'He was big and scary but I miss him now, do you think that he's really dead?'

Jele-Nai looked very grim.

'Jeepers buddy I hope not, we are not out of the storm yet'

The princess sped up her walk to scout ahead leaving her companions to struggle along the slippery tunnel.

'You'll protect me Fluke-Fluke won't you?

Tweakle-Ponk squeezed his hand tightly looking for some reassurance.

'Of course and don't forget about your brother, that guy will tear anyone apart if he sees you in trouble, isn't that right Spongley?'

He giggled and Spongley wrapped his arms around both of them.

'Yep! That's right Flukey, no one messes with my friends and family'

The trickling stream became loud now as it became a small river making it difficult to hear any sound above its splashing and echoing roar. 'I've found it! Lads we are nearly there! Just a little bit further!' Jele-Nai had spotted daylight casting a silvery shine on the end of the tunnel only a hundred yards away.

'Yippee! Out of the storm now guys, phew thank goodness!'

Their optimism was shattered by a far off moan and deep gurgling noise coming from behind them. Fluke-Fluke stared at Jele-Nai nervously.

'Fluke-Fluke get them going faster we can make it!'

The three younglings forgot their footing and sprinted as fast as they could towards Jele-Nai who had nearly made it to the end of the bright tunnel opening but the slime covered stones in the soil sent them all skidding along in a tumbling mess landing in front of the surprised but concerned princess.

'Right better to arrive in a mess than never at all, don't worry lads we will be long gone before those freaks arrive, all we have to do is walk down this slope into the valley and...'

She was peering over the edge of the tunnels end in shock.

'We may have to rethink our stratajeee!'

Fluke-Fluke stood up and scurried over to the edge of the tunnel. There was a large waterfall as he had expected but there was no ledge to walk around it and no way down to the valley floor except for leaping into the river. The waterfall was not completely vertical but still so steep as to be incredibly dangerous even for an acrobatic Gikkie Bokker youngling and the cliff face on either side of the waterfall was smooth and had nothing to grip onto. The moaning and gurgling was much louder now and they could hear the echo of fiend armour smashing awkwardly off the cave tunnels in the near distance.

'Fluke-Fluke! I'm heading back to give you some time, take Spongley and Tweakle-Ponk with you down the fall!'

'But what about you we can't leave you!'

A dark body swung in through the roof of the tunnel exit and landed on top of Jele-Nai sending her swiftly into the river. She swiftly righted herself and slipped out of the fiends grasp as her friends all screamed in terror. The fiend was followed by another one landing behind the upright Jele-Nai and pinned her arms behind her back. Her three companions

174

jumped onto the huge back of the first fiend attacking it desperately to keep it from closing in on the pinned Jele-Nai but the beast deliberately rammed its back against the cave tunnel wall leaving them in a daze after being crushed.

It now charged at the youngling princess who extended her talons on her clawed feet and stomped on the other fiend's feet causing it to hiss in agony. Its grip loosened and she ducked underneath the attacking fiends stabbing arms. The fiend was committed and could not slow-down in time and stabbed its companion in the chest, still carried by its own momentum it slammed into the other fiend and they both fell off the edge of the tunnel exit falling into the waterfall but not before one of them grabbed Jele-Nai's feet and pulled her in along with them.

Fluke-Fluke came to and leaped after her trying to grab her hand. She was gripping onto an old tree root partially submerged in the waterfalls gushing flow and below her two bulky fiend soldiers were hanging from her feet trying to climb up her to reach her friends. There was another loud moan and gurgle from behind him and he turned around to see two fiend soldiers blocking the way back into the cave. Jele-Nai's grip on the root was strong but the root started to come loose from its foundations.

She strained to kick the gripping fiends free of her legs but their vine like hands were firm and seemed not to tire at all. She looked up at Fluke-Fluke who had a startling expression on his face. There was a snarl on his lips and his eyes glowed fiercely. A little growl emerged from inside his chest. The princess had not seen the look on Fluke-

Fluke's face before, there was strength and a fierceness in it.

'No Fluke-Fluke, don't! Get me free! I will take them on!'
The youngling reached over his head and grabbed the two serrated fiend sword arms that he had strapped to his back and spun around racing towards the two fiend soldiers taking them by surprise.

'Nooooo!'

She screamed out in alarm for his safety. Jele-Nai could not see anything but she could hear fiend armour rattling and their weapons hitting off the cave tunnel walls and a growling and hissing from Fluke-Fluke that she had never witnessed before. The root came free and she felt herself in free-fall for a split second and then stopped suddenly as she was jerked up towards the cave tunnels exit. The sudden jerking motion shook free the fiend's grip on her legs as they wailed and moaned hurtling into the chaotic rush of the waterfall. She was being pulled up wards onto the river bank by Spongley-Mok and Tweakle-Ponk who had come to her aid after they had recovered from the crushing attack of one of the ghastly fiend's.

'Fluke-Fluke!'

She roared out in concern after coming to her senses and broke into a sprint as soon as her companions pulled her upright from the waterfall.

She disappeared from view into the cave depths screaming and growling in concern for him followed desperately by Spongley-Mok and Tweakle-Ponk. There was no sound of battle anymore only the loud rumbling of the waterfall nearby. The princess was sobbing to herself frantically searching for her awkward friend's body.

'You didn't have to do this at all Fluke-Fluke! Why did you have to go and act this way?'

She stopped in her tracks and made no sound at all while her two companions caught up with her. They were afraid to say anything and terrified of what she may have found but with a nervous gulp they looked over her shoulder and stared at what was in front of her. Fluke Fluke's back was facing them still brandishing the two fiend sword appendages and directly in front of him lay the two fiend soldiers who attempted to block their exit, laying lifeless and with battered armour fragments littering the area around his feet.

'You did not! How did ya pull this one off? I mean…'
The fiery princess was at a loss to explain it. The youngling turned to face her slowly with the fierce look still in his eyes taking his companions by surprise.

'Are you all unharmed?'
It was Fluke Fluke's voice but deeper and full of confidence.

'Yes! We are all fine, I got free thanks to these two, thank you, we did it buddy lets go and find a way out of here , I think there is a way down from the waterfall after all!'

Fluke Flukes eyes faded and he dropped his swords.
'Good! Because I'm really scared right now and I don't like fighting! I just want my mammy to hold me!'

He broke down into tears and bowed his head sobbing deeply.

Jele-Nai rushed over to him and placed his head on her shoulder.

'If your mammy is alive Fluke-Fluke or whatever way she is I swear that I will help you find her, you did great, come on we have a long way to go yet!'

Everyone surrounded Fluke-Fluke and ushered him back to the waterfalls drop. Jele-Nai asked Tweakle-Ponk to hold onto him as she raced back to the fiend carcasses and removed their stabbing arm swords to take with her. She soon reached her friends who were all calmly looking down at the waterfall.

'I know it looks grim but when I was hanging off a tree root I noticed lots more of them below me, lots! They are hidden under the waters flow! I reckon that's how we get down to the valley oh and here ya go, Spongley and Tweakle take these!'

She gave them a fiend stabbing sword each leaving her with two just like Fluke-Fluke.

'Let's hope we don't need to use them again except for evidence for the Aoes Shee in the youngling tree city'.

The day's events had taken an enormous toll on them and not a word was uttered as they carefully climbed down the waterfall, feeling underneath the water's surface for tree roots to hold onto. The daylight which fascinated them was fading and the slight faint disc of the moon stared down on the valley. Their dense water tight fur kept them well insulated but the lower they descended the greater was the wrath of the mighty waterfall's power.

They could descend no further as there were no roots left to hold onto but after looking around they spotted a small shelf of rock on either side of the waterfall. They managed to leap onto the narrow ledge and moved carefully across it to a modest overhang of rock and looked downwards.

There was only another one hundred feet or so to go before they reached the valley floor. Fluke-Fluke spotted a series of tree roots emerging from out of the cliff face below the ledge and quietly scurried down them followed by his friends. They swiftly climbed down to the ground and marched off on a quick pace along the east bank of the river terrified of giving their presence away to anything but the valley was serene and beautiful with no sign of danger. The lush green valley stretched onwards for miles in front of them and its end was obscured by a thick grey mist.

'What now Jele-Nai?' Asked a nervous Tweakle-Ponk.
'The river flows into the mist, we keep going, the youngling tree city has to be that way, let's hope that Zarn is there too!'

'I feel guilty! We should have climbed back up and back tracked to see if Zarn was alive in the fields!'

'Come on Spongley!, There where at least twenty of those fiends after us, we would only have slowed Zarn down, I feel awful as well but we are alive, even if he is dead we still have to warn the others or there will be countless dead in the coming days, knuckle down and suck it up, the tree city has to be near!'

As they marched they felt the soil along the river bank become soft and damp and they got bogged down in a swampy patch of deep mud hidden below a covering of long grass.

'This mud is disgusting, it stinks to the heavens, have you ever come across the like of it, just look at the state of it!'

Spongley-Mok picked up some of the mud in his hands letting it slide out of his grip. The mud left a black slime on his hands that made him wretch in disgust.

'You are a right plonker! Why pick it up if it disgusts you?, Let's get away from the river bank and get stuck into the undergrowth, we will still keep the river bank in sight so we know the right direction to take okay guys?' Everyone nodded in agreement at Jele-Nai and awkwardly freed themselves from the mud.

After flicking as much mud off of themselves as they could the younglings continued to march swiftly towards the misty end of the valley. As the friends relaxed Jele-Nai slowed down a little to stay by Fluke Fluke's side.

'You did great back there Flukey! Are you okay now?'
He looked up at her in surprise, she always acted proud and aloof around him unless she was busy giving out to him and name calling but this was genuine concern.

'I'm fine and thanks!' He kept on walking.
'Is there anything you need? I can carry those swords for you, they are a bit big for you ya know?' She playfully elbowed him in the ribs.

'If you want to help then please don't be mean to me anymore, it hurts me deep inside, lots more than carrying heavy swords, and it hurts even more cause I like you'.

The princess was lost for words and moved her lips to say something but nothing came out for a moment. She cleared her throat and started again and this time with no attitude at all in her voice.

'Well I er, I won't do that again… I'm sorry, listen I never asked you before but I'd like to know if it's okay, where is your mammy? Is there something I can do to help you find her? Is she on a secret errand for Vrool or something?'

'My mummy was taken away from me when I was really small'

'What? This is not known to me! How? And why?'

'My daddy was very bad, he scared mummy with his power and got into trouble with my granddad. He had a fight with Granddad and Granddad made him leave!, He kept coming back angry all the time scaring everyone until they both had a really big fight and granddad had to hurt him. Mummy had to leave to a safe place but when she left she never came back, nobody knows where she left except Granddad and he won't say!.... daddy doesn't come back anymore now, granddad searches for him sometimes to see if he is okay, that's all I know'.

Jele-Nai swiftly wiped the tears from her eyes trying to keep her sorrow at bay.

'I'm so sorry, why didn't you say something?'

'You were too busy making fun of me and calling me names, I didn't want to make myself look even worse, I don't feel normal and it hurts my belly deep inside!'

She couldn't help but hold his hand and her tears flowed unrestrained dripping off her face and onto his shoulder'

'I'm sorry, I didn't mean to wet your fur!' She sniffled.
'It's okay! You're my friend anyways, even though you can be a bit narkey sometimes!'

He turned to look up at her and winked with a hint of a smile. They kept holding hands walking behind their friends under the silver moonlight with neither of them speaking a word, the understanding that they had from a simple heart felt and honest conversation made both walk a little more lightly on the ground. The princess discovered a whole new depth to herself and her smaller friend, he was such a happy and go lucky personality on the outside but to learn that it was on the inside that her friend had a hidden pain pulled at her heart badly, she couldn't be the same person with him ever again, there would be no more hiding behind her cold exterior, she held his hand more tightly now and he returned her affection in kind. That moment was when Fluke Flukes heart smiled inside again for the first time in many a passing moon.

Chapter Fourteen – Battling the madness

She forgot her task at hand and briefly savoured the surroundings of the Spungle valley moving so fast she caused the nearby trees to sway from her slip stream. Smiling to herself she stopped at the place strongest with the Spungles energy, a clearing near an overgrown path to the Selfin Mountains. She waited for her king to catch up and examined the area.

A few parts of the overgrowth had been exposed, lifted off in huge chunks revealing an ornamental road way with delicately carved depictions of battle on its surface.

Vrool arrived alongside her and without a word quickly searched the area facing away from his queen.

'He has left here only moments ago but I cannot sense his energy beyond this place!'

He walked over to a massive sculpture towering over him, he smiled at it remembering fondly every event that was intricately carved and chiselled out of it.

'This was a great day, may we be blessed with further victories of this kind, but where have you gone my great warrior friend?'

'There is nothing of his presence this way either my love!'
'Thank you, my queen! I feel Vraarl's presence in the Selfin mountains, he seems calm, and no other presence other than Kurn and Bralnar, I feel they shall be with us soon, it is strange that the Morgannis cannot block our vision all of the time, she seems to block our vision at the moment of an attack, it must cost her vast amounts of energy!'

'Speaking of vast amounts of energy can you think of anywhere that

Eireannos could have fled to?'

'No realm would have him willingly, they do not trust his power, the only place other than the sealed off Wrathien realm would be the cradle of his ancestors in the realm of Daragnar Gulthume - the mountain cathedral! I fear that they would punish him, even destroy him as soon as he entered the realm!'

The earth below them rumbled deeply. Shard looked at Vrool with great concern.

'He has gone truly mad, he is trying to open the doorway to the Wrathien Realm! He will bring the wrath of his creators down upon us! Follow me!'

They hurried past the great sculpture and made their way into the centre of the Spungle village. At the dead centre of the village lay the remains of what was the largest of the ornate village huts, smashed to its foundations it revealed a large opening in the earth that contained a massive spiralling stone staircase.

'That's why we could not sense him, the entrance has a cloaking vex on it, It masked his energy, prepare yourself my queen, we may have to work together!'

After running down the staircase they entered a large underground arched hallway that contained a large intricately decorated semi-circular building with a giant set of silver doors, and smashing on the doors with all four dark fists was the crazed Spungle, all dark and unkempt fur in a violent frenzy muttering and cursing to itself but not making a mark on the doors.

'I want to be with my fathers! Bring me back to my people! Take me back to my creator!'

Its rage was ceaseless but the doors did not even mark or stain from the ferocious barrage of his huge fists.

'Settle your anger my old friend! See who you really are! A great noble warrior of mighty deeds, let us help you find the answers you so desperately seek!'

The barrage stopped and the frightening figure turned its head to gaze on Vrool and Shard.

'Ah Vrool and his Queen! You've come to share with me now the truth! A mere coincidence is it not that you hope to prevent me from entering my true home? Always a second meaning to your speech, you may fear the wrath of my creators but I do not, flee here now while you have a chance, I have no need of seeing your truth! I shall retake what's mine and renew my brother Kings Empire!'

It turned around to face the huge doors and resumed its attack. The giant hallway rumbled deeply sending harsh vibrations into the earth but the doors remained firmly fixed and immaculately pristine.

'You shall be punished by your ancestors if you continue, you know the bargain that was agreed between our races after we defeated the Morgannis, the Wrathien homeland had to be sealed off to ensure that the Morgannis could never use its facilities against us, you were not in a fit state of mind to be its lawful King, I pray for the day that you can take up your brothers crown but only if you master yourself!'

'Vrool! You self-serving pleaser of all races, never taking sides, you and your kind are a lost mongrel race so desperate to fit in that you will fight for the highest bidder! If you had any courage you would have found a new realm owned by no-one so you could settle down but you compromise yourself by being a puppet for your Siabhra masters!'

'My love! Do not react to his taunts, he seeks only violence for violence sakes, madness I fear may have transformed into evil, we should leave and let him face the consequences of his actions!'

'Ah the wise queen speaks! Ever the soother of your king's darker side! A side that should never have been suppressed, Vrool you are a killer! But you feel weak and forgetful now, this is not an accident, I sense a transformation within you! Whatever created you may be near, your masters calling is at hand and your body reacts!'

Vrool froze inside with the shock of the thought implanted in his mind, it could be only a mocking taunt at him but every Aoes Shee warrior and Gikkie Bokker youngling's deepest wish was to find their true origins and home.

'I try to help you and you harm my feelings with darkness! If you are so resolute in your convictions then why fear facing the truth that I offer you? Surely such a fearsome beast as yourself would not be scared of recalling his past in full?'

Shard stepped back behind Vrool sensing his power rise.

'Don't harm him my love, ease your anger down to a whisper and let him act first!'

'My past means nothing! I see clearly now, I shall open this doorway and reclaim the heritage that was swindled from me, then a new dark dawn shall break upon all in this realm with me as it's king, I give you and your kind three days to leave these lands, where you go I care not! Now go! Get out!'

He turned to fully face the Aoes Shee and took a massive swipe at Vrool with his left front arm. The Aoes Shee king stood rooted to the ground and let the massive fist collide with his body. There was a howl of pain from the Spungle as it leaned over clasping its fist in agony.

'I am sorry my friend your anger brings you closer to despair, stand down and speak with me as a friend'

The Spungle sat slowly down sobbing quietly and its dark fur lightened to a dull silver. Shard walked over to the beast and without a word it picked her up gently in the cradle of its hand and brought her close to its chest.

'The time has come dear friend, the time to heal!'
Vrool walked slowly towards them and reached out his arms to the beast.

'You are not a Spungle, the word is riddled with hate, your true name is Eireannos, and you have been fighting the memories that have laid waste to your spirit! Now merge with us and you shall see the full truth, it shall be hard for you, like your birth but when your true self is at one with the greatness of your name, you shall be healed!'

Shard whispered gently to the beast.

'It's time now, no matter how painful a vision you see, I am here with you, the memories come now, I feel them being called to you'.

Kurn and Bralnar arrived into the great hall amazed by the spectacle but Shard quickly gestured for them to stay put.

The beast became awake and shed its dark rage, its face relaxed and it looked down at Vrool. A large orb of glowing light floated from the Aoes Shee kings face and hovered in front of him. The orb became silver, then golden and appearing out of the orb was Vrool Gala's haunting eyes.

'Travel with me now to the truth our noble Dark Fist!'

Chapter Fifteen - The Flight of the Younglings

Tweakle-Ponk looked out at the river flowing by as she marched. The sound of its ponderous flow relaxed her. It had grown dark now and the moon cast silver highlights onto the river.

It would be nice to jump into that now and clean that mud off my fur properly, Ah well maybe later.

She kept marching but looked down at her feet, she noticed a muddy path behind her and looked closely at her feet.

'How are my feet dirty again? I cleaned myself off when I got out of the swamp!'

'What's that Tweakle-Ponk?' Asked Jele-Nai.

'Well I distinctly remember cleaning the scum and mud of my feet and it's back again and we couldn't have brought that much muck with us, I mean take a look for yourself!'

Jele-Nai looked down at Tweakle-Ponk's feet and the trail of black mud behind her. Quickly looking down at her own feet she noticed the same thing. Fluke-Fluke and Spongley-Mok did the same and they all observed that they had a dark muddy trail behind them.

The trails all fell back into the distance but seemed to be joining up some way off into one larger stream of dark mud.

'That's really weird the ground is not that swampy here. Right lads! Come on we can wash our feet back on the river bank it won't take that long at all!'

Everyone followed Jele-Nai over to the edge of the river and they all dipped their clawed feet into the river expecting a cool refreshing experience but the river was not flowing.

'It's still and Yuk! Slimy! And muddy ah this won't do come on we will just have to speed up and wash when we get to the tree city, come on lads!

Jele-Nai stood up and marched swiftly ahead in a huff with everyone else frantically scurrying after her.

'All I was hoping for was one little comfort, that muck is stuck in between my toe claws, manky dirty stuff, all right lets hurry up the opening out of this valley is not far off now, look you can see the mist swirling at the gap!'

She looked behind at the others to point the way but noticed something was about to join their ranks.

'EVERY BODY RUN!'

Her three companions looked behind themselves to see the familiar dreaded shape of fiends clumsily emerging from the muddy trail that was now alive and meandering rapidly towards them all. They all shrieked with terror and ran as swiftly as they could catching up with Jele-Nai.

A split second before they vanished into a large path of dense vegetation Fluke-Fluke spotted hundreds of fierce fiend soldiers leaping out of the now bubbling river bank bringing huge clods of mud along with them.

'We really need to hurry up, there's loads more of them jumping from out of the river!'

'Just keep moving Fluke-Fluke it's not long now even if the tree city is far off that bank of mist will help hide us better, keep going!'

There was a deep moaning and gurgling of frustration from the pursuing fiends as they awkwardly bungled against the dense vegetation which caught onto their jagged armour and seemed to be wrapping itself around their vine like limbs trying to entangle them deliberately.

The younglings dashed from out of the cover of dense vegetation and looked ahead to see the that the mist bank was only half a mile away, faint strands of mist already grabbed at their furry feet and became gradually denser the further they sped towards the misty gap.

The tortured sound of the fiends was increasing, it now seemed that there was a small army giving chase and a fiend shape stumbled out from the dense cover of vegetation and spotted the fleeing younglings giving a gurgling cry of encouragement to the rest of its numbers.

'They've spotted us Jele-Nai!'

'That's okay Fluke-Fluke you are faster than you think, look! We are nearly there!'

The mist was now waist deep all around them and thickening and the green valley's hue was changing to a silver grey from the faintly luminous mist. The mist bank itself lay only one hundred feet away now, densely undulating and swirling more akin to a huge storm system than a quietly creeping blanket of mist but a great roar stopped the younglings' dead in their tracks. The younglings' could spot a number of strangely moving shapes and shadows far off in the chaotic mist banks but the shapes were rapidly approaching and the ground underneath them shook from the vibration of a large force galloping towards them.

'We've been cut off! This was a trap all along, Fluke-Fluke ready your weapons, We stand and fight!'

Jele-Nai grabbed the criss crossing pair of fiend stabbing swords from off of her back and stood beside Fluke-Fluke and looked back out at the approaching fiends. Their number was massive and amongst their awkward stumbling numbers were a group of four huge master fiends, hissing and snarling and over one hundred feet in height. The pursuing dark mud flow had vanished after being used up creating the monstrous lumbering creatures.

'There are too many of them! Head into the mist, our odds will be better if we fight whatever is in there, we may even get them to attack each other if we get lucky!'

'Since when has this day been lucky Jele-Nai?'
Dark shadows gathered number amongst the turbulent mist and the galloping thudding noise shook the soil beneath their feet.

'Zarn will not have died in vain Fluke-Fluke, let's take a few down with us, what do you say little buddy?'

'I'm with you Jele-Nai!' He growled as he readied himself.
'Us too!' Protested Spongley-Mok and Tweakle-Ponk amongst the now deafening din of the approaching mist bound attackers.

The youngling and his sister extended surprisingly long claws from their hands and stood either side of Fluke-Fluke and Jele-Nai.

The youngling princess ignited a fiery rage in her heart growling loudly and sprinted blindly into the engulfing mist. Fluke-Fluke raced after her hissing and growling to give her support. Spongley-Mok and Tweakle-Ponk darted into the chaotic mist behind them shouting at the top of their voices with pride.

'We are the Aoes Shee younglings! Prepare to have your hides scratched to pieces!'

The mist was almost choking in its density and the light from the younglings glowing eyes illuminated deep into the swirling vortex of icy cold water vapour.

'Here they come!' Shouted Jele-Nai.

The great shadows of an approaching force were right upon them darkening the silvery mist. The terrified younglings closed their eyes as the ground vibrated so hard it nearly threw them off their feet. There was a deep roar from above them and the galloping thunder ceased for a brief moment creating a vacuum of silence and a great wind swept over their heads. The Galloping resumed with a deafening thud but came from past their ranks.

'What just happened? Didn't they see us?' Whimpered Fluke-Fluke.
'I hope so! Stay put and crouch down we may be able to give them the slip after all!'

Jele-Nai grabbed everyone's hands and brought her companions to a stooping position.

In the distance behind them erupted a huge clash of armour and screeching. It was a sound of surprised chaos. Gurgling moans and deep roars mixed with hissing steam like screams echoed in the depths of the chaotic mist.

'Are they are fighting each other! What a bunch of morons! Come on we should have a sneak peek!'

'Jele-Nai! Are you bonkers? We should be going away from them not be running back!'

Tweakle-Ponk scolded her but it was too late, the youngling princess doubled back on herself sneaking slowly out of the deep mist. Her companions looked at each other in disbelief but scurried after her with concern. The battle was still raging on wildly and the princess could see dark shadows of all shapes and sizes moving around swiftly. She ventured forward another few steps and the mist cleared enough for her to see a small section of the ongoing battle.

'In the name of! How is this happening?'

She gasped but her companions blinded by the mist could not see her and ran into her back causing the whole gang to topple over face first into the grass. As they looked up at the battle before them they saw masses of fiend carcasses littering the valley floor and perhaps one hundred remaining fiend soldiers retreating towards the riverbanks edge along with only one master fiend. Raising themselves slowly to their feet they saw that the attackers only numbered twenty and were mounted on top of golden armoured Fíochmhar steeds.

It was a small unit of Aoes Shee warriors and at the head of the formation was Zarn cleaving fiends in two with his twin swords and bashing away at a group of fiend's with his serrated twin shields as they attempted to jump onto his back. The younglings yelped and screamed in approval at the spectacle jumping in the air with joy. Out of sheer giddiness they all started to run towards the mounted Aoes Shee which attracted Zarn's attention. He quickly warded them off waving his swords in a warning to them. The retreating master fiend saw it's chance and swiped a great fist at Zarn's steed knocking it over onto the ground but Zarn leaped off the fallen creature and flung one of his serrated shields like a discuss towards the fiends neck severing the creatures head from its shoulders.

The fiend's massive body shook in surprise and started to topple over towards Zarn. His faithful steed rose to its feet with a concerned howl and dashed towards Zarn who grasped the saddle on its back and was pulled away from the crushing thud of the headless fiends awkwardly collapsing body.

The handful of remaining fiend soldiers froze in their stride as if paralysed and fell onto the ground with a feeble hiss. Zarn's soldiers rallied around him as he soothed his Fíochmhar steed, gently whispering to it and patting it softly on its massive shoulder.

Fluke-Fluke ran as fast as he could over to Zarn scurrying in and around the legs of Zarn's soldiers. Upon seeing the youngling Zarn's fearsome expression melted with relief, he picked the youngling up in his arms holding onto him tightly.

'You and your friends have proven yourselves today simply by getting to this place! But we must not linger the machine of war is gathering momentum! Zhan! Hylar! Take these younglings to the tree city immediately, I shall remain and dispose of any stragglers left from the fiend army, I'm afraid that our plans have changed we must find a way to contact our king!'

Two mounted warriors trotted slowly over to the younglings and reached out their arms beckoning the younglings to jump up onto their huge steeds.

'I've never been on one of these things, this is deadly!' Shouted out Spongley-Mok proudly.

'Well master Mok you shall become familiar enough with them on your stay at our tree city, I shall be with you soon, brief Zhan and Hylar on what has happened to you since we were separated, farewell for now brave younglings!'

Zarn mounted his steed and galloped off into the distance with his soldiers in pursuit to find any stray fiends. The younglings balanced comfortably on the rear saddles of Zhan and Hylar's steeds even though they were moving at great speed. The steeds moved like a cross between a fine race horse and a komodo dragon. On smooth terrain it galloped and on rougher terrain it sank low to the ground for greater grip and rapidly crawled and scurried. The creatures frame was akin to a well-muscled horse but much more powerfully built and the four legs were much broader and thicker but had hoof like pads on the bottom of their feet with three large sharp claws on powerful toes that spread its weight evenly on the ground. Sharp spikes protruded from its shoulders neck and legs and its tail was long and flexible with four dinosaur like spines at the end resembling a double set of antlers vertically opposing each other. The head was more dog shaped than horse like and a large horn protruded from its snout like a rhinoceros but there was also two large horns underneath its jaws that extended beyond its head. The mouth had sharp canines and incisors much like a big cat and its yellow eyes faced forward like a predatory bird. The whole appearance of the beasts were made even more formidable by the golden and bronze coloured armour that adorned its frame. Any creature that would be foolish enough to attack the beast would be severely injured from the armoured horns and blades protruding from out of the armours angular extremities.

As they galloped head long into the dense mist the creatures let out a low howl like a wolf. The younglings were captivated by the creatures.

Fluke-Fluke looked at Jele-Nai and smiled with amazement and they both looked over at Tweakle-Ponk and Spongley-Mok on the back of Hylar's steed. They were smiling broadly back at them with a satisfied sense of adventure.

'We are nearing the tree city little ones, you must hold on tightly!' Jele-Nai looked puzzled.
'We are holding on fine as it is, do we have to jump over a gate or something now?'

'Not quite!' Laughed Zhan. 'Look!' He pointed skywards and a massive dark grey shape appeared out of the mist. Jele-Nai gasped.

'It's huge!' The form of a massive hulking tree of otherworldly proportions gradually came into view from out of the mist, it resembled a gigantic sycamore tree, wide and sprawling at the start of its branches and gradually tapering to a narrower top.

'Where is the entrance? I can't see anything yet!'
Zhan laughed loudly as the hulking form of the giant tree trunk blotted out their peripheral vision. 'There is no entrance! We climb!'

He yelled out commanding his steed to leap into the air at the giant trunk of the tree and the steed rose up on its hind legs and jumped vertically out of the mist bank. Its powerful claws gripped the hard bark and the creature propelled itself upwards running vertically as fast as it did when it was galloping on the ground. It's legs were splayed apart like a giant lizard racing up a wall and the younglings dared to take a peek downwards at the mist bank and noticed that the gigantic tree was situated in another much larger valley but they all had to turn their heads back and face upwards to balance themselves. Fluke-Fluke shouted aloud in amazement.

'I've only heard about this place in bedtime stories, it's just as big as our mountain temple! It's some place just for a training ground!'
Zhan looked behind at Fluke-Fluke and smiled.

'The original youngling tree city was destroyed by the Morgannis! She hoped to destroy our race by targeting younglings like yourselves! But it hardened us and we grew stronger from her attack, this new city is more of a fortress and is shielded from even her vision. Vrool and Shard have this place protected with even more of their mana energy than that of the spire!'

The journey upwards lasted longer than the younglings had expected and the massive canopy of branches and leaves created a shadow upon them as if night had fallen. They had to adjust themselves constantly now as the massive steeds leaped and bounded from off of the giant trunk of the tree onto one massive branch after another, running horizontally on occasion then leaping vertically to grasp onto another branch until finally they climbed onto a gigantic branch which resembled more of a road way and started to trot along it's ascending path much to the younglings relief.

As they travelled up into the trees dense foliage they started to notice strange pods of wood hanging from the smaller branches. The pods were made from the same material as the tree itself but looked to the younglings as if they had been hand crafted. Each globe had one large circular opening that revealed a cosy interior of bedded leaves and grass that was lit from the inside by a golden lamp light. Each globe was easily large enough to hold a youngling inside but they could see no living thing in any of them as they passed them by.

The rustling of the leaves in the tree began to get calmer and a wonderful calm chorus of chiming clangs and tinkling noises sweetly echoed throughout the interior of the canopy. Then as they ventured ever upwards the branches all started to become more ornate and elegant. Even at a calm trot the Fíochmhar steeds moved swiftly and the younglings found it difficult to make out detail on the branches but the tree seemed to be becoming more engraved and decorated by delicate ornate embellishments as if the structure of the tree was becoming a living Aoes Shee City. They turned off to the left of the giant branch and jumped calmly onto another great branch that angled itself at a greater incline and the pace slowed down a little. Now parts of the enormous intricate structure of branches and foliage began to become more symmetrical as they began to venture further into the trees interior.

Tweakle-Ponk pointed with her hand towards a small clearing in the dense foliage.

'Parts of this place look like our mountain temple, look Fluke-Fluke over there behind those smaller branches!

I don't believe it! A water fall! That's going... upwards?'

The younglings craned their heads around their Aoes Shee riders so they could get a better view. There was a waterfall travelling upwards along the massive tree trunk and it had a snaking set of smaller tributaries that to the younglings astonishment flowed off of the trunk and snaked around some of the larger branches like a creeper vine would do utterly defying gravity.

'I'm beginning to like this place, it feels homey!' Sighed a relieved Tweakle-Ponk.

Trotting further upwards they started to encounter partially hidden buildings easily as large as the smaller buildings in the mountain temple, buildings that were all manufactured out of wood and were organically designed to fit in with their environment. All had openings to let light in and were illuminated by different hues of gold and green in the darker more densely leaved areas. They passed along the way a series of crafted open metal gates that had unmanned checkpoints or guard posts with elegantly crafted Aoes Shee weapons lined up neatly in wall mounted racks inside them.

After a few moments trot the steeds halted and Zhan and Hylar dismounted and gently placed the younglings gently onto the giant tree path. Hylar pointed to a large semi-circular shaped tree pod with the welcoming steam of hot cooking flowing from out of its windows.

'We shall rest in that structure ahead until Zarn returns, and well done for being so brave, partake of the refreshments in there but do not venture far away from us until we are inside the city!'

Fluke-Fluke scratched his head. 'I thought that this was the city?'

'No youngling it is not! The city is higher up still and closer to the interior, rest now!'

'But Hylar Zarn asked me to tell you what has happened! We really are in a huge pickle!' Hylar looked at Zhan in confusion.

'Pickle? We are in a pickle? What are you speaking off?'

Zhan smiled and slapped Hylar's shoulder reassuringly.

'Hylar these are the younglings that went amiss beyond the portal! They have adopted the slang speech of the humans!'

'Ah Zarn spoke to me about them briefly, my younglings we know what you have gone through and are pleased with your bravery, the Morgannis' power cannot pierce this valley so we are free to read

203

thoughts at will, we cannot however see out past the valley so must await Zarn to give us word on what takes place outside this realm, now enjoy your rest little ones!'

Spongley-Mok scurried up to Hylar inquisitively.

'Why can't she use her power here?'

'Because this realm belongs to her creators, the Banshees!'

Chapter Sixteen – The heads of the Hydra

The massive arched vault rumbled with the power of an Aoes Shee King and Queen infusing healing energy into their old ally.

'He is holding back! I can get no further, I have never seen such a massive vex on any creature!'

'Keep trying my Queen I will protect us, just keep delving, we must get to the source of his suffering, otherwise he is lost to us!'

Shard strained under the heavy energy of sorrow that engulfed the Spungle and finally broke through to the beast's inner mind.

The Spungle shook violently nearly unbalancing her precarious position in the beast's great hand.

'All of it now is light, I am there, prepare yourself my king he is about to face his darkest memories!'

Vrool summoned all of his reserves as the floating orb between himself and the beasts face projected the memories of suffering of the Spungle. Vrool and Shard felt the Spungle convulsing as it witnessed the source of its tormented existence. The orb displayed the terrible battle of Terun-nill-vath-doom but this time the Spungle beast was not alone, his vision was shared by his old friends, his body relaxed and a low sobbing and weeping replaced his convulsive shaking. He could see his march with his half of the battalion towards the old entrance to the mountain temple that was now a massive trap for the Morgannis.

His brother king Gelfedaron was high above him on the mountain top with his half of the battalion battling a dark cloud of fiend soldiers and he could sense the joyous fire inside him as he felt his brother tear apart vast numbers of the creatures.

Then his attention shifted to the rapidly approaching mass of master fiends bearing down on his half of the battalion. The battle went swiftly and decisively in his favour, he swept through their dark ranks with his companions searching for the Morgannis while his Siabhra and Aoes Shee allies held off a surprise fiend attack coming at them from the southern swamps.

Finally he located his old foe. She was lashing powerful streams of energy against the entrance to the mountain and as planned his forces held back slightly to let her think that she was getting the upper hand in her quest. He had to be mindful of protecting a much weaker force of human allies who were also near the door. They were led by a human called Henry whose job was to be bait to lure the Morgannis into making a hasty attack at the entrance.

She craved the energy of the mountain temples massive spire to what end no creature ever found out but the doorway was designed to open slowly under attack and shut rapidly after the Morgannis entered sealing her in forever guarded by the most powerful spell to be cast by any creature in the known realms.

And she took the bait, on Eireannos' command Henry ordered his soldiers to retreat away from the massive doors giving the Morgannis clear access to them. Under her massive barrage of energy blasts the doors slowly heaved open and she was escorted past the doors into a cavernous hall by her remaining master fiends. The Morgannis shrieked with delight at her apparent victory but quickly realised that she was being fooled. She attempted to escape but was blocked in by Gelfedaron and his army who had disposed of her forces that attacked the higher parts of the mountain temple.

The Morgannis used all of her energy to break out of the giant hall and hammered the king and his troops away from the still opening doors.

Eireannos prepared a killing blow with one of his mighty fists but was taken by surprise as a huge force pummelled him from behind.

His mighty bulk was sent hurtling to the ground by one of his own kin. 'Ulgathos what are doing? The enemy is upon us!'

There was a vile laugh and cackle from within the giant chamber doorway and the smell of dark energy on the air. 'I have prayed to my dark gods for so long to have this day, do you not think that I had suspected a trap all along? I may not best you in battle but a blow from one of your wretched kind will do more than that!'

As she spoke Ulgathos his old friend changed hue from a bright silver to a dark unkempt shadow and ran wildly at the fallen Eireannos extending his sword arms to kill his friend. The young wrathien's heart sank in sorrow at this inexplicable betrayal and rolled out of the way of Ulgathos' attack but his situation became more ghastly by the second as he fought back to defend himself he sensed his entire pack begin to turn.

'Come to your senses Ulgathos! She is a trickster! Do not let her turn you against me!'

His old friend sneered back at him and lashed out wildly forcing

Eireannos to lift the turned wrathien off his feet with a massive uppercut.

Before the young wrathien could regain his composure a dark mass of bodies jumped on top of him flailing away wildly stabbing at him with serrated sword arms but these were no fiends. The brutish mob was led by his own brother King Gelfedaron. He cried out in pain as he endured wounds that no wrathien was ever intended to bear but managed to break free and fell off the great path that lead to the doorway were the Morgannis was still trying to escape from.

Masses of his turned companions raced after him down a sloping decline that lead to part of the stout lakes. As he tumbled chaotically downwards he felt his battle queen speak into his mind. 'My son your companions are no longer in control you must defend yourself at any cost! You must help the Siabhra entomb the Morgannis! Fight back or all our realms will be slaughtered!'

He felt his glyphs darken and the furnace inside his eyes ignited red. Gelfedaron was seconds away from a killing leap to finish him off and his pack backed up by a small army of master fiends was eager to devour the remains. His back slapped off the lake shore and he pleaded one last time to his turned brother.

'My king the cost is too great to let you slay me, clear your mind and re-join me I beg you otherwise you leave me no choice!'

Gelfedaron leaped into the air with a horrible dark roar and landed on top of his younger brother stabbing and slashing wildly. Ulgathos followed right behind his king frantically trying to get around him to stab at Eireannos but found himself impaled by a silver sword that was protruding from out of Gelfedaron' back.

A bright burst of white light erupted from out of the wound followed by a huge fireball that engulfed the three battling wrathiens. The blast knocked the remaining wrathiens off of their feet and incinerated the pursuing master fiends.

Eireannos cried out in despair realising what he had done and staggered to his feet but his remaining pack gave him no time to mourn as they recovered and with renewed hatred attempted to slay him. As he met them in battle he felled dozens of them frantically trying to get back onto the stone path to assist the Siabhra and Aoes Shee in preventing the Morgannis from escaping. Even with the chaos of battle around him he could sense the Morgannis rise in power. After slaying another two of his pack he managed to leap above the remaining group and land back onto the path and raced up to the giant doorway to meet battle with the Morgannis. As he sprinted his heart ached in pain as he witnessed hundreds of Siabhra bodies littering the outside of the entrance. Only two warriors remained and another fiend army raced towards them to finish them off.

Before the fiends reached them a thirty strong force of Aoes Shee warriors hurled themselves into their ranks slicing the fiend army to pieces with blinding speed. As Eireannos reached the Siabhra the Morgannis broke free once more and circled high in the air above the battle. The residual aura of Eireannos' fallen comrades swirled upwards towards her and enveloped her pale body. The remaining wrathien pack had now caught up with him and he was forced to fight them off but he still kept his eye on the floating banshee queen.

She materialised a long dark sword into her left hand and let the slain wrathien' aura whirl around it turning the dark sword into the same silvery hue as Eireannos himself. Eireannos could keep his eyes on the witch no longer and in a desperate rage slayed four of his companions in one swipe, the resulting explosion of aura knocked the rest of the wrathien mob to the ground in a concussed mess.

'Well done my unwitting ally for now I have a living sword! Forged in the same energy as your vile race!' She cackled and started to attack Henry and his force of human soldiers with the silver weapon.

Henry took his foot soldiers and mounted cavalry down off the stone path and into the dense swamps to the north of the stout lakes hoping to conceal his forces from the full might of her power. Eireannos had to act quickly to save the humans. He leaped into the air and grabbed the silver sword from the Morgannis and landed back onto the earth.

The banshee queen cursed him and lashed a barrage of dark energy onto him. He felt the sword being grasped out of his hand but his eyes were blinded by the witch's energy attack.

He finally deflected the energy back onto the Morgannis causing her to hiss with anger and tried to locate the humans. The Aoes Shee were escorting them through the marshes and towards the direction of the portal entrance to the human realm.

He felt a stabbing pain in his spine and saw his own aura spew out around his own body. As he fell to his knees he managed to turn his head around to see Drevathius smiling and pulling the silver sword from out of his back. The sword had increased itself in size to suit the massive wrathiens hand. He felt a sharp pain in his eyes and his vision darkened but he forced himself to stay alive, only he could stop the witch and the consequences of him dying were worse than death itself.

'Go after the humans and slay every one of them then you can rule the rest of the wrathien rabble for all eternity!'

Drevathius looked up at the floating witch and smiled greedily and kicked Eireannos down onto the ground and ran off into the direction of the human army wildly brandishing the now giant silver weapon.

Eireannos could not endure the nature of this betrayal but knew the only hope of salvation was to find a way to get the witch into the tomb entrance, the humans would have to fend for themselves.

'My mother give me the strength from within to rise!' But he could no longer feel her presence. His frustration and sadness fused together brewing an awful unearthly dark rage, his faded silver hue now turned to a dark metallic sheen and he rose to his feet growling and ignoring the huge masses of fiend soldiers attacking him. He shrugged them off and long dark talons extended from his four dark massive hands, the remaining pack of turned wrathiens halted their impending attack on him and fled in terror. The young wrathien roared to the heavens in rage knocking hundreds onto the ground. He scanned the area and saw that the two remaining Siabhra and the Aoes Shee warriors had come back from escorting the humans out into their own realm and were slaying the remaining fiend forces. His dark rage was fuelled in hope at the heroic sight of thirty two figures battling thousands of dark freakish brutes and winning!

The Morgannis had ceased attacking the forces below her with a look of concern, he knew that look well enough from his last battle with her. She was preparing to escape. But he could not let her go, she would simply leave and in time cause another endless array of battles and chaos, utter annihilation was the only way to put an end to this.

The Morgannis lashed out one last bitter flow of evil energy from her hands at the battling forces below to cover her escape and even took out large parts of her own fiend armies in the process but Eireannos leaped through her energy blasts and slammed his gargantuan body into her sending her reeling backwards down towards the earth and right through the giant door way. He then flew like an eagle covering the distance in seconds and followed her through the doorway and pinned her to the ground inside the tomb entrance.

With a look of utter hatred he slayed her with one stroke of his sword arm creating a suffocating explosion of dark ash and smoke.

The Spungle relaxed even more as he recalled using his living armour to slay the banshee queen but he became agitated again as he now witnessed more of the unfolding battle as the Morgannis resurrected to the horror of all.

Vrool strained desperately to keep the Spungle focused as Shard delved deeper into its memory, the beast constantly fluxed from jet black to dark silver metal as its mood rapidly fluxed and changed. The raging chaos of the past battle still shimmered and glowed above them in the sphere that Vrool had created.

'Keep her entombed! Close the doors!' Roared out Vrool to his wrathien ally as a new wave of master fiends approached the pathway leading up to the mountain entrance.

The Aoes Shee king felt a huge slap against his chest and was flung through the air by a massive blast of dark energy from the resurrected Morgannis and he fell into the expectant masses of approaching master fiend warriors.

'No!' The Spungle remembered shouting out in concern for his dear ally. He leaped into the dark wave of master fiends along with the rest of Vrool's forces and started to dismantle the attackers. A fresh laugh filled the air even stopping the marauding fiends in their tracks.

'My transformation is complete, the dark magic and I are as one!' She cackled triumphantly and started to reform herself and made for the giant doors to escape.

Eireannos noticed another steely set of reflections coming from out of the dark masses of the master fiends. His remaining wrathien pack were now free of the Morgannis' spell and were charging and trampling through the fiend forces along with Vrool and his Aoes Shee warriors to assist him but before he could reach the doorway the Morgannis leaped from out of it but to his surprise the banshee queen seemed to rebound harshly off an invisible barrier and was flung onto the ground in confusion.

The last two Siabhra warriors left from the battle stood side by side with hands outreached deep in concentration creating a massive spell to block the witch from escaping. Eireannos' heart lifted in hope as he jumped into the air and used his unique gift of flight to sail past the Siabhra and force shut the massive doors.

He felt his chest erupt with a stabbing pain and saw a silver blade protrude out from the front of his body. The wrathien warrior known as Drevathius had returned from his mission to slaughter the human forces and had sent the enchanted sword of the Morgannis hurtling through the air into the back of Eireannos. Before Eireannos' companions could reach Drevathius the rogue wrathien warrior leaped high into the air and was scooped up by a huge monstrous stone coloured dragon that flew off with him in the direction of the Siabhra home world.

'You not only betray your own race but now you betray me in my time of need?'
The Morgannis shouted out aloud and rose to her feet and pressed back at the Siabhra's spell pushing the beautiful young warriors backwards and making them lose their balance.

Eireannos' life seeped out of his body but he stumbled forward and fell just short of the exhausted Siabhra and landed in a heap in front of the delighted Morgannis.

'You are at last dead!' The witch blasted the two Siabhra warriors off of their feet and floated towards the hulking body of a faintly breathing Eireannos with a gloating malice.

'The mighty dark fist has been outwitted and slain by his own kind! I told you that I would destroy everything that you loved before your cursed eyes and so it has come to pass! With you gone the balance shall sway in my favour but I think I have done enough this day, perhaps I shall send you on your way now to whatever useless gods that made you!'

She held the Siabhra's spell at bay and pushed back further while casting a deadly torrent of glowing energy towards the remaining Wrathiens and Aoes Shee forces. Laughing as she did so she materialised a silver knife coated in the aura of slain wrathien essence.

'And now my friend! Time to die!'

Eireannos sprang to life, reaching out towards her with one of his mighty arms he grabbed her and flung her back towards the tomb doors.   H e started to crawl weakly towards the doors to shut them forever. The spell was cast so that only he could secure the doors shut for eternity but he felt his life nearly at an end and the Banshee playfully laughed at his attempt to entomb her. Vrool and his forces had finished off the remaining fiend forces and closed in rapidly on the Morgannis and were about to leap past Eireannos and finish the job.

But the sky above them darkened and a massive winged beast the size of a small mountain appeared above them and Drevathius the rogue wrathien was sat upon the back of its massive head spitting out vile wrathien curses at the army below him.

The massive dark beast lashed out its gigantic tail at the wrathien forces sending them hurtling through the air and landing far way in the misty lakes surrounding the mountain temple.

Vrool and his sons Synar-Chro and Mil-Mil Ulthu were far too swift for the gigantic creature and evaded the beast's tail. The entire force of the Aoes Shee flung their serrated shields upwards towards the giant winged beast and knocked Drevathius off of the dark creatures head causing his massive body to plummet towards the earth and collide with the ground far off in the distance. The great dark beast seemed to lose its awareness and flew off into the distance towards the Selfin mountains roaring much to the joy of the Aoes Shee warriors.

Quickly they ran to the aid of the rapidly weakening Siabhra sisters who still pushed back at the witch but they were forced back along with the Siabhra from a deadly blast of energy from the Morgannis.

'Surrender! You are all beaten! There is not a wretched one of you that lives that can entomb me! Your plan has failed!'

The Allies felt themselves beaten down by an increasingly powerful banshee queen mystified as to the immense power of the dark energy that she had summoned. The sky grew black as night and with one last great effort the banshee queen knocked the Siabhra and their allies backwards into the air in a concussed heap littering the giant pathway leading up to the doors of the tomb.

As the rogue banshee queen floated towards the doorway for the last time her face brightened and she took out a long black comb from within her white robe and softly combed her long black hair savouring the carnage and destruction that lay in front of her.

'The land that was swindled from my time as a maid now returns as my enemies I do now slay! My dark union with he who has slumbered far away is growing stronger as the good in the land fades in decay!'

A beast cried out to the west of the Banshee, a sound that she had not heard in the realm for centuries. Eireannos' failing vision strained to locate the creature. Before his vision lapsed into darkness he saw a beautiful white horse leap up onto the massive white stone pathway leading up to the giant tomb doors and sitting atop the beautiful steed was the human known only to him as Henry.

His vision failed, he crawled his way toward the doors praying to himself that he would hold his course. His rapidly numbing body faintly felt the dead carcasses of fellow wrathiens and wounded Aoes Shee warriors littered around him. He was almost upon the doors, all he had to do was to reach out and push them gently but even this simple act was in jeopardy with his failing strength. He heard a startled screech from the banshee queen and the sound of a human roaring at the top of his voice and then a collision of some kind.

It had to be the human tackling the Morgannis. He knew he had no choice, the doors had to be slammed shut. If this was the last act of the wrathien he would give his life to accomplish it. He mustered all his remaining strength and stood up, completely blind he felt his body give way and start to fall. All he could do was to fall towards what he thought was the location of the giant doors. He reached out all of his arms and drew his last breath and committed himself to landing against the doors. As he fell he heard screams of alarm and the wailing of the vile witch, a vast wailing even more desperate than the last one that she had let out when he had first defeated her. As he let himself sink into darkness he felt a cold wind sweep over him and then a joyous elated roar of triumph echoed out around his body. He would let this triumphant chant of Aoes shee warriors and Wrathien pack soldiers carry him off to the other world secure in the knowledge that he had given everything that he had to ensure the survival of his race.

'Keep him still my queen you know what's to come if he survives this oncoming memory then he can survive anything!'

The giant hall shook so much that the walls started to crack and debris started to fall from the massive ceiling high overhead.

'Please my old friend stay your course I am here with you!' Shard looked over at Vrool with tears flowing from her eyes. 'I feel his sorrow, this is affecting me also!'

'My love I will protect you, make yourself as a mirror does as it reflects back what is cast upon it, we owe it to him to complete his reckoning with the past!'

The sphere was growing larger and spinning more rapidly creating a chaotic kaleidoscope of colours and hues in the massive hall. 'Be ready now! It comes upon him!'

Both Shard and Vrool felt as if they were now sucked up into the sphere of light. They were now part of the vision and yet outside of it as well. Being able to see the spinning orb with its reflections of the past and also feeling that they were beside the vision of the young wrathien inside the sphere.

The icy cold frost of a winter's morning gently tickled his body and a fresh wave of life rushed through his lungs setting his hearts to beat a gentle rhythm. His eyes were open but the darkness took some moments to fade from his vision. His body could not yet move but his awareness began to expand and he noticed that he was lying on his side underneath a blanket of rolling mist. Sensation began to stir more strongly in him and his body felt the texture of mountain stone beneath him.

Is this what I've longed for to find true peace? Am I in the vaults of my creators in the sky?

He felt a set of powerful hands on either side of him pull him gently onto his feet. He stood weakly at first, swayed by a cold mountain breeze. His body started to ache from the countless wounds inflicted on him by his own race.

'So I have not ascended, what is to be of my faith?'

As his vision was restored to him Grawd-Dun-Ulos the enormous guardian of the mountain cathedral came into view. He was a massive stone humanoid creature who sat upon a gigantic throne of rock and crystal. On either side of the gigantic creature stood the surviving members of the Wrathien pack all dwarfed by the massive guardian.

'Daragnar Gulthume - the mountain cathedral! The dwelling of the earthly gods of the wrathien race. How am I still alive? And why have you brought me here?'

The great grim looking stone creature looked down on him with heavy eyes and spoke.

'The Aoes Shee queen has revived you, she rests now in her mountain temple exhausted from the battle with the Morgannis. She protected the temple from harm while Vrool assisted the Siabhra and your remaining companions in the battle at the foot of An teampall sliabh barr an tsolais! You are here to answer to your kind for the murder of your companions!'

'Murder? They were all turned by the witch and attacked me! Every last one of them including the very ones who stand before me now!'

'Your account of the situation is honest but you slayed your own kind and this is a violation of your oath to protect your people, the penalty for this is death!'

'You let the Aoes Shee queen revive me so that you can then kill me?'
'You have to answer for your crimes and Shard was confident that she could save you.'

'I am sure that you neglected to mention that it was your intention to execute me after she had healed me!'

'True but we took the opportunity that presented itself! What have you to say for yourself before I carry out the sentence?'

Eireannos looked over at his companions. Each wrathien warrior had a look of dread on their faces. They seemed to be held against their will.

'Let my companions speak for themselves on the matter and not be mute witnesses for a creature that openly states that I should be executed with such haste that makes even a banshee inquisitor seem sluggish!'

'Your sentence is final I have spoken! Your execution shall be in your surface village! Take him to his final resting place so that he can see the full extent of his crimes!'

His companions led him away with a guilty look on their faces. Eight wrathien warriors left alive from all of the wrathien packs in his home-world, he could barely stand upright and shuffled along with the help of his surviving pack.

'What further crimes am I to be accused of? I wish to see my battle queen! Why is she not here to defend my actions?'

'Prepare yourself Eireannos, I can say no more under the law of this realm, I warn you! Say nothing until we reach the borders of our home!'

Grunthuuleon his former pack member spoke very quietly under his breath for fear of being heard. Eireannos had never seen this cowardly behaviour from any wrathien and it deeply disturbed him. A full day cycle passed without the wrathiens speaking until finally they reached the outskirts of their realm.

Grunthuuleon ordered the pack to stop and without warning they all circled Eireannos and embraced him. His weak body was overcome by emotion but he did his best to return each of his comrade's embrace.

'Forgive us mighty Eireannos we had no choice! The traitor Drevathius made his way to Grawd-Dun-Ulos and accused us of siding with the Morgannis during the battle and we spent many hours protesting our innocence but even after the guardian was satisfied that we were not traitors he would not believe that you were blameless!'

Eireannos struggled with the logic of what was being told to him. 'How can a wrathien traitor plagued with the stains of the Morgannis manage to convince one of our earthly god's that I am a villain? I sense the work of the Morgannis at hand, where is she now?'

'You entombed her along with the human protector of the Gikkie Bokker younglings, you saved us all, believe me when I say that you had no choice but to close the doors, the human sacrificed himself so as to give you time to seal the doors forever!'

'Then it is over! But why are you all so grim? We have lost much yes none more than I in the loss of my brother king but we shall rebuild our ranks once more!'

Silence greeted him at first but as he looked at each of his pack they began to weep.

'What are you not telling me?'

The young wrathien suddenly suspected the worst and ran down the massive footpath of his realm into his village. His pack stayed behind as if their legs were fused to the ground.

Grunthuuleon closed his eyes shut tightly as he did his best to block out the enormous roar of shock and sorrow that erupted from the centre of the wrathien village. Gradranos his companion attempted to run after the grieving Eireannos but was firmly stopped by the rest of the pack.

'Easy Gradranos he needs time! Do not interfere with his mourning!' The glowing sphere in the giant hallway began to show different sections of Eireannos' memory in a rapid sequence causing Vrool and Shard to strain hard to control the speed at which Eireannos was recalling his past. The wrathiens body shuddered and convulsed and tears fell from his closed eyes.

'What have they done to each other? How have our gods let this happen?' He roared.

'My brave Eireannos it was the spell of the Morgannis, it did not just affect us! It also turned our own families and darklings against each other. There was no living thing that could have prevented this, we can only thank our gods that she is now entombed forever!'

'Damn you and your gods Grunthuuleon!' Eireannos grabbed him by the neck and lifted him off the ground but quickly released him and fell to the ground sobbing.

'I have saved a world but my own has been taken from me, what good is my sacrifice now? Our race is destroyed! Where is my queen?'

His roar unsettled his companions and the forest valley shook with his rage.

'Hear us out Eireannos I grieve for your loss and we have had time to grieve were as you have not but we must hasten our plans!' Gradranos placed a comforting hand on his fallen companions shoulder.

'We are not executing anyone and more than that we are choosing exile to leave these lands! Our earth bound gods can be offended all they like yet they did not help us once in battle! We shall leave these lands and find a new home in secrecy away from their self-righteousness influence and fade into the shadows. This land is now dark and forever night! It is a curse left upon this realm by the hand of the Morgannis and the corrupted energy of our slain brethren! We have already taken our battle queen to safety, she is well and she left something for you!'

Gradranos placed a dark shiny orb into Eireannos' hand.

'It is a message for you and you alone, she has instructed us to leave you for now only saying that you have an important task at hand. I pray that we see you soon. Farewell for now mighty Eireannos!'

His pack all touched him on the shoulder as they marched back up the giant pathway leading out onto the Selfin Mountain's leaving him to quietly sob away to himself. Eireannos wept for days in the same spot and his exterior skin became dark and dull. When he came to his senses he buried his whole village in an underground tomb but did not look upon the message orb for many more days.

Vrool and Shard stared in amazement at the memories flashing before them on the floating sphere for they had never witnessed the full truth of what had happened to Eireannos. The wrathiens body relaxed again and went limp giving the exhausted Aoes Shee king and queen precious moments to rest themselves.

A final memory materialised from out of the glowing sphere and the massive hall ceased to vibrate and shudder. Vrool and Shard looked on with concern. Eireannos picked up the dark message orb and held it gently, reaching out into the dark ether as his battle queen had shown him as a darkling the orb glowed bright orange in his hand.

'My son you have done so well!'

He pondered the somewhat cryptic message from his queen.

'In spite of the great evil that had descended upon us all you were the only one who had the strength to overcome all of her trickery and defeat her. If it were not for you there would not be a single one of us left alive, there is always hope my son!'

He wept at the sound of his Queens voice longing to be with her wherever she was.

'I have another task for you, a task that no other wrathien is capable of! You must remain in this realm and guard it from intruders and ensure that no creature ventures near the tomb of the Morgannis. Protect the mountain temple and our village and seal off the entrance to our wrathien home world, let no entity either living or undead near it! We cannot afford for anyone to harness the power that resides there!'

'I will my queen, when shall you return my beautiful mother?'

'It shall be many planetary cycles before I can return, I am unsure of how effective the entombment of the Morgannis will be and I cannot afford to be exposed to her darkness if she does manage to escape again, it is better that I go into hiding with what's left of your pack and find a way to rebuild our forces in secrecy! Speak of this to no living being, the great realms all think that I am dead and I intend to foster this perception!'

'Please stay with me mother for a little while longer! The emptiness is my only companion! How shall I exist with a lifeless empty realm to look over?'

'You must be strong Eireannos my dark fist, I cannot afford to communicate with you any longer, I fear even though the Morgannis has been entombed she has allies that we cannot account for in these lands, further sharing with you through the dark ether is a risk that we cannot afford to take. We must keep up the deception that there are no more of us left. The traitor Drevathius is still roaming wild and unchecked and with a weapon that can slay a wrathien, do not seek him out or let him fool you into pursuing him out of your realm but if he trespasses slay him. Remember me son for I shall return and we will rebuild our realm!'

The messaging orb faded back into its original hue. He wept to himself with the pain of his wounds from the Morgannis as his only companion. Shunning every living being in the great realms he became dark and unkempt. The more time passed the more he forgot the ways of the great realms, his speech became rough and mean and he showed no respect to any creature. He defended the realms over time more from habit than from remembering any oath of allegiance and became a lowly beast aimlessly patrolling the borders of the Aoes shee realm and the Forrest valley of the Wrathien realm.

Vrool and his queen wept at the memories shown through the eyes of

Eireannos that appeared from out of the floating sphere and they slowly eased the wrathien out of his dream like state. The sphere slowly faded into thin air and the exhausted Aoes Shee stepped away from Eireannos contemplating the revelations that they had discovered by the sharing of the wrathiens thoughts.

'If this is true my love there is the possibility of another wrathien home world!'

'Perhaps my king but Drevathius and his dishonest dealings with Grawd-Dun-Ulos could have seen to their destruction! We cannot chase whispers and shadows! We need to focus on Eireannos and heal him quickly!'

They turned to the deathly still wrathien and gasped in surprise. The body of the massive Eireannos was turning deathly pale and a milky coloured lattice of slimy cob webs was growing all over his body.

'We need to bring him to our mountain temple! I have never seen such a process at work on any creature in our realm, the power of the mountain can save him!'

Without a word Kurn and Bralnar raced over to help their king and queen drag Eireannos' lifeless bulk out of the giant chamber and up the massive spiral stairway.

Vrool spoke aloud to Kurn and Bralnar as they all pulled Eireannos' body up the giant stairway… 'We must seal off this entrance with every tool known to us! The humans Harry and Diarmuid are still in our realm and must be summoned to this cause. I sense that Lidana and Orofey have awakened our sleeping warriors! My connection to them has been restored for the moment, welcome news for a very dark day!'

'Yes my lord I shall call for them as soon as we have dealt with Eireannos!'

'Thank you Kurn! When you have summoned the humans go and take command of the guard at the entrance to the tomb of the Morgannis and my brave Bralnar I need you to leave for the Selfin mountains and check on Vraarl Uldunjen's progress with the Heratii refugees! I will concentrate on restoring strength to the awakening Aoes Shee warriors in the mountain temple and Shard my love use all of your prowess to heal Eireannos!'

Vrool's Aoes Shee warriors nodded in agreement but Shard did not reply. Instead the Aoes Shee queen began to chant a healing spell very softly almost under her breath into the left ear of the giant wrathien warrior but the massive beast did not respond and the slimy trail of milky cobweb grew even denser over his frame.

Vrool stopped suddenly with fright letting go of his grip on the wrathiens body. He fell to his knees in shock as Shard let go of her grip on Eireannos and ran over to him.

'My love what is it?'

'I can sense them again! My sons! And Hugo! They have no idea what they are walking into! They are all in great danger!'

The Aoes Shee king tried to reach out and warn his sons and their allies through the dark ether but the vision swiftly vanished.

Chapter Seventeen – The buried ruins

He deeply inhaled a sharp chilled lung full of damp air. As he gasped from the shock a great clawed hand pulled his limp body from out of the suffocating mound of clay and mud that he was trapped under and he stumbled out of the dirt.

'We were all dead! How did we make it out alive from this?' Hugo staggered onto his feet awkwardly and his eyes strained to make anything out in the gloomy dark. His eyes recovered and he saw that he was standing in a pale green mist strewn tunnel of dirt and rock. The two Aoes Shee brothers stood in front of him observing him closely, their heads almost touched the roof of the tunnel.

'You are very fortunate son of Henry to be alive!' Synar spoke softly and slowly.

'Well I don't feel very fortunate mate... Ah listen ya didn't deserve that! I'm just very sore that's all, are you guys okay?'

'We are faring well Hugo, the amulet that our father gave you has saved your life, its power will now grow and flow into you, I fear that you shall need it soon! But your friends were not so lucky!' The Aoes Shee warrior pointed to the pale bodies of Yardal and Larrymond half-submerged in the earth.

'Ah no, they weren't evil they didn't deserve to die!' Hugo groaned painfully.

Mil-Mil Ulthu placed a hand onto Hugo's amulet and closed his eyes in deep thought.

'We could not revive them, I am very sorry! But we must move!

Hugo! Your amulet! It will talk to you soon enough, so do not be alarmed if you hear voices inside you.'

'Ye Wha? Not more bleedin voices for goodness sake!'
The Aoes Shee warrior opened his eyes slowly and moved his hand onto Hugo's shoulder.

'Come Hugo, free your earthly companion for we must move.'
Hugo looked to the other side of the tunnel and saw Reginold's upper body stuck in a mound of loose soil his legs wriggling to get free. He walked over to him and grabbed the old man's two feet and pulled hard. Reginold landed in a heap cursing to himself and spitting out pieces of soil from his mouth.

'I think death may be preferable to being with you lot, what on earth happened?'

'We protected you as best as we could earth dweller! But we must move onwards or risk facing another collapse of stone and earth.'

The four figures marched along the tunnel and it started to decline steeply and they all became soaked in the cold green mist.

'Any idea where we are my boys?' Asked Reginold.
'They are no longer with us Reginold! I am sorry!' Replied Synar in a soft voice.

'My poor old friends! I've done this to them! Please forgive me!' Sobbed Reginold as he ran as fast as he could.
The ground started to rumble shaking loose large lumps of soil and stone loose.

'We must hurry! The time to grieve fully shall come in time! Come now Reginold, Hugo! Follow us quickly!'

The Aoes Shee brothers ran further down the tunnel but slowly enough to allow for the wheezing and panting Hugo to keep up with them. The tunnel was widening but the rate at which loose soil and dirt was falling from the tunnel roof was worsening. The tunnel's slope declined suddenly taking the four allies by surprise and they all stumbled out of the tunnel and onto a dark cliff face.

'What on earth? This can't be possible!'

Hugo peered out in amazement at the unfolding landscape that he overlooked. Below the cliff face and stretching out into the gloomy distance was a huge spacious cavern bathed in eerie green mist. At the far end of the cavern there was a small mountain of white sharp rock with a large path that spiralled gently upwards to the top of the mountain top which was almost touching the roof of the mighty valley cave. In between the mountain and the cliff face that they all stood upon was a gloomy valley floor, a chaotic mix of hillocks of grass mixed with sharp white rock randomly jutting out from the earth at different angles and in the centre of the valley was what resembled a large make shift grave yard with a wooden church overlooking it.

'We must keep moving Hugo, come with us.'

Synar grabbed Hugo and place him onto the back of his neck and took an almost suicidal dive of the edge of the cliff face and scrambled vertically downwards towards the valley floor. Hugo screamed with alarm and held on as tightly as he could shutting his eyes tightly to block out the view of the rapidly approaching valley floor.

'Calm down you fat hairy man!'

Hugo opened his eyes and looked at the back of Synar Chro's head.

'Did you just call me a fat hairy git?'

'Man of earth I have not spoken to you just hold on tightly!'

As he was rocked about on top of Synar's neck he looked over his shoulder at Mil-Mil who was closely behind his brother with a terrified Reginold holding onto him.

Nah, definitely not your voice either! I am imagining things!

'No you are not you thick blob! You woke me up and now we are stuck together!'

'Vrool if I ever see ya again I will give your furry head a slap! A talkin amulet wonderful! Just wonderful!'

Synar reached the end of the cliff face and leaped onto the ground and let Hugo off while Mil-Mil raced ahead of them in a blur of speed to scout for any danger.

'Did you know about this Synar? Talkin bleedin amulets?'

'Yes! We can talk later but we need to find cover, be very silent and follow me.'

'Aha so I am not the only one who hears voices in my head then?' Reginold shouted out.

Mil-Mil Ulthu glared over his shoulder at Hugo's companion.

'Be silent old man we have no knowledge of this place, our enemies may be near.'

Hugo and Reginold shrugged their shoulders and grunted as they followed the Aoes Shee. The ground was damp and grassy in places and littered with large mossy boulders. The terrain did not match anything that they had ever encountered on their hunting adventures.

As they moved deeper into the valley cave they met the first of many graves with worn but unmarked tombstones awkwardly jutting out of the ground. The soil looked like it had been freshly overturned and smelled of pungent decay. Randomly littered everywhere lay a bizarre mix of battle worn pikes, swords and shields. They all stopped short of the rusty iron boundary fence leading up to the wooden church and looked around. The green mist cleared enough for them to see further in the distance. Past the old church grounds and before the small underground mountain was a green lake split into two by a long stone pathway that lead upwards into the winding mountain trail. There were two stone towers nested into the base of the small mountain, one was almost upright and the other one had collapsed in front of it.

'This place is really weird, parts of forest mixed with hills of dirty mossy grass and then huge boulders sitting around like a giant just threw a few around for sport. It's a complete mess! What happened here?'

'Hugo go into the church with Reginold while we scout further on.' The voice was from both Aoes Shee warriors and was sent into Hugo's mind. He shuffled angrily into the ruins of the church grounds. The church itself was constructed from old dark wooden planks and was clumsily put together. It was as if whomever had built the structure was either drunk or blindfolded. He walked right up to the church and examined the structure. The dark planks were solid and very hard.

'We can hide up in here for a while until we figure out what to do, Do you still have your gun with you?'

'Why in fact yes I do but I've only five rounds remaining.'

'Better than nuthin Reginold, let's see if we can get into that church.' They walked towards the double arched doorway and grabbed the simple black iron handles on it and to their surprise the doors effortlessly swung open. As they walked in the green mist outside seeped into the church giving off enough glowing light so that Hugo could make out the detail inside. The inside had everything a regular church would have, pews statues and an altar but it was deserted. The windows on closer inspection had no glass but had very thick cruciform frames that let four openings of dim light in from the outside. The statues were carved out of rough stone and quartz and a large crucifix stood upright behind the altar. Hugo walked outside into the grounds and picked up a handful of the best pikes and swords that he could find from the rough graves and brought them back inside. He nearly tripped over a large piece of quartz and stone that had broken off of one of the statues and picked it up.

'Best to get to work and sharpen a few of these until the scruff bags get back'.

'Yeah sharpen the weapons for all the good it will do for ya! Can you not smell the danger around ya?'

Hugo spun around to face Reginold in surprise who in turn was looking back at him in astonishment.

'Reggie! Did you just hear that as well?'

'Yes! Yes I did, and look! Your amulet was glowing as I heard the voice.'

'So is yours!'

'Well well well! So you pair of paddy geniuses are starting to figure it out at last!'

This time the sarcastic toned voice was heard aloud startling the companions.

'That sounds like a young Gikkie Bokker! Hugo it has that unmistakable multi toned pitch to it! Go on and show yourself you young cur!'

'Easy now Reggie, if it is then at least we know that it's friendly.'

'Friendly? I ain't your friend you pair of scaldy nosed maggots!'

Hugo had endured enough of the taunting and took his amulet off and placed it onto the church floor and started to study it closely. The amulet that Vrool had given him was changing. The gold and silver metal that it was made from was flowing almost like a slow liquid and the form of the engraving of the two Siabhra warriors crossing swords over the portal beneath the moon started to disappear and was flowing into an entirely different shape.

'Reggie! Take your amulet off and place it beside mine quick.'

The skinny old man did as Hugo suggested but his amulet was not changing at all. After a brief moment of flowing metal the design of Hugo's amulet morphed into the face of a Gikkie Bokker youngling.

Then it blinked its eyes and spoke aloud.

'Better get used to me buddy cause I'm your conscience from now on!' It laughed in a mocking tone. Hugo squinted and a nervous twitch of frustration was starting to develop in his right eye.

'Why you manky mangy flea ridden messer, I'm not putting ya on my neck again, ya can stay in me pocket from now on!'

'Easy now my good fellow I am sure that there is an explanation for this!' Said Reginold in a soothing voice.

'That's easy for you Reggie your amulet doesn't talk back to ya! We just survived and god knows how a huge land slide and are lost in an underground grave yard and for what? To have a snivelling runt of a Gikkie Bokker haunt my amulet?'

The double doors opened slowly and the Aoes Shee warriors walked in towards Hugo and Reginold. They both carried a bunch of pikes in each of their hands and placed them down at the men's feet.

'Take a stone and sharpen these, we shall set up a perimeter within the church grounds.'

'Synar did ya know that this amulet of mine has a talking Gikkie Bokker on it?'

'Get used to it Hugo, that amulet is a one of a kind! Treat it well as he can save your life!'

'He? Ah no I got a feeling I've more questions to be asking, why can't my stupid set of diaries open like they are supposed to so I can know about all of this stuff in advance?'

The bound leather diary of his ancestor Alastair fell out of his inside jacket pocket and opened neatly on the first page the moment that it hit the church floor.

'Ah, well now at least that much went in me favour!'

He bent down and picked the diary up. Examining it carefully he read the inside title.

The lost lore of the other people – Diary two, Alastair MacNiadh.

'At Last!'

He ignored his amulet and attempted to read the next page.

'Ya could of said thanks for me opening the smelly book for ya!'

He looked down at his amulet in surprise.

'You opened it? If ya did then thanks, now just let me read over a little bit will you?'

Mil-Mil dragged Hugo to his feet.

'Sharpen the weapons first and create a perimeter within the church grounds as we have requested, then you can read.' Hugo sniffed at Mil-Mil cheekily but grabbed a set of long pikes and left the church leaving his amulet behind.

Reginold picked up his amulet and placed it back around his neck and reached down to pick up Hugo's talking amulet.

'Get your skanky hands of me ya lanky scarecrow!'

Reginold recoiled in surprise and quickly picked up a set of pikes and left the church in a nervous stride.

Reginold stepped outside. The air was growing colder still and the green mist became more luminous and seemed to be flowing faster along the earth. He took a deep gulp of air but then coughed out loudly momentarily forgetting about the putrid stench from the huge graveyard beyond. He looked for Hugo who was at the front iron gates and walked over to him.

'A perimeter eh? What are these Gikkie Bokker warrior things getting up to now?'

'Don't know Reggie! I guess they are as in the dark as much as we are on this and plan to dig in and think things over with us.'

'Perhaps, these weapons, you know they are of the same fashion as the pike weapons of the seventeen hundreds?'

'No Reggie I didn't know that, what's the significance?'

'Since I put on my amulet information of all varieties has seeped into my mind, events that seem like my own memories but they are not yet I feel like I am there when I remember them! Most strange! Anyhow I saw a great battle and amongst the carnage I remember seeing a small army of humans fighting alongside the Gikkie Bokkers and also that Spungle beast and his companions. The thing that stuck most in my mind is the weapons that they used. These are exactly the same as I remembered in my visions, just older!'

'Terun-nill-vath-doom! The last great war!'

The voice boomed out from across the church grounds. Synar-Chro stepped towards them after placing the last set of sharpened pikes facing out towards the direction of the graveyard.

'And you are correct old man of earth, these are the very ones! Come with us inside earth dwellers! We must talk now!'

They all sat down along the steps of the altar, the inside of the church illuminated by the Aoes Shee warriors glowing eyes. Synar was the first to speak.

'My brother and I fought alongside your kind hundreds of your earth years ago. Most of your forces were slain! Only a handful remained after Henry's brave sacrifice. During the course of the battle the Morgannis set a wrathien traitor by the name of Drevathius loose upon your retreating human forces armed with the deadliest weapon that has ever been wielded in any battle. Your forces made it out beyond the portal but shortly afterwards Drevathius returned to meet us in battle boasting aloud to us in a vile taunt that he had destroyed your kind. And here we sit just a short distance away from an arsenal of scattered weapons that exactly match what was used against the Morgannis by your forces!'

Hugo and Reginold shuddered with the cold wrapping their arms around themselves to keep the warmth of their bodies from escaping.

Mil-Mil Ulthu took notice of them and spoke aloud an incantation. 'Lumenar-brom-scald' He commanded as he pointed his hand towards a stone statue nearby which began to glow with a steady heat.

'We suspect that this place contains the remains of our human allies that were killed by Drevathius all those years ago but as to why they are buried in this strange place is a mystery to us. We need you to stay here while we travel to the mountain in the distance and see where the path on it leads to. Hopefully to a way out of here for I have already tested the waters below it and they lead nowhere!'

'Okay Mil-Mil we can stand guard here but will you tell me what's up with this talking amulet of mine before you go?'

'We have no time, we must reach the surface soon, there could be open war raged upon the surface by now and our king will have need of us all so I suggest that while you are here Hugo read the second diary of Alastair! I am sure that it will appease your curiosity!'

'Marvellous! I feel like a school child that's just been given an answer by a snotty nosed teacher, meh!' The Aoes Shee warriors stood up and made their way out of the church.

'Right then might as well read a bit, Reggie get some sleep I will fill you in on anything that I learn from this diary!'

'I can help I can help!' The voice came from the rear of the church were Hugo had set down his amulet. He threw his eyes up in the air with frustration at the irritating voice.

'What do ya mean smart ass?'
'You can read and I can send the story into your skinny friend's mind cause he has an amulet as well, go on and give it a go!'

'And why should I want to do that when I could just as easily ask you what's in the diary?'

'I don't know what's in the diary you mutton headed freak! You've got to read it first! Then I can send your thoughts into the amulet for your friend.'

'Well that's mighty obliging of ya!'

'You woke me up when you died and I had to save you and now I can't go back asleep! I might as well do something while I'm up!'

'I died? Wait a minute how did that happen?'

'Just read the bloomin book will ya? I am up for a lark!'

Hugo sighed and looked over at a bemused Reginold who eagerly motioned for him to start reading the second diary.

Chapter Eighteen – The other people

Saturday, the twenty seventh of August eighteen hundred and three.

It has been just one week since we have arrived back in London to be reunited with our lovely Miranda. We are all well and overjoyed, the hug that I gave her after I had spotted her waiting for us at the train station in London spoke more to her than our choked up words could ever have done. She knew instantly from our hugs that our trip was far more of an ordeal than was expected and it took a great amount of explanation from us all to convince her of what had happened. She still looks at me in a funny way from the corner of her eye as if we have made it all up but is letting things pass because she sees the sincerity in all of our eyes. It has made our home life a little uncomfortable as she told me she thinks that we may have imagined it all due to the stress that we were under during the voyage which has upset Bobbert and Emily a little.

Every night when I tuck away Bobbert and Emily they ask me why mummy does not believe us and all I can do is to reassure them that it takes time for her to understand because our adventure was so stupendously enormous. This eases the tension somewhat. In time I am tempted to bring her along with us on a return trip to Ireland and introduce her to our furry friends but something is holding me back, I feel it is not the right time to do so and our home life is much more important a thing to stabilise right now after having been separated for so long. Every night I hold her in my arms and thank god that I have such a lovely caring and beautiful wife and when she falls asleep I spend a little time looking out of our balcony out across the Thames River and reminisce about our adventure. When I see the moon it brings me right back to how the creature's eyes looked, hypnotic and spell binding, and hearing the starlings call or the Magpies warbles brings me back to the unearthly speech that they use.

I feel torn right now as if two worlds are competing for my presence as if a bigger force is at work shaping our destiny, very strange and dream-like but I have resigned myself to the belief that one would naturally be inclined to feel this way after having experienced such a fantastical voyage. Emily has made a few woollen dolls that resemble the creatures and Bobbert plays around the garden mimicking their calls. All in all things are settling down as best as they can. I do miss them all so and would love to find out how they are fitting into their new home.

Thursday, the sixth of August eighteen hundred and three.

Miranda and the children called into the royal society of gentleman adventurers club this afternoon to see me but Miranda was in such a fluster that I had to usher her into a private room to get a coherent answer from her. She saw a tall grim looking man follow her into the local market and all the way up to the club. It takes a lot to frighten my dear Miranda and I ran downstairs and out onto the street to find the ruffian and there he was, bold as brass standing across the other side of the street looking into the doorway were I had just emerged from. A very grim looking individual, tall and pale with a sour bitter look on his face and a ghastly pair of steel blue eyes nested into a balding skull. I approached him and demanded to know what he was up to but before I could finish my sentence he lashed out at me with a powerful fist and almost floored me with a right hook. I managed to regain my balance and retaliated against the brute with a short uppercut underneath his protruding jaw that staggered him backwards and made him smack into the red brick wall of the local pub. It was only then that I recognised him. This was the brute that called himself 'Iron Knuckles' from Bokwana Island, I did not recognise him from a distance with a gentleman's clothing on and I got such a surprise I nearly fainted.

I was fortunate to get the attention of a local police officer who arrested him for assault and disrupting the peace. As he was taken away he made no sound but looked over his shoulder at another man who was lurking outside the entrance to the lane way beside the gentleman adventurers club. I attempted to approach the man but he quickly made off down the alleyway and scaled the wall at its end.

I returned to Miranda and the children and let them knew that everything had been taken care of and they were greatly relieved. I however felt very concerned but hid it and made my way to the police station and requested an audience with the arrested Iron Knuckles. Despite his up market tweed clothing his awkward shifty gait and mean personality refused to be hidden. His finger nails were long and untrimmed and yellow with rot and his breath smelled of alcohol and he stared at me slyly as if comforted by some dark thought. I was permitted to question him on why he was following my family but only replied to me after being threatened with a more lengthy incarceration. He simply said that he had powerful friends who were looking to get back his property on his behalf. Then he remained silent and would not respond at all. That night I received a telephone call from the police station that the wall of the cell that he was in was ripped open from the outside and Iron Knuckles had escaped.

I immediately locked and bolted every door and unlocked my arms chest and loaded up my revolver and shotgun. I knew what that brute meant by his property but powerful friends could mean anyone. I kept Miranda and the children upstairs and patrolled my grounds almost relishing the idea of finishing this brute off but he did not turn up that evening at all.

Tuesday, the sixth of December eighteen hundred and three.

Life very much went on as normal with everyone forgetting about our troubles and settling into normality with ease until two days ago. The man who Iron Knuckles had looked at as he was being arrested showed up outside Bobbert and Emily's school this morning. I caught him by accident as I was leaving in my carriage. I gave chase but he disappeared into the crowd at Old Street Train Station. I contacted Inspector Belmont and arranged for a police patrol to keep an eye on the school from now on and have hired a private body guard to keep an eye on our house when I am away. I managed to get a good look at the rascal so he is a marked man. He was as tall as Iron Knuckles and quite like him to think of it but slimmer, much older and far more well-groomed but his eyes were jet black and had a degree of sharp wittedness about them. I don't know what to expect next from these people but I fear for my family more than I do for myself.

Yesterday Malcolm our private body guard did not show up for work in the morning and our ground floor was burgled. The entire floor was turned upside down and wrecked but nothing was taken and yet the police patrol spotted nothing. Today I am going to rent out a few rooms in a hotel in Devon to keep Miranda and the children safe while I keep patrolling our home and face down these villains.

Thursday, the eight of December eighteen hundred and three.

My family has been kidnapped! I got a note in my letter box this morning only a day after sending Miranda and our children to the Restful Pines hotel in Devon. The kidnappers have demanded that I return what's rightfully theirs to them by the end of the week or I shall never see my family again. That monster Iron Knuckles and whatever gang of criminals he has teamed up with shall have no resting place if they harm my loved ones, the kidnappers did not mention a way to even contact them or even a place to return The Gikkie Bokkers to but no matter I have no intention to return to Ireland and place these creatures back into the custody of these vile men. I informed the police and a man hunt is on but I am not hopeful of this being resolved soon.

Friday, the seventh of December eighteen and hundred and three.

I cried myself to sleep last night and then had a strange dream. I felt the Gikkie Bokker creatures reaching out to me. They spoke to me in my own language and comforted me and sounded very sad and concerned.

Two stood out from the group that I saw, a male and a female, both had amazingly haunting eyes and were taller than the rest. The image of them stayed with me a few moments after I had awoken.

Despite policemen patrolling my grounds another letter was delivered through my letter box this morning demanding that I leave their property at an abandoned warehouse on the local docks on Sunday morning. I am now panicking as I have no idea what to do. Even if I was to hand over the creatures it would take more than a couple of days to do it. I am going to patrol the surrounding area tonight in hope that I can locate one of the ringleaders lurking about.

Saturday, the eight of December eighteen hundred and three.

I managed to get an hours sleep last night after an intensive patrol and had another dream. The same Gikkie Bokkers appeared to me and told me to get ready, that they're coming! I am unsure if this means that the kidnappers are coming or that the Gikkie Bokkers are coming but I have resolved to myself that if I simply show up at the abandoned warehouse alone then I can reason with these people and work something out.

Monday, the tenth of December eighteen hundred and three.

I write this piece with thanks to god for the wonderful outcome that occurred yesterday morning but also I shall have memories of sorrow that shall go with me to the grave. I turned up at the old warehouse and walked inside through a rusty torn opening in the huge sliding doors. It was a perfectly chosen place as there was so much old disused machinery and scrap littering the entrance that it would make any policeman's job extremely difficult to navigate safely unless they were familiar with the area. The warehouse itself was extremely dark and the scrap and debris inside was arranged to create a narrow pathway leading further on ahead into utter blackness.

I slowly made my way through the passageway which lead into a large opening that was surrounded by more rubbish and old wooden crates which created a circular barrier. For a moment I almost thought that I was inside the makeshift coliseum that the villagers on Bokwana Island had created for their vile tournaments. I was grabbed from behind by two large burly thugs and held still while that horrible man that was spying on my children appeared out of the shadows in front of me. As similar to Iron Knuckles as he was this evil excuse for a human being had an aura about him, I wished to have plunged myself into the Thames to cleanse myself of his dark presence after one look up close at him.

He introduced himself as Mister Ilgrim Borglum, philanthropist of discerning tastes and worthy causes. I remember losing myself to intense anger and breaking free of my thug escorts to get a hold on his throat but Borglum pointed his finger at my head and an unseen force brought me swiftly to my knees. I could not raise my head to meet his accursed face but I did see Iron Knuckles walk from out of the gloom to stand beside him. Iron Knuckles began to demand his property back but was speaking to Borglum and not myself. Borglum silenced the brute and raised me upright onto my feet again and demanded to know where were the Gikkie Bokkers. I was shocked as he used the name itself and he smiled when he noticed the look of dread on my face.

I pleaded with him that a few days was not enough time to bring them back to London and I offered to give him information on where they were if he promised that he would leave the creatures unharmed. His face became even colder and hollow looking at my attempt to bargain and he made a gesture to a group of henchmen half concealed by the shadows to my left. As soon as he did so I heard my Emily scream with fright. Borglum seemed to enjoy the suffering he was causing and I became enraged with a power I have never felt before. I threw off the thugs that were restraining me and raced towards the direction of Emily's scream. Borglum reached out after me and I felt his power grip me but the sheer single minded will power I had to protect my loved ones was greater still and I leaped into the darkness at the partially shaded henchmen and knocked them all unconscious. Before I could reach were I thought Emily was a series of bright lamps flooded the warehouse with a harsh dazzling light which blinded me for an instant and I felt my body collide with a large metal object which knocked me off of my feet.

As I came to I was swiftly tied up and made stare at what I had just collided with. It was a contraption almost exactly like the one that Iron Knuckles had made to crush the Gikkie Bokker Younglings eggs if they did not fight for him in his arena. The only difference was that this was much larger and instead of a compartment for eggs this device had my whole family inside it.

Borglum was not grinning anymore, his face seemed shocked at how I managed to break free from whatever power that he wielded but he composed himself swiftly and ordered the mouth gags on my family to be removed so I could hear them whimper and cry. This man is good at what he does, like he has had plenty of practice at such tasks in the past but my family to his surprise made no sound despite their predicament and it gave me that extra bit of resolve to keep my own composure.

As I desperately looked around to find a way out of my predicament I noticed that the warehouse was full of not rough henchmen but nearly one hundred well groomed middle aged men much resembling my own appearance or any one of my companions at the gentlemen adventurers club. The one unifying feature of all of them including Ilgrim Borglum was a black sash draped across their left shoulders with three white calligraphic letters on it. B, M and H, I believe was the initials and as best as I can make out the letters were resting upon a graphic emblem of a marsh or bay. Before I could act the local police including one Inspector Belmont arrived in force through the narrow opening and faced Borglum and his men.

To my horror they turned around to face me and joined ranks with

Borglum's followers. Inspector Belmont pleaded with me to hand over the creatures as he was powerless to stop Ilgrim Borglum. I would have dismissed him outright if it were not for the fact that Belmont has been my good friend for a number of years. How much power and influence had this man and how had he amassed it? I was lost and bewildered at my situation and Borglum sensed it revelling in my predicament. At that moment in time I was seriously giving thought to letting him know the location of the creatures, anything to save my family and it was at that moment of utter despair that they arrived.

The old skylights in the rusting roof above us shattered into tiny fragments and a group of claw bearing fur covered silhouettes dropped down and landed amongst Borglum's followers. Utter carnage followed as the finely dressed followers of Ilgrim Borglum drew swords and pistols and attempted to attack the creatures but all that I could make out as I rushed over to the contraption that trapped my family was the blur of human bodies hurtling through the air as if they were rag dolls amongst the unearthly battle cries of the creatures.

As I got to Borglum's invention I saw Iron Knuckles and Borglum race over to the other side of the contraption and pull a set of levers. Three of the Gikkie Bokker younglings saw what the humans had done and leaped through the glass panel where my family was and pushed them out of the compartment but the huge dangling steel spike that was poised above my family came hurtling down too swiftly and crushed the three younglings beneath it.

There was a painfully sharp cry of grief from the remaining Gikkie Bokker Younglings who had by this time rendered all of Borglum's men unconscious. The whole event was a blurred mess as I raced over to check on my beloved family but I knew deep down that they were fine and my heart grieved so for hearing the cries of my fur covered companions it aches inside me so deeply I still have trouble sleeping.

As I tended to Miranda, Bobbert and Emily I noticed the creatures were that bit larger than when I saw them last, each one standing about four feet high except for the male and female that I had seen in my dreams who stood at least five feet high and were much more muscular and fierce looking.

I heard the clatter of old decaying planks and toppling crates as Ilgrim Borglum and Iron Knuckles made an attempt to escape. They had already made some distance from us but the look in the male Gikkie Bokkers expression frightened me. His wonderful expressive and kind eyes swiftly changed to the most terrifying look of anger that I have ever seen in my whole life. His body grew larger still until the creature was at least as tall as I was and he moved so swiftly from where he stood that he became a blur. The creature must have cleared over eighty feet in one second as he blocked off the humans means of exit and picked each of them up in one arm apiece and hurled them into the air were they landed roughly right back at where I had met them. When the male youngling sped back to where we stood he roared with tears in his eyes in grief and spoke an incredibly deep barrage of speech at the humans.

He raised his clawed hands to execute the men but his female companion stayed his hand and pleaded with him to relent. The male creature looked at my Emily and Bobbert crying and his face softened and he raced over to the wrecked contraption and tossed aside the huge steel spike as if it were a match stick to him. All of the Gikkie Bokkers silently stood over the crushed younglings motionless. Bobbert and Emily ran over crying and tried to pat the youngling's fur to comfort them. I started to hear a soft chanting, sweet and lovely to the ear and it felt as if the sound came from within my chest. Two of the younglings started to breath but the third could not be revived, its injuries were too great. The sound of weeping and sobbing from these creatures is an experience that shall never leave me.

We turned our attentions to Borglum and Iron Knuckles who were badly injured after the male youngling hurled them through the air. Borglum's power had no effect on the Gikkie Bokkers but his aura scared my family so I left them with the startled ranks of Inspector Belmont's police force who were still motionless in shock at what had happened. I am amazed at how the younglings never attacked the policemen in spite of their reluctant siding with Borglum but they are not bad men so perhaps they felt the same as I did. I demanded that Inspector Belmont and his men renounce whatever oath that they had taken to assist Ilgrim Borglum and side with us. A stern look from the male and female younglings was enough to see the men agree heartily. Belmont took Borglum and Iron Knuckles and their henchmen to jail in private cells to keep them away from everyone until we could all decide on what further action to take. Over the next day I did my best to communicate with the Gikkie Bokkers as I sneaked them out of the old warehouse and back to my family home.

The female had the dead youngling in her lap the whole time and her male companion never left her side even while we tried to communicate with each other but there was no sense of anything morbid in her actions, there was some purpose in what she was doing.

Wednesday the fourteenth of December eighteen hundred and three.
They want us to return with them to Ireland. Borglum, his men and Iron Knuckles in spite of their actions and the fierce protests of Inspector Belmont were freed yesterday by a group of solicitors claiming to be acting on behalf of an organisation called B-M-H Acquisitions. Whatever legal nonsense that was presented to Belmont unfortunately seemed to hold water and an entire sect of evil men were set loose out into the world again.

The creatures seemed to understand this and the female touched me with her eye stalks and I felt myself floating in a dream-like state but I could feel everything that they wanted to do rather than hearing it being spoken aloud. They know that my home is no longer safe. I spent the next few days arranging for my family to go to Ireland secretly while the Gikkie Bokkers said their good byes to me and vanished, I do not know how they got to London or how they shall return to Ireland.

Belmont promised to keep my London home in good repair and I have given him the house as his on provision that he remain loyal to our cause. All that is left for me is to hand over the keys to Belmont and I shall leave this very evening for Ireland.

Wednesday the twenty first of December eighteen hundred and three.
I have had little time to write as I have been so busy acquiring a splendid mansion house overlooking the very bay that our ship was stranded upon on our first visit to this area. A beautiful but gothic house built upon the hill that overlooks the Irish Sea on its front garden and its back garden faces towards the magical bay. I am impressed by this place but puzzled at how quickly it was built, it has only been two months if even that since our first visit concluded here and there was not even a foundation on that hill. The builders must have been numerous and extremely hardy to accomplish such a feat. The land owner who I bought the house from said that the house had a great many parts pre-assembled to allow for a speedy build but could not keep the house because his fortune had run out. He was a pleasant chap and I bought the house for a just and honest price. Our wrecked ship has vanished without a trace but everything else is as it was on our first journey here. Our Gikkie Bokker friends arrived the day after I purchased the house to the astonishment of Miranda and are spending time with Emily and Bobbert. I feel that the large male and female want me to come with them this evening but I do not know why.

I do not remember them when I was on Bokwana Island, their features are not the same as the group that I rescued and they seem much more serious than the others. I still am amazed at how quickly the male turned so aggressive when fighting but they are not dumb beasts, he was simply protecting his kind from Borglum's henchmen just as I had done.

At mid night the large male and female arrived at my doorstep and reached out their hands to me. I gently accepted their hands and they slowly lead me down out of my mansion and out onto the old dirt path overlooking the mist covered bay. As soon as I touched their hands I could feel their sorrow at the loss of one of their kind seep into me but it felt like they could feel my awareness of this and they appeared moved by my sympathy. They brought me close to the edge of the path with a wide view of the bay in front of me. A wonderful bright white aura flashed in front of me and Eimhir and Brianag the two beautiful protectors of the younglings materialised from out of the light and approached me. They both embraced me at the same time and brought me through the white light with them. It took me a few moments to orient myself as when I walked into the light I found myself stepping out onto the bay but yet it was not the bay. Every colour and feature of the pace was more intense and lush and the size of the moon was immense filling nearly one eight of the sky above us. My old wrecked ship lay in exactly the same spot as when it ran aground, there is strange magic or physics at work here. We spoke at length about how I was and what had happened over in London and they explained a great many details about our furry friends. The younglings sensed that Miranda and the children were in danger and left to help me and apparently swam over to London without a bother to reach us. Eimhir and Brianag were not allowed to leave their lands and had to stay behind. I learned that the ladies are gate keepers – guardians of the entrance to their hidden world and have been busy training and educating our Gikkie Bokker friends to help protect their realm.

Their race is known as the Siabhra who are a mix of warrior and priestess sworn to protect a sacred city far beyond the mountain.

They asked me to help them by taking an intricately detailed amulet that would enable me to access their world at will by simply speaking an incantation. I said that I would need time to think about such a commitment as all I was focused on was settling my family back into a comfortable and safe life.

I ventured with them deep into the misty marshes past a series of lakes and hills up through a dense forest that lead out onto a plateau that had an amazing set of luminous gardens at its end that was overlooked by a tall forested mountain with a large pointed spire at its top.

There were hundreds of women just like Eimhir and Brianag working away just below the spire on an intricately stacked mountain city that was radiant white in appearance. The city was a new home for the Gikkie Bokkers in thanks for coming to the rescue of Maeve the Siabhra queen when she was ambushed by some deadly enemy that none of the Siabhra seemed comfortable to talk about in any more detail. I seemed to be held in high esteem by all that I encountered because I saved the creatures from the horrors on Bokwana Island.

I found out that the large fierce male youngling was named Vrool Gala and the feline like female was called Shard Gala - his life mate.

The Siabhra did not know how large the younglings would be when fully grown so allowed for plenty of extra height and width in their construction of the city and it was a wondrous site to behold even partially completed. I learned that the younglings had difficulty understanding language as they took words to be completely literal which took time to overcome and were fantastic mimics of any sound that could be produced by any living creature. I asked about the eggs that I had found and what came out of them and to my surprise I was told that the eggs hatched Vrool and Shard along with three tiny sons. It made no sense to me as this male and female were clearly leading their kind despite being hatched by the others that I had freed from Bokwana Island. But even the Siabhra had no idea as to why this was and when they asked the younglings they said that they cannot remember anything other than simply knowing that these eggs were to be protected at all costs. The Siabhra use a strange language which is a mix of old Celtic, Latin and other terms and words that I cannot place from any language that I know and I have been studying language as a hobby for many years. The youngling's use their own speech as my son has documented but the male and female speak something entirely different as well that is much closer to the Siabhra's tongue. Why they even need language is a mystery because the Siabhra quickly realised that the Gikkie Bokkers are telepathic and can share experiences from the past and present as well as near future events or at least the impression of impending danger which gives their already lightning fast reflexes an incredible boost.

The Siabhra gave the Gikkie Bokkers a term in their own language, they refer to them as the Aoes Shee which loosely translated means 'The Other People' or 'The Lost Race'. Every youngling even the smallest and most timid are incredible fighters having an uncanny sense of timing and unearthly speed and flexibility but Maeve the Siabhra Queen is concerned by Vrool and Shards development, their features are changing to something much fiercer than the cute and scraggly younglings and even she cannot read the minds of the creatures. Maeve instructed Eimhir and Brianag to keep a watchful eye on the Gikkie Bokkers in spite of being told to adopt them by their higher powers who are known as The Resplendent Ones or The forces of Light.

It's as if the Gikkie Bokker creatures don't obey the natural laws of mother-nature or can cheat the normal physical laws that constrain us all. I am also unsure if these Resplendent Ones are Gods or just a different or higher form of life but I have yet to see them or feel their presence or hand at work.

There is so much knowledge that I have absorbed that it's difficult to make sense of things so I requested to leave until I can settle my family and then return to learn more. The Siabhra have extended their welcome to my family and I to venture into their realm in times of need with the use of their amulet. I gratefully accepted and they escorted me back to my family. Time in the magical realm of the Siabhra and Aoes Shee is not in synchronicity with our earthly measurements as I felt that I spent days with them yet when I returned to my family I had only been away for a couple of hours.

Friday the twenty third of December eighteen hundred and three.

Miranda and our children had a wonderful day preparing for Christmas and placed decorations about the entire house, we really are fitting in nicely here. There is nobody for many miles around and I am home schooling Emily and Bobbert for the time being. I am glad of the rest and letting the knowledge that I have learned process in good time.

Sunday the twenty fifth of December eighteen hundred and three.

Our Christmas morning was wonderful and full of joy and our Furry friends arrived after breakfast and asked us in muddled English to follow them over to the bay. They all have the ability to summon the portal of light that leads into the Siabhra realm using a wonderful musical chirp and Eimhir and Brianag were waiting for us on the other side. Brianag handed me an ornamental walking stick of unrivalled beauty and crafting as a gift and Eimhir presented me with a beautifully engraved silver and bronze plate while Emily and Bobbert both received a heavy hooded silk green and silver cloak from the Siabhra. We were then taken on the backs of the loveliest white horses that I have ever encountered and travelled around the great forest of the Aoes Shee and past a deep lush valley which lead up into a range of wonderful mountains covered in mist. As we descended we trotted down to a long bronze and silver bridge which arched over a huge sparkling blue river that lead out onto a vast golden and green plain. After a brief rest were we were provided with a refreshing picnic and took in the amazing view.

When rested we were lead up to the outskirts of a huge golden and bronze city with huge elongated ornamental towers and battlements that was flanked on both sides by golden dolmens. It was difficult to make out a lot of the intricate detail in the city outskirts due to the amount of reflected glare from the sun. We reached a bronze road that lead to a large cathedral like building that had a large set of broad steps leading up to a square for people to congregate.

At the front step stood Maeve the Siabhra Queen flanked by two guards. She presented me with the same intricately detailed amulet that I was offered when I arrived from London. I accepted it and was instructed that it was a gift of friendship and that I was not to wear it unless I was sure of becoming a guardian of the portal along with Eimhir and Brianag. It feels amazing in my hands, a sensation of calmness washes over me, even when I hold it now as I write it seems to emit a sense of serenity all around my study. As we were leaving the Siabhra outskirts we heard a shrill cry in the air that seemed to come from the distant forests to the west of the Siabhra vale. Within moments our Siabhra escorts doubled and our Gikkie Bokker youngling friends appeared from out of the golden grasses. They had followed us the whole way over and back without a sound and they chirped and danced merrily along with us on our way back to the Aoes Shee forest. In the evening we parted ways at the portal entrance and made our way home to a most peaceful slumber.

Monday the twenty sixth of December eighteen hundred and three.

I began the morning by staring at the amulet that Maeve had presented me with enthralled by its design. During breakfast Miranda and I were taken by surprise by a shadow outside my front door. The female known to me as Shard Gala stood outside and begged to be let in. Her use of the English language was far more evolved than the others and she clearly explained to me that she studied constantly the lore and magic of all the living creatures in the magical realms. I was unsure as to where Shard was going with the conversation until she asked to see my amulet. I politely handed it to her and she studied it closely.

After a few moments she explained that she had learned of a means to revive the dead youngling who was crushed by Borglum's dreadful contraption but needed a magical artefact that could contain the creature's spirit. I suspected what she wanted to do and asked her to consider the kind of life a youngling would have if it was trapped alive inside an amulet. She then told me of the importance of not letting the younglings spirit wander lost in the lands of the Aoes Shee. She explained to me that if a creature belonging to this land was killed its spirit would roam for weeks aimlessly through the realms and could be captured by a number of ghastly powers bent on using it for horrendous plots and schemes before it had time to ascend to the forces of light. She begged me to let her make use of the amulet to store the soul of her dead friend until she could find a way to restore the spirit to the youngling's body.

When I looked into her eyes I saw only sincerity and love with no shadow of deception. That evening Shard brought the younglings body over to my study and I let her go inside with the creature after handing my amulet over to her. After an hour of uncertainty Shard emerged smiling and handed my amulet back to me and she caressed my cheek with her hand and kissed me tenderly on my forehead. Miranda looked surprised as she studied the amulet. The intricate design of two Siabhra warriors brandishing swords under a crescent moon was changing slowly into the face of the dead youngling Gikkie Bokker. 'Hello there' it chuckled to us and I nearly dropped it onto the floor. We held conversation with the creature for over an hour. It was so excited Shard could not get a word in edgeways but the chirpy little face had no difficulty explaining what had happened and what we were to do.

'Only wake me when you need me, I like sleep so until Shard gets my body I will sleep!' I had to laugh at the little fellows pluck, after being crushed to death and transferred into a magical amulet the defiant little youngling was very positive. Shard was overjoyed and advised me to treat the amulet as it was before she transferred the youngling's soul into it and not to directly communicate with the youngling inside as it will rest until she can find a way to place its spirit back into its body.

Wednesday the twenty eight of December eighteen hundred and three.

I have lived up to my end of the arrangement in that I never talk to the younglings spirit but as for it resting until Shard finds a means to restore it that part has not come to pass, the little mite will not shut up, not even at night, it spouts off about everything and anything which delights Emily and Bobbert and it has them in stitches calling me names and mimicking my voice around the house but saying silly things that I would never utter in the wildest of fits.

Even Miranda who was quite timid around the creatures has been in tears of laughter at the irreverent humour of it. The local Parish Priest paid us a visit this morning and was a lovely kind old man who had spent some time in getting to our remote location so we sat him down for tea and pastries but the youngling must have sensed him from my study in which I keep him stowed away in my old storage chest and mimicked my voice to deliberately cause chaos with the old man. For a few moments he thought that I was going to switch our faith to a deity called Molombo the mighty god of all cabbages and start a cult following in his parish.

I had to invent a yarn about a series of delirious relapses of Malaria that I suffered from due to my adventuring in Africa which seemed to allay the priest's fears. I politely ushered him out of our home and wished him well before the youngling could think of further mischief to inflict upon him.

Thursday the twenty ninth of December eighteen hundred and three.

I had a vision last night, Shard appeared before me and told me to not venture into the lands of the Siabhra or the Aoes Shee as it was not safe anymore, she refused to speak of it any further and vanished and then the youngling in the amulet started to cry. She told me not to speak to the creature but how could I not? My heart would not permit it and I spent the early hours of the morning comforting it.

During our talk I found out the creatures name was Ookle-Tonk and he spoke to me about his life playing around the stout lakes and running under the Siabhra's feet as they helped build the Aoes Shee mountain temple city. He is very much a fun loving child and I swore to myself from that evening on I would find a way to return his soul to his body after all he saved my family with no thought of his own safety.

I prayed that evening to Shard and begged her to contact me but I got no response. Ookle-Tonk appeared to be resting and there was no magical aura from the amulet, it looks like we are cut off from the Aoes Shee and Siabhra realms for our own protection but what is causing them so much trouble?

Friday the sixth of January eighteen hundred and four
– The Siabhra City.

I am so tired and barely able to write in my current condition. The day after I had the vision my house was attacked by a gang of vicious thugs masquerading as lost delivery men. They were charming enough to get

268

past my front gate but then they tried to rush me at my front door but I held them off and they retreated for a brief moment only to let a hideous dark beast from out of a large wooden crate on the back of their horse and cart. I shut my doors as they set the dark creature on me but it knocked the double doors down onto me like they were made of paper and it walked over me cracking my ribs running off into the house after my Miranda and our children.

I was clever enough to have a locked gun chest by the door and I crawled over to unlock it and pulled out my loaded shotgun. I heard a huge commotion in the kitchen and crawled along the corridor and caught the dark creature swiping at our service hatch for the dumb waiter. It's a device we don't use but works fine as a micro elevator that you can send a prepared tray of breakfast up into for the upper guest bed room. The creature had ripped the door off its hinges and was trying to place one of its huge arms up into the shaft. I could hear my family struggle and scream and thank goodness they were smart enough to hide in the dumb waiter shaft rather than a room as it offered the only real protection from the creature.

I let off two rounds into the beasts back and it stumbled backwards gurgling and moaning but it slowly got back to its feet and turned its attention to me. It had a serrated set of sharp stabbing pincers on its huge forearms and I knew if I didn't load my shotgun fast enough I would be seeing them much closer. I managed one well timed head shot as it leaped onto me that dropped the beast instantly but its huge frame fell on top of me and damaged my ribs even more. There was no sign of the thugs inside the house as I crawled free of the dead creature but I shouted to Miranda to stay put in the shaft and I slowly got to my feet and made my way outside. I spotted the men walking towards the house with loaded shotguns and I limped back into my study and grabbed the amulet from out of my old storage chest.

I pleaded with Ookle-Tonk to awake as I held onto the amulet like it was one of my children, I felt that the youngling was also a part of my family now and would protect him with the same ferocity that I protected Miranda and the children. There was no reply and I resigned myself to face down the thugs alone but as I turned I saw the shadow of the great beast flick across the hall outside, it seemed to have repaired itself, the wounds in its head were almost gone and it sped into my study and attempted to stab me with both of its pincers.

Out of instinct I hunched myself low to the ground and hit the beast as hard as I could with a powerful body punch forgetting that I had the amulet in my hand. The beast let out a huge bellowing roar of pain and collapsed into a heap on top of me. I had accidentally stabbed it right through with the amulet and the creatures body started to rot away in front of my eyes leaving only a few pieces of dark armoured husk. As I freed my arm from the rotting remains the amulet glowed a golden hue and Ookle-Tonk's face appeared on it. He squealed and shouted at me that the thugs were breaking in from the rear of the kitchen to take me by surprise. I limped out of the study into the hallway amidst the sound of breaking glass and screaming and I made my way to the dumb waiter service hatch to free my family but they were gone. I became enraged but spotted the thugs dragging my family away from the smashed windows but they blasted at me with their shotguns to keep me at bay.

I forgot about my own safety and leaped out of one of the broken kitchen windows and landed badly out on the grass yard. Ookle-Tonk begged me to place the amulet around my neck and I barely managed to while two of the thugs closed in on me to finish me off while the remaining four made off with my family. I could see them sneering in triumph at me but as soon as the golden chain of the amulet rested upon my neck my body surged with life and vitality and I rose up right in front of my attackers.

I took them by surprise and their over confidence became their undoing as they came so close to me that I disarmed them both after a few well timed blows to their scruffy faces. Ookle-Tonk was yelling at me to get to the front of the house grounds to counter the remaining four thugs so I grabbed the ruffian's two shotguns and raced out around to the front of the garden. They had already passed the garden and were hastily making their way down the hill towards their horse and carriage but as I bore down on them another carriage in the distance was travelling down the dirt road towards us. I ran as fast as I could but the remaining henchmen had already placed my family into the back of their cart and were about to make off with them. Ookle-Tonk's mimicry of sounds was put to good use as he imitated a startled horse bolting which cause the henchmen's black stallion to bolt sending the cart lopsided and throwing the henchmen off of the cart. It gave me the time I needed to render the fallen thugs unconscious with the butt of my shotguns.

As I freed my family the other carriage was closing in and was close enough that I could spot four more henchmen and a set of four large wooden crates in the cart. Ookle-Tonk screamed at me to take my family over to the entrance of the portal entrance and he would plead with Shard to open the portal. Even as I made my way towards the portal entrance I could see two of the henchmen start to break open the wooden crates in the cart and my heart sink with despair. I reached the area were the Siabhra and Gikkie Bokkers appeared from and roared into the air above for Shard to appear and save us. Ookle-Tonk began to chirp and speak in his own language lending me support as I saw four dark beasts leap from the still moving cart and sprint towards us.

We had seconds before the creatures would reach us but the amulet started to glow as a flashing aura of white light erupted from out of the thin air above us. We all jumped through the light and vanished from the side of the bay that we stood upon. Seconds later we fell over each other in an untidy mess onto the other side of the bay into the magical Aoes Shee realm.

To our horror we found ourselves amidst a great battle between the Siabhra and a huge army of dark creatures that looked exactly like the beasts that were about to attack us outside my home. I made Emily grab the children and duck under a small overturned tree that had fallen partly into the marshy swamp water and I followed them doing my best to remain still.

The battle was being won by the Siabhra but the numbers of the dark beasts were being replenished by an enormous black husk of an object that loomed menacingly in the distance. Hundreds of the dark beasts ran out from the huge gaping hole at the front of the massive object every few seconds but the Siabhra held their ground fighting with a deadly precision that was almost hypnotising to watch.

My amulet started to glow as Ookle-Tonk kept shouting out a word that I was not familiar with...

'Eireannos, Eireannos' he shouted aloud. I urged him to remain silent but he could not contain his excitement. I started to feel a distant rhythmic rumble that began to cause small ripples in the marshy water which increased gradually over the next few seconds. The dark beasts started to notice the waters that they stood in as the ripples gave way to small waves.

The Siabhra immediately retreated towards the shores of the largest lake to our west ignoring the dark beasts who seemed confused as the waves became more intense. One half of their army started to march after the Siabhra while the other half marched towards the giant dark husk like object to the east of the lakes. The great object was still spewing forth large numbers of beasts from its opening, a truly mighty and beastly sight but the entity that leapt from out of the dust and carnage of the ongoing battle was even more impressive.

A metallic silver hued humanoid at least one hundred feet in height had appeared from behind the giant husk and stepped on top of the object and raised four powerful arms over its head and crushed the dark object into dust with such ferocity that the entire force of dark beasts paused to look at the massive creature. It then began to step on the remaining beasts that fled from the wreckage and started to look out across the lakes towards the rest of the divided dark army. We all stayed put waist deep in the warm swamp waters spell bound by the spectacle.

The nearest half of the dark army charged wildly at the giant creature but the massive humanoid did not move. Instead its metallic fur seemed to elongate and it calmly grabbed a small tuft of silver hair on one of its massive forearms and cut it free with a massive dark claw.

Then the humanoid rubbed the hair clippings between its massive fingers and inhaled deeply. It pursed its dark lips and blew the metallic hair clippings from out of its fingers towards the attacking dark army.

What was a tiny piece of hair clippings to the great creature was the size of a small spear to a dark beast and the metallic hair spread out and sliced through hundreds of the dark army ripping them apart.

The metallic projectiles did not stop after slicing through one group of beasts, in fact the hair strands seemed to be guided and swept around and attacked wave after wave of desperately retreating dark beasts until none remained, the hair strands speeded back to the huge creature and reattached themselves to its silver fur. The remaining half of the dark beast army turned away from pursuing the Siabhra and attempted to surround the massive humanoid to overwhelm it but the plan backfired on the beasts as the humanoid punched the water below him with such force it created a shock wave of such intensity that it tore the attacking beasts apart.

We were fortunate that our position was sheltered and remote as the shock wave passed swiftly over our heads flattening trees and foliage for miles. The Siabhra cheered triumphantly but surprisingly raced past the massive creature and hurried into the forest beyond the lakes up towards the temple mountain. The silver beast bowed its head as they raced by and slowly followed as if curious.

As I examined the massive life form I noticed its face was very expressive, this was no mindless terror at work, it was highly intelligent and sympathetic to the Siabhra. Then I realised that the Aoes Shee were nowhere to be seen and I suspected the worst in my heart.

We struggled out from underneath the fallen tree and made our way across the lakes after many hours marching. We met two Siabhra rangers at the shoreline of the Aoes Shee forest who summoned two horses for us to carry us towards the temple mountain. As I left them they could not contain themselves and started to weep but they would not say why. As we made our way past the beautiful ornamental gardens on the plateau overlooking the forest we passed by a few token Siabhra guarding the area, all weeping. We finally made our way up through the mountain and finally reached the partially built Aoes Shee city. The city was empty until we reached a large set of wonderfully decorated silver gates that lead into a large descending courtyard with a huge tree in the middle but one half of the tree was charred black and still smouldering. The greater part of the Siabhra army had encircled the tree looking down at the earth silently. I asked Miranda to keep Bobbert and Emily away from them until I could see what was happening. As I approached the Siabhra let me pass through and Maeve approached me slowly noticing my amulet and did her best to smile politely and embraced me.

She then quietly stood aside and I witnessed what had happened. Shard was standing over a charred body sobbing quietly and flanked on either side by ten small Gikkie Bokker younglings. As I walked towards her and out onto the courtyard I could see the full extent of the slaughter.

One hundred Gikkie Bokker Youngling bodies littered the courtyard in different positions. It looked like they were thrown from the charred tree by an explosion. As I turned my head towards Shard and wiped the stream of tears from my eyes I looked down upon the body that she stood over. The eyes and facial features were unmistakable despite the massive damage done to the body. Vrool had been slain.

'This tree was the play school for our smallest younglings, what place could be safer for them than in our own city' she whispered under her breath. 'He gave all he had to save me and the ones you see before you from the creature'.

A huge sigh came from far over our heads. As I looked over behind me I could see the huge Silver humanoid towering over the entrance gates peering down onto the courtyard. I swear I could see it weep diamonds from its eyes and it remained silent. The remaining younglings saw the humanoid and ran past us and out of the court yard towards the great beast. After a few moments they emerged out of the entrance to the temple mountain and climbed up onto the humanoid who remained motionless. They all rested on his massive shoulders and seemed to be softly talking to the great creature who was gently nodding in agreement with them. Bobbert and Emily got free of Miranda who raced after them but she could not stop them in time from seeing Vrool's body. This day had turned to a nightmare for us all and I can do nothing to ease my children's grief.

That evening we chose to stay with Shard and Maeve in a private quarters overlooking the courtyard. The Siabhra had wrapped Vrool's body in a golden shawl and placed him onto a marble slab decorated with pretty flowers in the courtyard at the exact spot where he was found. I noticed that the clouds high above us began to grow darker and then noticed something else, a trail in the sky, like the smoke from a firework but fainter. The trail seemed to be moving independently of the wind and I was compelled to follow it. I walked over to the bay window overlooking the lands to the north and saw the source of the trail.

Many miles in the distance a faint object circled slowly over a dark mountain range leaving a dark trail in its wake. Shard stood by my side and whispered slowly. 'It has no name and did not explain its actions, it went after the younglings first then Vrool stood in its way. He injured it badly before it killed him'. It appeared to be harvesting electrical energy from the mountain range it circled over as lightning arcs shot from the mountain tops up into the object. 'There may be a race who knows what it is' offered Maeve. As she finished her words Eimhir entered our quarters to inform us that we had visitors from two different races in the courtyard. She seemed unsettled.

We all arrived into the courtyard and passed Brianag who seemed very grim as she stood silently in front of a tall dark figure who did not speak a word until Shard arrived. It bowed its elongated triangular head respectfully but Shard had a look of dread on her face the moment she placed her eyes on the creature. I was not sure if the creature had an elaborate set of clothing or that the detail on it was actually part of its unsettling body.

It had six shiny black eye slits and a strange mouth that had four diamond shaped segments that acted as its lips that almost reminded me of a crustacean's mouth piece. But the rest of the creature resembled more of a fusion between man and crow. It announced itself as Lug, Chief Inquisitor of the Fomori and said that Vrool was to be taken for the trials. Shard looked puzzled and horrified all at the same time and insisted that her life partner was dead. The creature disagreed politely and stated that Vrool was close to death but could still be revived.

It said that Vrool's actions in battle had aroused the curiosity of his race and they wanted him to go for the trials and be given an opportunity to ascend to a higher form. Shard refused but Maeve reminded her of the laws of Siabhra realm. I had no idea what she was talking about and the atmosphere grew very tense. Shard wept and left the courtyard in a terrible state as the creature picked up Vrool's body and floated into the air with him until it vanished from our sight.

Maeve was about to run after Shard but the second visitor chose to materialise in front of her blocking her way. It appeared as a tall slim woman in glowing white shawls with jet black hair and cold piercing eyes. She stood over twenty feet tall and her feet never touched the ground. In her right hand she carried a long black comb and in her left she held a braided wrist band that she politely presented to Maeve.

Maeve bowed and accepted the gift and they spoke at length without acknowledging me in an old form of Gaelic that I could not follow.

The floating woman then turned its gaze onto me and I froze as if planted into the earth. She introduced herself as Eevul the Banshee queen and told me that my family line was destined to do battle with the creature that had slain Vrool until one of my descendants could find a means to defeat it. Eevul explained to us that the entity that killed Vrool and the younglings was Morríghan, once a great queen of the Banshee race until she was exiled for exploiting the dark arts for her own selfish gain and stripped of her powers. She carelessly dabbled in the dark arts and corrupted herself becoming an entity known as the Morgannis and was defeated by the Banshee army but Eevul had no knowledge as to how the outcast queen had returned and become so powerful. She also stated that I must protect the Aoes Shee and prevent Vrool from losing his self to rage if he survived the ordeal of the trials at the hands of the

Fomori Inquisitors or chaos would descend upon the all the realms and spill out into my world.

Eevul gave me her races blessing and floated out of the courtyard in search of Shard. I spent the next few days recovering from my wounds with my family under the care of Maeve and Shard. I did not miss my mansion at all during my stay but Shard arranged for a group of younglings to scout out my home and repair the damage by Ilgrim Borglum's henchmen.

Ookle-Tonk was very quiet during our stay but I could feel that he was content and resting. Before we left I promised Shard that I would be her protector till the end of my days and I would pass my diaries down to my descendants to keep my heritage strong. She told me that it would be some time before she would see me again as she planned to leave with Eevul the Banshee Queen to study under her and investigate how the exiled Banshee Queen had managed to return. Eimhir and Brianag were to take control of the Aoes Shee city until she returned and the giant humanoid Eireannos was permitted by his race to patrol the borders of the Aoes Shee realm and bring Vrool's sons with him to train them in the art of war. Eimhir and Brianag came with us to our mansion and after scouting for any signs of Ilgrim's henchmen we talked all evening about the tragedy that had haunted us all. They explained a great deal to me of the nature of the Banshee race and of the Siabhra. They also spoke of Eireannos the giant humanoid that so effortlessly wiped out an entire army of those dark beasts. His race are called Wrathiens and they at one time lived amongst our world as gods but found a new home here growing tired of the human race and its squabbles, they patrol their borders and readily assist any realm in need of protection from evil as battle is in their blood. In spite of being the perfect warriors they have a strict sense of duty and honour and have even helped the Siabhra build their bronze and gold city.

Eireannos himself seems fascinated by the Gikkie Bokkers and visits them as often as he can. He told Eimhir and Brianag that he sees so much of himself in them and is curious as to how their features are very similar to his own race.

The beasts that attacked me are simply known as Fiends and are known throughout all the realms but have been extinct for thousands of years. It was said that their numbers used to blacken the horizon and they turned on their creators long ago and ran unchecked wiping out entire races but the Banshees finally obliterated them but they could not explain what had resurrected the ones that attacked the Gikkie Bokkers lakes and forest a few days ago.

Our thoughts then turned to Vrool and Ookle-Tonk and Shards research into transferring the spirits of dead Gikkie Bokkers back into their repaired bodies. Both Eimhir and Brianag expressed great concern over this issue as they feared that could of been what the fiend's creators may have been trying to do themselves at one point and ended up accidentally creating a hideous army of undead killing machines that turned upon them.

Eimhir and Brianag told us upon leaving that they were sending scouts to set out after the tracks of Ilgrim Borglum's henchmen left in the dirt road and capture them and asked us to consider moving into the Siabhra city instead of our mansion at least till they had investigated Ilgrim's secret organisation.

After my family being exposed to so much terror and sadness I really had no choice. I would visit the house every other day but make a temporary home in the Siabhra city. I requested that I be trained in their combat arts so that I can deal with whatever comes my way as effectively as possible.

I sit here now amongst furnishings that are beautiful and plush with my family soundly asleep and calm. The Siabhra city is spectacular and peaceful. The outside is clean lined and almost surgical in its precise architecture but inside the protective battlements and walls is the most beautiful green environment that I have ever seen, squares of lush green trees and a small forest leads out to a glistening waterfall overlooking a golden valley and river that is itself raised high above an unfolding mist covered landscape. I have made a great many friends and am nearly well enough from my wounds to learn their combat disciplines and they are all so loving and caring to Emily and Bobbert. My beautiful Miranda fits in very well with them as she would easily pass for one of them if she wore the appropriate attire.

I miss my youngling friends. A great deal of the ones I rescued from Bokwana Island were amongst the slaughtered and it is impossible to accept that any entity would be capable of carrying out such an evil deed. I spotted what looked like the one that was fighting in the arena being thought how to wield Siabhra weapons in a secluded courtyard this evening, it looked very determined and focused. I am so sad that its innocence was shattered by the Morgannis' vile actions, these creatures have had no time at all to settle down in peace.

Friday the twenty ninth of March eighteen hundred and five.
So much intense training and learning has been placed upon us at such a frantic pace that it was impossible to keep my diary updated. However it has been by all accounts a highly rewarding experience. All of us are well versed now in a number of Siabhra combat disciplines and I have been thought how to use the full power of the magical amulet to enhance my strength, vision and healing.

Shard has only returned twice in all of the time that has passed and has grown even taller and more beautiful with an aura of power about her that is incredible to experience. There have been ten minor incursions of Fiend beasts along the Siabhra borders in the last six months which were swiftly quelled by Maeve and her forces but there has been no sign of the Morgannis creature itself. Also curiously there are no men here. In fact the only men like race that I noticed were a small force of nomadic travelling people that traded with the Siabhra at the end of every lunar month. I don't feel yet that I have the courage to ask Maeve why this is so. The Siabhra are human in appearance but their powers both physical and magical are anything but human so I may enquire in time as to how they came to be but not just yet.

The Fomori Inquisitors have yet to return Vrool's body from the trials and at this point I do not believe that he has been revived by them. I suspect deeper hidden motives to his absence but no news has reached us as the Fomori homeland's location is a well-guarded secret. I asked Maeve as to why they can appear out of nowhere and take any creature they wish if it arouses their curiosity. I was told it was because they engineered the magical divide that separated these kingdoms from the world that I was born into and in tribute to their mighty craftsmanship they are free to choose what they call Champions, any gifted creature they see with the potential and ability to further the survival of their race can be chosen at any given time. But there is an initiation and a price for those chosen to be champions. A series of ghastly trials is tasked upon those chosen, challenges and ordeals designed to ascend them to more efficient warriors or kill them in the attempt. Trials so deadly and horrific that even if a creature is powerful and lucky enough to ascend to a champion it is never the same again.

I asked her how many have become champions amongst all of the realms. I learned that over thousands of years mere hundreds were chosen to face the trials but only six creatures became champions. I remember her voice faltered with emotion as she named them.

'Dhuul-Grun-Chrom-Hellwrath, Gelfedaron-Hellwrath, Drevathius-Urndragor, Brianag Ó Deoráinil … Eimhir Ó Deoráinil… and myself!

Maeve Ó hAllmhuráin, the others are all dead! Only three bodies of the hundreds chosen had enough remains to be buried upon their return by the Fomori!'

I was unsettled for days after our talk at such a ghastly practice, no matter what the principal was behind it. I recruited my entire family to spend time in the Siabhra archives of knowledge to learn as much as we could about the processes and technology at work that concealed these realms from the ordinary world of man. My aim is to find a way to mask these realms from the human race without the need for paying tribute to the Fomori Inquisitors. Maeve is deeply moved by our commitment to the research and has joined us with a number of her council to aid us in the task.

We search through endless parchment scrolls and calligraphic books every day for answers. We know nothing about magic but with the aid of Maeve's assistants they guide us through anything that we find too difficult to comprehend. They are all pleased at the way we go about the research as we look at things in a different way to them which has unearthed some revelations as to how the Fomori technology works.

The best way to describe what I mean is to state clearly in this realm that a word in itself is a mere sound with a certain amount of energy attached to it. In this realm I have found out that sound travels faster than light does and even more startling is the fact that the Fomori know how to infuse their force of will into a sound and make it carry out a specific task. It took us weeks to translate old documents to unravel this but now at least there is a beacon of hope, a clue that entices us to delve deeper in search of a solution.

Saturday the seventh of June eighteen hundred and five.

Emily unearthed an old scroll today that was partially buried under an old rotten pile of books but it caught my attention for some reason. It had no relevance to our cause but was a fascinating read. We are all adept at the Siabhra language now and can also partially read a few other older languages from the surrounding lands and we eagerly translated this little piece of history and to our surprise it was written in old Gaelic which was a far more recent language than any speech used in these realms. It told the tale of a cursed witch who battled a large force of men and women villagers who rose up against it. The battle took place in the large ruins of an old church ground and the witch crushed the rebellion leaving only a young woman alive to act as a witness to its terrible power.

The witch's power brought the villagers back from the dead. Enslaved to her will she commanded them to burn down the neighbouring village as a sign of her power. But as soon as the resurrected villagers attempted to leave the church grounds they were stopped by an invisible barrier preventing them from escape. The witch realising that the holy ground prevented the undead from doing any more harm destroyed them and fled the area. With her power greatly diminished as part of her essence was trapped in the holy grounds she could never again wield such terrible power and was never heard of again.

It's interesting that the witch had power over anyone it killed but the holy blessed earth of the church grounds prevented the undead from doing any harm outside of its boundaries. The way the tale was written made it seem like a fairy tale rather than a factual event but it made for an entertaining diversion from our research.

The rest of my notes in this diary shall contain more of the technical nature of how the Fomori are concealing the magical realms from us but the only steady fact in all of the lore and history that I am exploring is that there is no reference anywhere so far of where the Fomori come from. I have read dozens of manuscripts and scrolls with references to them and other races that dealt with them but nothing about the Fomori race itself.

In the meantime if I ever find myself confronted by an army of resurrected undead in a church yard at least I know I will be safe if I step outside its boundary walls but I doubt that will ever be the case for me or anyone of my bloodline.

The book leapt into life and shut tightly closed startling Hugo who let it drop from out of his hands. 'Why did you do that Hugo? That was very rude! I was quite enjoying that!'

'I didn't do anything, the creepy book just did that itself, and it's not letting me open it either, is that you're doing you amulet bound ruffian?' The spirit of the Gikkie Bokker barked back in a serious tone. 'Time to get up human thingy's, danger is about, danger is about!'

The air began to get colder and heavier as the two men rushed outside the old church and scanned the area for Synar and Mil-Mil. Hugo felt the need to securely fasten his amulet around his neck as he raced his eyes across the eerie landscape in search of his Aoes Shee companions.

'You are Ookle-Tonk aren't you?' He asked softly to his amulet. 'Yes I am, get ready to throw some punches as I can feel them coming!'

'Who? Who do you feel is coming? And where is Mil-Mil and Synar?' 'They are fighting on top of that mountain top! Prepare yourself and your skinny friend!'

'What? How is that happening?'

The dark soil beneath Hugo's feet burst open and a pair of skeletal hands grabbed his ankles and attempted to drag him to the ground. 'What the? No you don't take your freaky mitts off me!' Hugo counter grabbed the bony arms and snapped them off and started to bash the emerging rotten skeletal creature on top of its head with them. As he dispatched the rotting creature he swung his head towards Reginold who was smacking the butt of his large gun against the partially rotten head of another creature. Hugo rushed over to his friend and helped him destroy the reanimated corpse.

'Thanks Ookle-Tonk, much obliged!' Hugo patted his amulet softly in appreciation. 'Eh? Don't get so cosy with me old man that's only the beginning!'

The earth below their feet started to gently rumble and the mist was getting denser as thousands of undead started to slowly emerge from out of their graves. 'Ah! So this is why Synar and Mil-Mil told us to sharpen the pikes! Come Hugo on let's get back inside the church!'

'No way Reggie, that's our last port of call! It's a dead end at least we can move around in the open air! Mobility is our best weapon! Let's stay inside the church grounds as long as we can pal!'

Reginold did not respond and held tightly onto a single handed sword and took the safety trigger off of his powerful gun. 'Best to make every shot count! Only five rounds remain!' He mumbled to himself as dense mist started to clear a little and revealed masses of undead humans picking up swords and pikes from around the graves that they had emerged from.

The undead slowly stumbled towards the two men only yards away from the makeshift defences that the Aoes Shee warriors had constructed as a barrier. 'Ookle-Tonk! Are these the warriors that helped my father Henry in the Great War against the Morgannis?'

'They are Hugo but make no mistake they will hunt you down to the ends of the earth if you don't defend yourself but... Wait! Something is strange here! I can read their minds, Hugo! They are friendly to us!' An old rusty spear raced out of the green mist and narrowly missed Hugo's head. 'Whatcha mean friendly? Did ya just see what happened there ya mad thing?

'Hugo just defend yourself if you have to but try to keep out of their way, I think I can speak to them!'

'Well bleedin go on then and speak to them will ya? Those pikes we stuck up are not going to hold them for long!'

Masses of the undead stumbled slowly up to the perimeter created by the pikes and started to press against them while masses more of the undead bungled their way over the shoulders of their companions falling awkwardly over the shoulders of the first wave of undead and clumsily landing beyond the perimeter defences. 'There's that many of them good god we are in for it now Reggie!'

As the second wave of undead rose up off the ground and made for Hugo and Reginold another wave replaced them landing almost at their feet. 'Right Reggie! We get stuck in now or we won't last long! Come on! Let's put some manners on them!'

Hugo raced towards the undead warriors feeling Ookle-Tonk increase his strength using the amulets power. Reginold felt a surge of power race into him from his own amulet and he joined Hugo as they clashed into the clumsily moving mobs of undead that had penetrated the perimeter defences. 'Ookle-Tonk how is your chat going with our friendly zombie villagers? Anything to report?'

'Just keep defending yourself Hugo, it's been a while since they have spoken, takes a little time when bits and pieces drop off of you ya know!' Hugo sighed and gave up on the idea of a peaceful way out of the predicament. Reginold fell back a few steps and with a well-timed aim took out four undead with a single shot from his gun giving Hugo time to cleave in two another mob of attacking zombies. But the numbers were building up rapidly inside the perimeter and there was no sign of the Aoes Shee warriors. 'Reginold it may well be time to go inside the church! Go on and I will hold them off. Get ready to barricade ourselves in as soon as I am through the door with you!'

Reginold nodded and raced as fast as he could into the old church taking out another four undead with his gun before he disappeared in through the doors. Hugo's amulet transferred more magical energy into his body to heal his wounds and keep his stamina from failing as he destroyed wave after wave of the undead villagers. 'Hugo he understands! It's okay!'

'What?'

'It's alright their leader can understand me now and he is friendly!'

'Ah thank god I am knackered!'

'No Hugo don't stop!'

He ducked his head in time as three spears nearly ran his head through. 'You told me that he was friendly, they nearly killed me just now!

'Ah yes, well they are friendly but as long as we are in their territory they will keep trying to kill us! It's something to do with a curse that's on them!'

'Well thanks for clearing that up, any ideas what's not their territory?'

'No idea! Perhaps the church?'

'Ah for the love of…'

Hugo broke away from fighting the oncoming hordes and sprinted into the church as Reginold closed the heavy doors after him.

'Reginold this Gikkie Bokker inside my amulet has said these guys are friendly but are fighting against their will! As long as we are in their territory they won't stop attacking us!'

'Yes Hugo my dear chap! I know! My amulet sees what your amulet sees, we need to create a diversion and escape into some place outside of their grave yard!'

'Right then!'

Hugo grabbed an old wooden bench and placed it against the wall furthest away from the undead army and placed it underneath one of the window openings. He climbed up the bench and used his sword to knock out the thick wooden frame in the window giving him just enough space to get out of the window opening. 'Reginold, I am going to run around and flank them and get them to follow me, as soon as you see them take the bait, climb out of the window and head up towards the old path leading up to the mountain!'

'But Hugo! What's facing us there could be worse than here! That Gikkie Bokker thing said that Synar and Mil-Mil were fighting up at the top of the mountain!'

'Then that means that you've got the rest of the mountain to hold up in! Come on Reginold! Start to think positive will ya?'

'Right Hugo, your argument holds water! Good luck old chap!'

The old man winked at his friend and started to reinforce the barricaded doors with more pikes as it was harshly pounded upon by the unrelenting undead army.

Hugo took a deep breath and leaped from the window opening falling gently onto the soft marshy earth. As he stood up he peered slowly around the corner of the church to see the undead hammering and scratching against the heavy church doors to get inside. He briskly walked as fast as could without making noise away from the church and slipped quietly by the flank of the undead army.

As soon as he was in position he started to yell at the flank of the undead to get their attention. 'Well hello there ya rotting mess of gizzards and guts! Fancy a brisk afternoon stroll? Ya all look like ya need a wee bit of exercise! There's not a pick of muscle on ya!'

The undead army turned around slowly and stopped pounding against the church doors and started to hiss and moan and bash their swords and shields together in rage at being outwitted.

'Ookle-Tonk Ya better be still talkin to their leader cause we are running out of options! I'm leading these critters towards the cliff we jumped off so as soon as we reach there that's it! It's all over! Understand little fella?' But Ookle-Tonk did not reply.

'Ookle-Tonk! Ookle-Tonk! Ah forget it go back asleep!'

Undeterred Hugo started to jog away teasingly in front of the undead army leading them as far away as he could from Reginold who had already made his way past the graveyard grounds. Hugo was amazed at how fast he could run with the help of the amulet infusing magic into his body and he reached the looming cliff face sooner than he had expected.

'Ah well done Hugo you've lead them astray! Their leader is really nice, I just had a great chat with him and he knows your ancestor Alastair!'

'Listen fur gob! Get me to a safe place away from these limping gits or find a way to get their bone headed leader to stop attacking me or I'll melt you down into a set of ear rings for me cleaning lady!'

'Your fine now Hugo! Look how far we are past their fence!' The undead army had stopped, neatly arranged in an orderly line just behind the ruined fence of the grave yard. 'Can ya see how Reggie is getting on? Is he alright?'

'He is fine, he is waiting at the bridge near the base of the mountain stairway and he can hear Synar and Mil-Mil fighting but can't see them. It must be a hum dinger of a battle cause they are nearly at the top of the mountain!'

'All right then now tell the leader of this rabble that I want to speak to him!'

Hugo walked towards the masses of the undead and stopped just short of the boundary fence so that the undead could not harm him and tried to spot the leader of the army. As he inspected their ranks without danger of attack he observed that they all wore Irish Kilt Tunics with a saffron undershirt that were more well-preserved than their decaying bodies.

All had a quiver of arrows and a long bow as well as a short sword and shield and the larger of the undead brandished heavy long pikes. Far off in the masses there was a small shuffle and disturbance as a much taller undead creature made its way slowly but confidently to the front of the ranks.

Dressed the same as the rest of his undead followers but a full head height taller than the largest of them he stepped as close as he could to boundary fence and spoke aloud.

'Is é mo ainm Fionn Ó Conchobhair cad is ainm duit?'
Hugo looked in surprise at the undead man.

'Aha, sorry pal, Irish is it? Give me a moment I'm a little rusty at it, er let's see… Okay here I go… Is é mo ainm Hugo MacNiadh agus ba mhaith liom a bheith do chara!'

The leader of the undead paused for a moment, half his face only a skull bone but his lips began to attempt to smile as he looked back at his army and spoke aloud in a booming voice.

'Cén cineál amadán bhfuil ainm cosúil MacNiadh? Ní mór a mháthair gur tugadh rogha bocht na fir a roghnú as ina laethanta súirí!'

His whole army laughed aloud whole heartedly some nearly falling over and losing bits of loose flesh off their bodies. Then the undead leader known as Fionn turned back to face Hugo and smiled.

'I know your name, how you got it must be a yarn worthy of a drink

296

or two but that name is honoured amongst us none the less!'

Hugo strained to see Fionn's face, trying to recreate it in his mind as if there was no decay and rot on it. 'You're the spitting image of that uptight muscle bound freak of an army man that came in from America a few days ago!' Fionn looked confused.

'I do not know of who you speak of but listen to me carefully! Let this be known to you so that you can tell the tale to all you know! We are the Gaelic knights of the order of the Aoes Shee! Sworn in allegiance to their noble ranks we served under your father Henry during the battle of Terun Nil Vath Doom! The battle went ill for us and we were ordered to retreat into the earthly realm but a Wrathien traitor named Drevathius followed us out of the portal and into this grave yard were we were taking refuge in. He wielded a dreaded weapon of supernatural power.

He slayed us all but the power of his weapon was so great that it caused the earth below us to collapse. We are under his spell because of his accursed sword but what he did not expect was that the blessed earth that we were slayed upon prevented us from venturing outside of it to do his bidding. Not even his other worldly sword could counter that magic! But as you have learned, if you venture into the land where we were killed we are cursed to carry out his bidding. For that we are all sorry!'

'I understand Fionn, I'm sorry for fighting your men too!'
Hugo looked beyond the undead army towards the pale mountain at the end of the massive cavern as brief flickers of light and what seemed like fire balls randomly erupted from its peak which briefly illuminated the

cavern ceiling above it.

'Fionn! I have to get to my friends! One is at the bridge over the river and the other two are in battle with an unknown force at the top of the mountain!'

'I cannot help you! Our curse prevents us from doing any action other than killing intruders on our land, I am sorry!'

'Very well fellas well if I can find a way to help you all I will but right now please excuse me, I need to skirt around your territory and make my way over to that mountain and help my buddies!'

Fionn bowed politely and his army broke rank at his command and started to slowly make their way back to their tombstones. Hugo sprinted as fast as he could towards the mountain keeping a watchful eye on the graveyard fencing so as not to venture to near to it.

'Alright Ookle-Tonk here is the deal, I don't know what my mates are up against and don't even know what to do once I get there!

Do you have any insight as to what is going on at the top of that mountain?'

'Not alive Hugo!'

'What do you mean not alive? Is it more of these undead zombie guys?'

'What's up there Hugo is not alive but it's not undead, I can't feel any life at all!'

Hugo sighed and kept running. Once in a while he occasionally trespassed across the boundary fence to the massive graveyard and was given a brief hiss of contempt and the odd rotten hand sprung out of the earth trying to grab at him. But his problems were about to get more complicated. At the end of the huge graveyard he noticed that its corner neatly met flush with the cavernous wall creating a dead end. It was impossible to notice this from far away due to the dense green mist and it meant that he would need to sprint for over half a mile right through the graveyard once again to get to the bridge over the river.

'Ookle-Tonk! Can you do anything other than talk? Do you have any powers at all?'

'No Hugo! I can only do what you've seen me do before!'
Hugo thought about what Ookle-Tonk had said and smiled. 'Buddy can you mimic other peoples voices and throw your voice so it appears like it's coming from somewhere else? You know like you did in Alastair's second diary?'

'Ah yeah that's easy! I love doing that!' He giggled.
'Right then, I'm making a break right through their land again, we've got no choice, when they start going after me, copy Fionn's voice and create a diversion!'

'Ha ha yeah Okay!' Ookle-Tonk giggled.
Hugo inhaled a deep breath and ran like he never ran before, using the amulets power to increase his sprint he would clear the distance to the river bridge in a short time but not quickly enough to avoid the undead army who immediately resurrected and leaped from the earth even faster than they had done the first time. 'Get ready buddy, they are going to head me off at the exit!'

'All right Hugo, wait till they get a load of me!' Ookle-Tonk sniggered. The Gikkie Bokker Youngling concentrated as hard as he could to remember Fionn's voice as a dense wall of undead warriors blockaded the corner where Hugo had to run through.

'Cease your attack there is another intruder at the far end of our land, come with me!'

The voice seemed to come from the heavens and the undead stopped for a moment in confusion as they recognised the voice but then kept closing in on Hugo who narrowly dodged a flurry of arrows whizzing past his head.

'He speaks in Irish you idiot! They don't understand you! Speak the same thing in Irish!'

'Aha! Sorry Hugo, give me a minute, Okay here goes! Scoirfidh do ionsaí go bhfuil ionraitheora eile ag an deireadh dtí ár talamh, teacht liom!'

The undead army stopped and rushed around Hugo towards what they thought was their leader's voice from far off in the distance. It took them minutes to realise that they were mistaken as an outraged Fionn possessed with the curse roared at them to turn around and attack Hugo but it was too late. As soon as Hugo had cleared the grave yard grounds the curse ended and Fionn grinned broadly on his half decayed face.

'Well done Hugo, well done!' And Fionn walked slowly off back to his tomb stone grave.

Hugo could see Reginold in the distance waiting at the end of the bridge on the other side of the river as the sounds of a chaotic battle raged on high above them on the mountain top.

'Hugo my boy my amulet showed me everything that you just did, that was a splendid piece of quick thinking on your part, well done!'

'No time to dally me auld mate lets be getting up that mountain top to give our friends a lending hand! Any idea what they are fighting?'

'Not the slightest I'm afraid but I hear explosions and you can see the flashes of light for yourself. I don't know if we are ready to take on that banshee creature if she is there!'

'We have to be ready whatever it is Reggie, Synar and Mil-Mil saved our lives in that landslide, we owe it to them to lend a hand even if we are not up to the task!'

'Agreed!'

The two former enemies sprinted along the mountain pathway as fast as they could armed with only a sword and a pike. The mountain path spiralled steeply upwards to the mountain top which was being illuminated even more fiercely than when Hugo spotted it off in the distance. The crackling boom of explosions sent a shudder throughout the mountain that the men could feel under their feet and small landslides of debris crumbled off the mountains edges blocking parts of the great spiralling path. They were moments away from the last turn which would bring them up to a much steeper and linear stairway at the top and as they turned around the huge summit they bumped into the rear of Synar-Chro and Mil-Mil-Ulthu who were battling a huge force of fiends dropping down from a large opening in the cavern roof in their hundreds. But there was also another threat. Every few moments the cavern roof illuminated brightly as projectiles shot from various directions out of thin air at the Aoes Shee warriors who deflected the blasts with split second timing away from themselves creating huge concussive explosions that rocked the mountain.

The explosions knocked Hugo and Reginold off their feet but the powerful frames of the Aoes shee warrior brothers stood firm and protected the men from the full brunt of the explosion. 'What is shooting at you two?' Roared Hugo who got to his feet and sliced an approaching fiend warrior in two with his sword. 'Devices of your world Hugo using a technology that was not earned by your kind!'

We must destroy them all, there is a reason for them guarding this entrance!' Mil-Mil turned back and decapitated three fiends with one swipe of his arm. 'Observe their arcs of fire and see if you can trace their location, then we can destroy them!' Hugo ducked to the ground with Reginold and waited for the bursts of fire to start again. Both came from the left of the Aoes Shee warriors behind a set of fallen boulders acting as cover. As soon as the Aoes Shee deflected the explosive projectiles the men used the cover of the explosion to race past their friends and raced over to the boulders two hundred yards in the distance.

A group of fifty fiend warriors attacked the men but Synar picked up a large sharp fragment of one of the projectiles and flung it at the mob of Fiends slicing through them leaving them awkwardly collapsing on top of each other. The two men reached the source of the projectile attack and examined the area and accidentally bumped into an invisible object. 'It feels like a tank my boy but it's masked from our vision! Get up on top of it Hugo, there has to be a turret where the thing is firing at our friends!'

Hugo climbed on top of what appeared to be thin air but every time he made contact with the object its outline became barely visible as if a hand gently disturbed a reflection in a pool of water. As Hugo got to the top of the object he waved his hands in the air and roared out at Synar and Mil-Mil. The Aoes Shee then let out a deafening battle roar and charged through the masses of fiend warriors ripping them to pieces as they closed in on one of the cloaked tanks. Hugo could only see a blur coming at him as the Aoes Shee charged through the invisible vehicle causing the machine to uncloak and become visible in an explosion of sparks and billowing smoke. He toppled off the top of the tank but his fall was broken by Reginold who was observing the location of the other tank as the explosion caused by the Aoes Shee warriors attack reflected off of the other vehicle. 'There my boys, over there right at the base of the last few steps!' He pointed frantically at a shimmering distortion of the air around the vehicle. The partially invisible machine let out a last desperate volley of explosive projectiles but it missed its mark as the Aoes Shee warriors hurled themselves into the machine and tore it to pieces with their bare hands.

'Well done boys!' Gloated Reginold proudly as he ran the last fiend warrior through with his sword. 'You have both done very well dwellers of the earthly realm!' Smiled Mil-Mil.

'Well now, thank god that's over with!' Gasped Hugo who sat down on a small boulder to rest himself.

'No humans aboard this vehicle it was controlled from afar by other means!'

Synar-Chro picked up a piece of the wreckage and examine it closely before spitting on it and hurling it to the ground. Hugo walked over and examined the piece of charred panel.

'*B-M-H*' That sounds familiar, where have I come across those abbreviations before?'

'In your ancestor's diary you mutton head!' Scolded Ookle-Tonk.
'B-M-H acquisitions! The guys who saved Ilgrim Borglum's ass from a stiff jail sentence. Is that a coincidence? And what does B-M-H stand for? And what are they doing fighting alongside Fiend warriors'

'They're scum that's what they are!' Snarled Ookle-Tonk.
'Better explain yourself little fella!' Sighed Hugo as he stood up slowly.

'I'm sure Alastair has written something on them for you later on in your diaries but I know enough about the name. B-M-H! The Black-Marsh-Hunters!'

'Black Marsh Hunters? Sounds a bit odd for an organisation that can afford futuristic and advanced weaponry! Do you have any idea why they are called that?' Asked the highly inquisitive Reginold.

'They are the people who kidnapped your ancestor's children and made that machine that killed me. I remember the emblem, it was on the machine!'

'And they hunt Gikkie Bokker Younglings!' Snarled Synar.

'And so far we have been fortunate in that we have lost only one of our number to them!'

'Larn!' Whispered Mil-Mil softly.

'Our father rescued him but whatever they did to him during his incarceration set him on a course that ultimately resulted in his exile!' Mil-Mil winced from the recollection of the memory.

They lurked at our portal entrance for years to try and catch any inquisitive younglings that used to venture out into the outside world but Vrool and Henry your father had enough of them after our brother Larn was turned wicked and they tracked them back to one of their hideouts and destroyed their organisation. Now it seems they are back!'

'And have made an allegiance to the Morgannis it seems!' Added Reginold.

'Don't be so sure!' Countered Synar.

'The Morgannis is pure deceit and trickery, it's more likely that the Black Marsh Hunters have been themselves deceived. Whatever end she is using them for she will destroy them as soon as they are no longer of use to her!'

'We can rest no more! We must make our way out of this place and reseal it until we find out what our enemies plans are. I feel the dark ether more clearly now, the nearer we are to the surface. The Morgannis is no longer blocking it. We may be able to contact our King!'

'No Mil-Mil! We cannot afford to make use of it, remember the false skewed vision that the Morgannis placed in our minds when we were looking for Hugo's diaries in his mansion? We must travel quickly and speak in person to everyone from now on!'

'Well said brother! Let us leave here at once!' Mil-Mil Ulthu placed the wreckage of both tanks together in a pile and stacked them on top of each other so that Hugo and Reginold could walk up onto it to reach the opening in the roof of the cavern. The Aoes Shee brothers then leaped out of the opening and pulled the men up into the open air. Hugo and Reginold stood upright and took a deep breath of fresh air savouring the sensation. They had emerged out onto a flat plain of dried mud and sharp jagged rocks miles away from the far side of the huge Aoes shee mountain temple.

Hugo looked around at the tracks of foot soldiers and heavy machinery and grunted.

'They created an opening in the earth and were about to do what exactly?'

'I am unsure Hugo my boy but they knew the location of this place as there are no signs of them exploring for the opening in other areas and what about Fionn and his army? How do we free them?'

'Reggie I think it's best to seal off this opening and get back to Gikkie Bokker Mountain, we can worry about this later!'

The stillness of the air was shattered by machine gun fire. Glowing tracers streaked by them as the humans ducked for cover behind the nearest pile of sharp rocks while Synar and Mil-Mil burst into a blindingly fast sprint head long into the machine gun fire. There was a sound off in the distance of a brief struggle and then the Aoes shee warriors returned with what looked like a human soldier in each of their four powerful arms and flung them roughly to the ground in front of Hugo and Reginold.

Synar growled menacingly at the dazed soldiers. 'Hugo! Ask our guests what are they doing in our lands? If you don't get an answer I will eat them!'

The soldiers had strange bulbous helmets with strange antennae like appendages protruding from the top but everyone could still hear them whimper and moan with fear. There was light electrical charges flickering over their bodies from their antennae and their bodies faded away to an almost invisible state then faded back.

'Easy now brother! Tame your rage! I cannot see into their minds! Hugo take their helmets off and let's see if we get the same result!'

Hugo and Reginold took the helmets off the eight soldiers and sat them upright on the ground while Mil-Mil Ulthu stood over them closing his eyes and extended his eye stalks from above his nose. 'I see distraction! Tedium! Sluggishness! They are awaiting orders! They feel empty and useless without their master's word!'

Reginold felt a shudder pass through him. 'Brain Washed! Like their minds have been programmed! Hypnotised soldiers! These antennae must be used to make them invisible and keep a connection between themselves and whoever commands them!'

'I sense that there were more of their kind in this place not long ago but they have left! Hugo and Reginold, make your way towards the mountain temple and find Vrool and Shard! We shall catch up with you shortly, we need to seal off this opening and conceal it! Tell our King and Queen to dispatch a battalion to secure this place until we can discover what these human soldiers are doing!'

'Alright then Synar were off! Good luck!' Nodded Hugo respectfully and he ran off side by side with Reginold. 'Hugo that man in Alastair's second diary, Borglum! I felt a sense of dread every time that he was mentioned. I feel like I know him well, I can't explain it!'

'Well he sounded like a spooky auld git all right, I'd say he would freak out anyone!'

'No Hugo! Vrool asked me how I came to get inside the Gikkie Bokker realm along with Yardal as I had no amulet and I could not remember. I remember intending to follow you there but the act of crossing over to the other side, well I can't recall a thing!'

'I did hit you over the head with me flashlight pal! It could of messed with your memory and you were crushed to death by the Spungle! Give yourself a break auld buddy!'

'Hugo I appreciate the sentiment but every time I think of that evening when I followed you into the Gikkie Bokkers realm I have an image of this Borglum fellow stuck in my mind's eye! I think I have met him before!' Reginold started to stumble as the terrain changed to dense bushes and trees as they travelled closer to the Aoes Shee forest.

'Reggie me auld pal! I think it's time we stopped second guessing ourselves and take the fight to these guys!'

'I fear we may not get a chance to!' Reginold gasped and pulled Hugo down into a dense patch of tall grass.

'What the? Reggie what are ya up ta?' Protested Hugo.

'Look but don't make another sound!' Whispered Reginold.

Hugo slowly parted the grass in two with his hands and slowly peered through the opening. The moon's silvery light was partially obscured by cloud but he could still make out an enormous army of Fiend soldiers blanketing the land all the way up to the west of the Aoes Shee Forest. The dark army were untypically silent and motionless.

Hugo crept back into the long grass in shock. 'How did they manage to get here without being seen? And why are they not moving?'

'Because they are asleep!' Whispered Ookle-Tonk. 'They've only just been created!'

'By who?' Asked Hugo.

An evil high pitched scream shrieked across the air and the entire mass of Fiend soldiers jolted into life creating a hideous ripple throughout their ranks. Moments later the whole force started to march into the Aoes Shee forest with a familiar gurgling moan.

'Why isn't Vrool doing anything? I don't understand!' Cried Hugo.

'Maybe he is!' Ookle-Tonk replied.

'Then whatever it is I hope he knows what he is doing! How are we going to reach him with that mob blocking our way?' Reginold whispered.

'We need to backtrack to the opening in the earth and skirt across the other way to the front of the Aoes Shee forest!'

'Hugo there is no time for that! What about that little fellow in the amulet? Wake him up and see if he can help!'

'Alright Reggie, Ookle-Tonk! Up ye get, come on and wake up I've a question for ya!'

The amulet bound youngling squeaked to life in annoyed surprise. 'What is it now old man?'

'Easy with the old man stuff little fella! Look over there and tell me what we are going to do about it. How do we get past them and warn your King?'

'I'm a freakin amulet bound Gikkie Bokker not a fortune teller! How would I know what to do? You would need to fly to warn Vrool in time!'

'What about the amulets power? Why not contact him directly?' Asked Reginold.

'No Reggie! The Morgannis may be able to sense communication through the dark ether and will alert that Fiend army, we need another way to warn him, hold on! Let's make our way back to where we were attacked by the soldiers, if there is a live shell or a few spare bullets in their encampment we could let one off but it needs to be big enough for the Aoes Shee in their mountain temple to see!'

'Perhaps they are already under attack from another direction and our warning distracts them instead of aiding them?'

'We have to take the chance, better to alert them to this force now rather than later!'

Both men raced off to where Synar and Mil-Mil had tackled the *B-M-H* soldiers and hurriedly searched through a small camouflaged encampment.

'Hurry Hugo I sense something nearby!' Warned Ookle-Tonk.
'Don't Worry little fella we are done here, Look! Flare guns Reggie! This will do the trick!' Hugo picked out a small steel case full of them and ran out of the tent only to run straight into the serrated stabbing sword of a fiend soldier.

Reginold leaped out of the tent and took the dark soldier by surprise with a powerful swing of his sword and cut the Fiend's head off. The dark soldier's body collapsed onto Hugo covering him from view but twenty more Fiends emerged from the long grass and surrounded the old man. He could hear the Gikkie Bokker youngling crying underneath the fiend carcase and rushed over to the black shelled creature and overturned it to reveal a panting Hugo.

As the fiends closed in he looked down upon Hugo's face who was gasping for air but with a hint of mischief in his eye placed his hand on a loaded flare gun he had pulled out of the steel box. Reginold smiled and expecting his next action to be his last on earth grabbed the gun from Hugo and fired it into the air. A bright red streaking flare hurtled vertically into the air high above the fields of long grass and forest outskirts illuminating a significant portion of the invading fiend army. Reginold closed his eyes waiting for the Fiend's to finish him off but a swift dark blur swept across the approaching creatures who collapsed upon themselves from the unknown attacker.

Reginold diverted his gaze to Hugo who was trying to sit up as Ookle-Tonk scolded him for being so careless. The old man smiled to see the amulets power was healing the wound and expected to see one of the Aoes Shee brothers standing in front of him. There was an uncomfortable silence after the attack and Reginold looked up at what he thought was Mil-Mil-Ulthu, but it was not who he thought it was.

Standing over him was an Aoes Shee warrior, dark and brooding like Mil-Mil but even larger, closer to Vrool's own stature and very silent.

'Thank you! Whoever you are! We must warn your King! Your forces are under attack!'

The dark warrior did not reply, instead it looked down upon Hugo and pulled him to his feet harshly and pulled the amulet off his neck to the shock of both men.

'I have no king! And no loyalty to his forces, go and warn them if it pleases you, I am leaving with this, if you try to stop me I will kill you both!'

Ookle-Tonk screeched out aloud in protest as Hugo attempted to approach the Aoes Shee creature but collapsed from his partially healed wound. 'Get your hands off the little guy! He is harmless!' As his knees hit the ground he could feel the rumbling of an approaching force.

'Harmless perhaps, but useful!' Replied the dark figure as he became a blur and sped off into the distance.

'Come back you scallywag! Hugo I promise you we will get that little critter back this is not over by a long shot!'

A small deployment of Siabhra scouts on thirty white horses stopped their gallop in front of the two men and two of the fully armoured warriors dismounted and came to Hugo's aid. As they reached Hugo the front face plate of their battle helmets retracted revealing the welcoming smile of Eimhir and Brianag.

'Who was the creature that saved you and took off with your amulet?' Asked Brianag.

'Eimhir I do not know! That amulet has the spirit of a youngling inside it!' Wheezed out Hugo in reply.

'It can only be Larn!' Sighed Brianag. 'Come we will bring you to the temple mountain, you have done well! An Aoes Shee scout saw your warning signal and the Fiend army is being attacked even as we speak!'

Hugo couldn't help smile at successfully warning his friends and stood up slowly as the two Siabhra sisters carried them on the backs of their steeds and galloped off towards the eastern entrance to the Aoes Shee Forest.

'How are you here ladies? I mean weren't you supposed to be looking after General Drake? Has he left and ratted us out?' Hugo snarled expecting an affirmative reply.

'No Hugo, he didn't leave! He is resting at our home and after a lengthy talk with us is trying to decide on the best way to approach his leaders to ask for help!'

'Well that's welcome news! Maybe General Square Head ain't so bad after all!' Smiled Hugo.

'Perhaps, but his actions shall define him now not his sentiments! We however are faced with a series of grave perils that are shortly about to befall us! Our Siabhra homeland is about to be attacked and we have been sent to meet with Vrool to beg for help! Then you raised the alarm but we have little time, you and Reginold have been summoned by the Aoes Shee King to his battle council!' Hugo did not respond but instead gulped with fear.

As they galloped towards the forest outskirts they could hear the sound of battle on its western side. A few rogue Fiend soldiers fleeing from the battle unexpectedly crossed paths with the mounted Siabhra and were destroyed. The lady warriors made swift work out of negotiating the terrain leading up to the Gikkie Bokker gardens beyond the plateau and were met by Vrool and his scouting party. The great King embraced Eimhir and Brianag and made his way over to Hugo and Reginold.

'We owe you much for your brave deeds! And thank you for not attempting to use the dark ether to communicate with us, now we are on even terms with the Morgannis, she has to do battle the same way as we do now but where are my sons and your two companions?'

Reginold's eyes were still moist from sobbing, 'We were all buried alive thanks to that witch and as for Yardal and Larrymond! They did not make it! I swear to you Vrool that creature has a lot to answer for!'

'I am sorry my friend if we survive this ordeal I shall recover their bodies for you! Now you both need to come with me to An teampall sliabh barr an tsolais! The Temple Mountain! Harry Corbett has fully recovered and is longing to see you Hugo! And he has an insight into the Morgannis and her actions!'

The humans made their way with the Siabhra through the upper mountain forest as the Aoes Shee warriors escorted them running along on all six limbs with an unearthly grace. They made their way into the courtyard of the Temple Mountain and Hugo got off his horse and walked purposefully alongside Vrool up a flight of stone steps and in through a large set of engraved silver doors. Reginold and the Siabhra forces followed closely behind until everyone reached a large dark chamber with a suspended throne high above them.

Vrool waved his hand and a large oval table made of quartz rose from the centre of the room as he beckoned his allies to stand around it to converse. 'The fiend force that is being intercepted to our eastern forests is a diversion for something much larger! General Bralnar has returned from meeting with Vraarl Uldunjen in the Selfin Mountain's where he has spotted a fiend army only miles away from the Siabhra Vale!'
The huge Aoes Shee warrior stepped forward from the shadows and stood beside his king.

'The force is as large as that of Terun Nil Vath Doom! But the fiends move differently now, they are more mobile and organised. The good news is that Vraarl Uldunjen has convinced the Heratii Refugees to stand alongside him to defend the Selfin mountain pass until all of our

Aoes Shee warriors are fully awake and ready for battle!'

Vrool looked over at Hugo and Reginold with a remorseful look upon his face.

'My sons Synar-Chro and Mil-Mil-Ulthu have not returned from concealing the opening into the sunken ruins of Fionn Ó Conchobhair but I cannot wait for them to return if they are still alive that is… And you my friends, in spite of the suffering that has befallen you we now need you for another mission while I prepare the full might of our entire army to rise!'

'But ye won't bee goin alone me lads!'
The mischievous frame of the white haired Diarmuid O'Weirdaun shuffled into the room behind Hugo and slapped him heartily on the back. 'I've been getting ready a few gadgets and gizmos for us to bee of help ta these furry scoundrels!'

'And let's not forget a strong will is also needed to keep the whole plan on track!'

Hugo looked over his shoulders as a smiling Harry Corbett entered the room. 'Harry ya mad git! Ah it's good to see that your well mate! Welcome back to the real world my friend!'

Harry was completely recovered from his sharing his pain with Vrool and looked twenty years younger, his frail body had become strong and his manner was decisive and resolute as he gave Hugo a great bone breaker of a hug.

'My only wish Hugo is that I should have recovered earlier to be with

318

you but I had so much healing to do from the pain that I was suffering from! But now listen to our plan!'

Harry took his place beside Diarmuid and Vrool spoke again.

'Eireannos is undergoing some sort of transformation unknown to us and my beloved Shard is overseeing his recovery so we must count him out of our plans. The Siabhra homeland is moments away from being attacked and I suspect a splinter force of fiends shall probe the defences that Vraarl has in place at the Selfin mountain pass. Colonel Kurn and Captains Lidana and Orofey are leading a force to defend the Morgannis Tomb and a quarter of our forces shall go to Vraarl Uldunjen's aid in the Selfin mountain pass as soon as they are ready! Now as for you my brave earth dwellers, your mission is to skirt by the oncoming battle and reach the Youngling Tree city and gather our remaining forces! That is if Zarn Hurad is still alive! Please follow Diarmuid and Harry who will prepare you for the journey! Eimhir and Brianag! Take your warriors along with a quarter of my forces when they are ready and make as much of a mess of the fiend army looming along the Siabhra Vale as you can, I will come to your aid as soon as I have dealt with The fiend army attacking our eastern flanks!'

The council convened and made their way out of the chamber. Hugo paused for a moment almost hypnotised by the walls of the chamber as the quartz table reflected some outside light onto the walls as the wood carvings of battles moved to form different battles and events. A huge fine fur covered hand stopped him leaving the chamber until the others had left.

'Hugo! My Grand Son Fluke-Fluke and his friends! Please find them! The first part of your journey will be very close to the path that they should have taken to the Youngling Tree City! I fear I may have already lost Synar and Mil-Mil and now I hear of Larn's appearance and of his theft of Ookle-Tonk the youngling's soul! To what end is a mystery to me. But please no matter what happens for good or evil do not contact anyone through the dark ether! Even if you believe it is one of our forces please ignore the messages that you may get as I have instructed all of our forces not to use it as the Morgannis will almost certainly use it to create distraction and lies!'

'Vrool auld buddy I will do me best to find them! I love the little fella! I am sure he is fine! Take care for now and see ya on the battle field!'

Hugo marched off to catch up with his team leaving Vrool to ponder upon the whereabouts of his sons. As Hugo marched out of the chamber he saw Reginold, Harry and Diarmuid at the far end of the court yard being dressed in Siabhra battle armour by Brianag and Eimhir.

He sniggered as all of his friends barely fitted into the beautiful silver and golden attire. He could not contain his mirth and roared out across the court yard to them.

'All right fellas! Those breast plates look a little bit too tight on ye all me thinks!'

'Shut your trap Hugo!' Scolded an indignant Harry Corbett, you have to wear it too you know!' Hugo's face soured a little as he made his way over to his friends.

'We made this armour especially for you all! Please forgive us if it is a little uncomfortable at first! I will ensure that it fits snug as soon as I have you all properly equipped!' Brianag smiled as she finished fitting out everyone except Hugo.

'Now my friend it's your turn!' She winked at him playfully.

'Ah Brianag you know that I'm not accustomed to wearing strange garb, I mean look at the state of that lot!' He pointed at his companions who all looked like school children who were forced to wear a rough wool sweaters and ill-fitting boots.

'Just put it on Hugo, We are going to war you know!'
He sighed to himself and took the armoured parts off her and after endless moaning and sighing managed to put it on as awkwardly as possible. 'Look at the state of us, the fiend's are definitely going to be running away from us in terror now, or maybe fall over and die laughing at us!'

'Hugo it has not settled on you yet, give it a moment!'
'What do you mean?'

'Our armour is forged from slivers of Wrathien hair, living Armour! That can also infuse itself with magical spells, the armour that you wear is alive!'

'Ah now ya tell me, get it off me! I had enough of that little fella hiding in my amulet and now I'm wearing living clothing?'

'Hugo MacNiadh shut your mouth and get on with the task at hand!'

321

Harry's voice was exactly as Hugo had remembered when he was a small child listening to Harry speak aloud his sermons at mass. Harry Corbett was definitely his old self again and Hugo stopped speaking and looked up sheepishly at Brianag and Eimhir who smiled.

'Thank you Harry! Now gentlemen prepare yourself as the living armour becomes aware of you!'

'Ye wha? Becomes aware? How does..'

The armour started to buzz and in a split second fastened itself perfectly onto each of the men's bodies perfectly fitting their every contour. Diarmuid smiled in amazement.

'That's snazzy! Aye like it a lot! Feels very snug!'

'And what about the weapons! Give us a sword or two will ya?'

Grinned Hugo.

Eimhir looked sternly at Hugo - 'Easy now Hugo! Before we hand them over to you understand that they are also forged from slivers of Wrathien hair, they can slice through anything! I mean anything Hugo, even the slightest pressure on our swords against solid jade will slice it in two like a warm knife through butter!'

'All right then I will keep it in mind! Anything to tell us about the shields?'

Brianag tossed a black diamond shield into Hugo's hand and it instantly shrinked to suit Hugo's stocky frame. 'Just be careful Hugo, we spent a humans lifetime studying weaponry and combat, respect your weapons they are more than dumb tools, they have a life force within them and they want to protect you!'

Hugo's smug grin faded away as he realised the great gift that he was receiving.

'Thank you ladies! I'm sorry I wasn't taking you seriously before!' Eimhir relaxed and handed weapons to the rest of Hugo's team.

'Now Hugo! Last but most important is your helmet! Prepare yourself when you put it on!'

Hugo timidly placed the sleek golden helmet over his head waiting for something to happen. Eimhir handed helmets to the rest of his friends and waited for them to put them on.

'What now Brianag? Does it shrink? I mean it's tight already!' Complained Hugo.

The helmets buzzed to life contouring to the humans head and a black diamond visor slid down over their faces. Hugo refocused his vision as he felt a surge of energy flow through his mind. The black visor showed the world in a startling way. The world was black and any detail in front of his eyes appeared to be a light shade of grey or a strange complete glowing white.

As Hugo looked around at his team they appeared as almost a glowing chalk line drawing that was clearly standing out from the background. As he focused on a single person the detail increased the longer he stared. The intensity of detail was too much and Hugo quickly took the helmet off.

'Ugh! I can't get used to that I feel sick!'

'In battle against endless droves of Fiend's it will give you the edge in perceiving the most immediate danger! You have no choice Hugo, If you go on this mission despite your orders being to avoid the Fiend forces you will most definitely encounter a great many of them! Their numbers are unlike anything that you have encountered Hugo, your mind and your friends minds will have great difficulty coping with them unless you relax and fuse your mind into the weapons that you wield!'

Hugo put his helmet on without a word and tried again. This time he breathed in deeply and exhaled slowly. The vision changed again and the detail became comfortable. He started to notice symbols beginning to contour over his team mates, ancient Gaelic and older symbols flowed slowly over them but Hugo steadied his resolve and concentrated. The symbols started to change slowly morphing into words. The words were still unrecognisable for a while but he decided to focus on one person instead of the whole team to see if he could resolve the detail. As he focused on Harry the words became his own language.

'Holy Mary mother of..! This is amazing!'

The first words that he recognised was *Harry – Friend and Guardian*, then he focused on a passing by Aoes Shee warrior, words flowed around the Aoes Shee creature, *Grar-grar-Ulshune - Aoes Shee warrior*, he became speechless as he now focused on the world around him taking in its detail as he saw it reborn in front of his own eyes.

'You all will adjust as your life comes face to face with grave peril for I sense that it is now near us! Our quarter of the Aoes Shee army has fully awakened and are prepared. You will follow our flanks until we finish off the straggling Fiend army that attacked us on our eastern forests then we are moving onto the main force of Fiend warriors that are massing on our Siabhra homeland! You must break off from our forces when we reach the end of the Morgannis Tomb! Then you make your way through the golden plains and over the waterfall into the great valley that leads to the Giant Youngling Tree City! Harry knows the location and it will appear on your black diamond visors!'

Hugo and his friends nervously took a deep breath in preparing themselves for the oncoming onslaught as Brianag brought over four amazing creatures that resembled a cross between a horse and a Komodo dragon with armoured spikes.

These Fíochmhar steeds are awarded to you, nothing moves swifter in these lands than these creatures, as long as you wear the armour we have given you they will obey you. The living armour shall ease you into controlling the beasts. Treat them well I raised each one and would die myself to protect them!'

'Oh Brianag I don't know what to say, I promise that I will..' She interrupted him with a stern hand on his chest.

'Your time to talk Hugo has ended! We move now, follow the flank of the Aoes Shee and fight with a pure heart! Good luck!'
She turned away from him as her helmet visor covered her face and she joined her sister as the courtyard flooded with Aoes Shee warriors who surrounded the Siabhra sisters and her small band of Siabhra warriors.

As Hugo stepped back to let the massive Aoes shee warriors into the courtyard he heard the sisters cry aloud in unison.

'Mo chairde mór dúinn a fuair bás i ngach arm eile, ní mór dúinn slumbered fad a cneasaigh ár wounds ó an brón de cath, ach seasamh dúinn le chéile anois mar deartháireacha agus deirfiúracha, tá tú mo theaghlach agus tú a shábháil mo bhaile ó terror agus iarr mé tú anois a shábháil arís agus chuige seo olc sin tuairisceáin sé riamh, bleed liom, a chur suas arm agus troid ar son ár saoirse!'

The Aoes Shee roared like an army of lions in unison and raised their serrated semi-circular shields over their heads with fiery passion. Eimhir willed the courtyard gates to open and the allies raced down through the Aoes Shee forest towards the first of the Fiend armies.

Even with their helmets on the sound was deafening to Hugo and his friends. Within seconds the courtyard had emptied leaving Hugo's team alone with the mighty beasts given to them for their mission. 'How the hell do we get onto these things?' shouted Hugo desperately. 'Just do it!' Shouted Harry as he closed his eyes and took a blind step onto golden stirrup and effortlessly mounted his armoured saddle.

'Now then that was not so bad!' He uttered in amazement. 'Aye this is great craic altogether me boys!' Laughed Diarmuid who got onto his armoured steed swiftly. 'Ah for janey sakes ya loada show offs, lets show them Reggie how it's really done!' Hugo stepped clumsily onto what he thought was a stirrup but was actually an armoured spike protruding from the creatures ribs and the mighty beast shrugged Hugo off like an elephant shakes off an ant. Hugo slammed to the ground and strained to get up. 'Ya bleedin mangey plank of a beast!, Let me up on ya or you'll be sorry!'

Reginold was busy placing strange containers on the sides of Diarmuid's Steed but with a slight chuckle he finished his task and walked over to Hugo and helped him onto his steed.

'There my boy you are well on your way to being a prime jockey!' He winked playfully at his old friend and then with ease mounted his own mighty steed.

Harry took the lead effortlessly trotting his beast to the front of the team. 'Hugo if we get into battle you take over but I know the way so till then follow me, now come on and get going! Yee-Aah! , Harry bolted out of the courtyard and vanished down into the forest.

'Ya over confident oaf! Come on let's get goin horsey! Come on!' Hugo was having great difficulty getting his steed to move as Reginold and Diarmuid galloped after Harry vanishing from sight. 'Come on Hugo me boyo!' Roared Diarmuid.

'Right! Giddie-Yup! Move! Come on out of that, will ya bleedin well move ya thick creature!' The fearsome beast flicked its head behind to meet Hugo's visor covered face and snorted, bearing it's huge canine fangs it bellowed out a great deep guttural roar and exploded into a gallop out of sight leaving a small group of Gikkie Bokker younglings to seal the gates behind him.

Chapter Twenty One - Facing your demons

The Fíochmhar steeds moved so swiftly and gracefully it seemed at times that the men were in a vehicle rather than a living thing as their armoured bodies cleared away any obstacle in their path. Hugo was desperately trying to catch up with his friends as he could hear the sound of a commencing battle. Seconds later his Steed ducked its head and lowered its body to evade four dark Fiend warriors who attempted to leap at its head but Hugo got the full brunt of the collision and went hurtling off into the air landing against a tree and landed awkwardly on top of two of the fiends whose bodies were broken from the impact.

Hugo's steed skidded to a halt and galloped back up the incline to reach him slaying the other two Fiends with its massive bear like claws. 'What the? Well thanks big fella! Much obliged!' He slowly got to his feet and got back on his steed as his dark visor indicated where his friends were. He could hear a group of men grunting and roaring off in the distance and his visor flashed the form of three mounted humans on a steep decline battling amongst a hoard of the enemy. He finally broke upon the fight and took the Fiend's by surprise slicing through four of them with his magical sword. Moments later the mob of fiends was slain and the group reunited.

'Hugo we need to move or we will mess this all up! Now follow me like it was your last act on earth!' Shouted Harry who bolted past them down the decline.

The group smashed through masses of the now routed enemy and eventually caught up with the Aoes Shee and Siabhra's flank, being careful not to overtake them.

There was a huge growl and then a roar of triumph as the alliance of Aoes Shee and Siabhra destroyed the first Fiend army. The swiftly moving force then swung around and headed east of the Aoes Shee forest and was moments away from the well-guarded Morgannis Tomb.

'Get ready Hugo! We are splitting away from them and heading into the golden plains!'

They swiftly galloped past a large force of formidable Aoes Shee warriors guarding the tomb of the Morgannis who passionately cheered them onwards.

'And Now! Follow me!' Harry raised his arm to signal his team to split away.

'Good luck my friends!' He roared out to the flank of the departing Aoes Shee and Siabhra alliance who all raised one of their mighty arms in reply.

'Oh my god Hugo! Look!' Warned Harry.

Hugo peered out into the west were the Siabhra's lands lay beyond the Selfin mountains and saw the horizon growing darker by the moment.

'There is no sun and no sunset in the land of the Aoes Shee, what's blotting out the lower horizon?' Shouted out Hugo.

'That's the real Fiend army Hugo, to see it from here means the force is in its millions!'

'And the Siabhra and the Aoes Shee are heading right into them!' His heart sank with the certainty that his friends would be slaughtered.

The fields raced by under the moonlight which began to fade away quickly into a golden dawn as they ventured out of Aoes shee territory and away from the curse of Terun nil vath doom. The visor in Hugo's helmet started to display a strange set of arrows pointing to just ahead of them. 'Guys please slow down I am seeing something here!'

'Hugo we have no time we need to combine all our forces!'
'But these signs on my visor! I think it's pointing to a series of trails left behind by someone, it could be Fluke-Fluke and his friends!'

Harry sighed but relented. 'Very well Hugo we shall slow down but only for a short time.

Hugo reached into his steeds mind and asked it to slow down a little and the steed instantly responded.

This is it! It's definitely Fluke-Fluke, and something much bigger, looks like an Aoes Shee Warriors tracks alright and something else. The visor confirmed his fears… Younglings, Aoes Shee, Fiends!

'Oh no! Please!' Hugo feared the worst but could see the tracks disappearing for over a mile but his visor picked up the trial leading past a dense forest and over to the end of the grassy plain into a valley. Hugo and his friends had to stop abruptly as the grassy plain ended in a cliff that had a waterfall just below the ground that they stood upon.

'Hugo's visor showed a trail partially obscured by the waterfalls torrents that lead down into a slowly flowing river that split the green valley into two.

'They were heading the right way anyhow but the tracks of the Aoes

Shee warrior that was with them have vanished!' Shouted out Hugo.

'Hugo if you calmed down a bit you would have noticed that we can all hear you fine these helmets keep us linked somehow!' Scolded Reginold.

'Yes your right Reginold! Hugo stop getting so worked up, I love Fluke-Fluke dearly and will fight to the death to protect him but we need to keep a clear mind, we don't know what's waiting for us in that valley ahead!'

'All right Harry I get it! Sorry lads!'

'Alriote then howe are wee goin ta get dowun there then? Luks ah bit steep ta me!' Observed Diarmuid.

'Well I guess these critters are nimble enough to...' Hugo could not finish his sentence as he was forced to hold on tightly as his steed raced off the waterfall's edge and scurried down amongst the torrential water like a lizard climbing down a wall. His friends all followed amazed at the agility of their steeds. As the level ground rapidly approached them Hugo cast his eyes out towards the green valley and picked up more tracks leading out of the valley.

'Guys we are nearly there get ready!' Hugo readied himself as his steed leaped away from the waterfall and splashed into the gushing river and swam out onto the river bank.

'The path! I can see a trail!' He shouted as his visor focused on tell-tale signs of Gikkie Bokker youngling tracks. But there were also masses of fiend tracks and as his friends caught up with him and ventured through the valley floor their steeds had to jump over carcasses of Fiend soldiers and four huge Master Fiend remains. This looks like it's leading up to a last stand! I'm dreading what I'm going to come across next! Hugo thought to himself.

He spotted in the distance a gap in the valley that was covered in dense swirling mist as Harry took the lead again and swiftly headed straight for it.

'This is the opening to the new Youngling Tree City! Shard forged an alliance with Eevul and her Banshee race to protect the younglings from any harm after the Morgannis nearly killed all of the Younglings including Vrool!'

'I didn't read far enough into the second diary to find out how the Fomori revived Vrool.

'Vrool was not revived by them! He revived himself and the Fomori amazed at his resilience placed him into the trials without giving him a chance to regain his strength. His were the most severe of all the trials!

At first they were curious as to how as a youngling that he was able to badly injure the Morgannis but they became afraid of his potential power! It was as if the Fomori did not want to make a champion out of him at all. Even after he had passed the Fomori Inquisitors insisted that he stay for further study but of course he refused. They tried to stop him by force but in the process of putting the Aoes Shee king through the most hideous trials of combat and punishment they caused his physical body to ascend and Vrool walked out of their homeland after destroying half of their kingdom. After he returned he would not permit even Shard to approach him for fear of what he was capable of.

He locked himself away in the depths of the mountain temple until he learned a way to master his rage. Vrool walks a fine line between his physical self and spiritual self. He is afraid of evolving further and has learned ways to suspend his full ascension until he fully understands what the Fomori plans are!'

Hugo listened intently as they all raced towards the misty gap in the valley and started to notice Fíochmhar steed tracks everywhere.

'That sounds like he could take on the Morgannis without blinking! He defended us all brilliantly when she appeared in my world, so your saying that that's not even his full power being used?'

'Don't you see Hugo, he fears if he lets himself go fully into his ascension that he will be unable to control himself and may become even worse than the Morgannis! Until he learns more of the Fomori and their plans he chooses not to progress further with his powers! Ah we are nearly here, prepare for a steep climb my friend and it's time for you to take over, because fighting is what's on the agenda for today and it's what you do best my friend!'

Hugo's visor retracted letting his face feel the cold mist sweep past his face. He could only think of how much power Vrool had and could it be used to free Henry his father from the Morgannis Tomb. He could hear a clarion call in the distance that brought him back to his senses and slowed his steed down to a trot. Moments later Zarn Hurad appeared on his huge steed and welcomed the men.

'You are the son of Henry! It is my privilege to meet you! His sacrifice gave us valuable time to build what you are about to see!'

Hugo looked up and saw the faint shape of a massive tree slowly being revealed by the chaotic mist. 'Listen Zarn thanks for staying away from the dark ether it's levelled the playing field for us but we need all of your forces to mobilise and come with us to flank a huge Fiend army that's about to wipe out the Siabhra realm!'

'And who will defend this place if we all leave?'

'Zarn leave a token force if you wish but most of your forces have to come, this is a Terun nil vath doom sized army at least and it may already be attacking the Siabhra city!'

'Very well I shall leave one hundred of my warriors here to look after our tree city and the younglings!' Hugo's faced brightened up in surprise.

'Younglings? Fluke-Fluke? Is the little fella here?'

'Yes Hugo! He rests in the heart of the Tree city with his friends. All are safe. He is a very brave fighter but you have no time to see him yet! I will call my forces now and we shall leave here to protect our allies!' Zarn turned around and galloped off into the mist.

Hugo made his steed trot closer into the huge mist bank to get a better look at the youngling tree city with his friends following closely behind. The mist bank cleared quickly as they ventured forth into the second valley and they all gasped at the vast shape of an enormous tree looming over them like a great mountain.

'It's absolutely beautiful!' Said Harry. 'I have only learned of this place over the last few days it has been kept so secret!'

'Aye suppose it had ta have beeeen! It's protecting their future!' Observed Diarmuid.

Hugo grinned broadly. 'To think that he is up there and safe please me no end! That little Fluke-Fluke fella is a brave little critter!'

Another clarion call broke the silence and Hugo could see faint pin prick sized lights rushing down the huge tree towards the ground. 'That's a big force being mobilised!'

As the faint lights reached the ground the Fíochmhar steeds could feel the earth underneath them start to gently tremble from the gallop of their own kind. They started to become excited and their breathing became faster as they anticipated the arrival of their companions in a vast formation.

The gently trembling vibration turned into a rumble that Hugo and his friends could feel in their chests and within minutes tens of thousands of mounted Aoes Shee warriors galloped out of the mist towards them led by Zarn Hurad. Harry looked on in amazement.

'I've never seen such a large force of Aoes Shee, not even in the Temple Mountain! And adorned in living armour as well! I can feel the magical power emanating from them!'

'This is going to be one hell of a fight lads!' Beamed Hugo proudly as Zarn's huge force stopped in a massive formation directly in front of

Hugo and his friends and saluted them proudly shaking the earth with their battle roars.

Chapter Twenty Two - My Enemies Enemy

The tall American general slowly rose from the old sofa in Eimhir and Brianag's living room and finished his mug of coffee. The sun light embraced his face and he could feel his wounds starting to heal. He had spent so much time thinking through his next course of action that it began to dawn on him that simply showing up to his superiors and being honest was really the best course of action to take. He took his battered smart phone out of his jacket pocket and tried to turn it on.

'Fried alive by that witch!' He sighed and threw the device onto the sofa in disgust. He looked around for a phone but could find nothing electrical except the light switch. 'Stay here and think it through they said! Ah jeez what do I do next?' He sighed.

'But she sure was cute!' He smiled to himself thinking of Brianag. He got restless and made his way to the front door to get some fresh air. He could see the shadow of a small statured man standing in front of the door about to knock. He got to the door before the man had a chance to knock and opened it ready to give the fake story given to him by Eimhir and Brianag about him being an American tourist looking for his ancestral Irish roots.

As soon as the muscular general opened the front door the small man smiled politely and took out what Drake thought would be a business card but instead the man had a taser gun in his hand and unleashed a violent electrical charge into Drakes body causing him to double over in pain. Four much larger men rushed through the doorway ahead of the little man and grabbed the stunned General and placed him roughly onto the sofa.

The small statured man looked around the inside of the house and took out another device from his black overcoat and started to point it around the inside of the house looking for something but after a few moments he sighed to himself and placed the device back into his overcoat pocket. Then the man spoke in a soft American accent... 'It's all fine in here sir! You may enter the premises!' A tall man with dark almost black eyes slowly entered the house and made his way over to General Drake and pulled over an old wooden dining chair.

'You are a very important man Mister Andrew Drake! Very important! You have a number of things that I want and I always get what I want!'

Before the tall man got a chance to speak another group of four men dressed in US Army uniforms entered the living room and stood over the restrained American General.

Three of the men were in their twenties and broad and sturdy while the fourth was in his sixties and portly with a bald head.

'I'm commander Tenison and you are walking a very fine line between hero and traitor my friend. We know what you have been doing. How long did you think you could pull this off for? Don't get me wrong your alien friends are very good at what they do and if it were not for this man here we would be none the wiser to what you were getting up to!'

Drake tried to free himself from his captors but the small man in the dark suit injected Drake in the arm with a serum. Drake almost flopped back down into the couch from the power of the serums contents.

'I am no traitor! There are no aliens around here! I don't know what you are talking about!'

'Our friend thinks otherwise! You are coming with us back home for a court martial then you are going to tell us exactly what's been going on here under your command general!'

The small man took out his taser gun one last time and stuck it into Drakes chest rendering him unconscious.

The burly soldiers then raised the unconscious general to his feet and dragged him out of Eimhir and Brianag's house and threw him into the back of a large black jeep.

Everyone left the house as the small man rearranged the furniture to the way it was before they had forced their way in. 'It's all taken care of Commander Tenison!' Assured the small man as he walked past the portly commander and into the jeep.

The tall man approached Tenison and towered over him... 'Now remember I want him handed over to me after his court martial, there is a lot of research I have to do on him, I have paid you good money for your troubles!'

'Do you want him alive or dead?'

'Bring him to me alive! I want to finish him off myself, besides some of my experiments require that he is conscious for the... radical procedures that he will undergo!'

'And what address am I delivering him to once I finish with him?'

The tall man looked into the back of the sturdy black jeep at Drakes unconscious body and smiled.

'Seal him in a wooden crate and mark it for the attention of one Mister Ilgrim Borglum, chief CEO of *B-M-H* Acquisitions, Corporate Head Quarters, Flavel Island, Antarctica!

THE END

TO BE CONTINUED ...

343

IF YOU HAVE MADE IT THIS FAR

Then thankyou. If you read and enjoy my Gikkie Bokker Books then I consider you a friend. The adventure continues in 'The Gikkie Bokkers Book Three - The Talon Guardian', arriving soon on this side of the magical portal.

Made in the USA
Lexington, KY
29 November 2016